IT'S ABOUT TIME

Hillary Gauvreau Oat

Copyright © 2024 Hillary Gauvreau Oat

All rights reserved. No part of this book may be copied or reproduced in any form without permission in writing from the author, except by a reviewer who may quote brief passages for review purposes.

This is a work of fiction. The names, characters, businesses, places, and incidents in the book are either a product of the author's imagination or used in a fictitious manner. Any resemblance to actual persons, living or dead, or actual events is purely coincidental

Cover design by John Oat Studio

Bridebrook Press

I dedicate this book with love to my grandchildren—
Jonah, Estelle, Octavia, Norah, and Callahan.

ACKNOWLEDGMENTS

Writing this book was the most fun I have had in a long time, and I owe it all to Patty Chaffee who is an award-winning writer, poet, and friend. After I attended one of her writing workshops, she encouraged me to keep writing, and I will be forever grateful.

I also want to thank Joanne Moore for the title suggestion of the book and her exceptional feedback as we shared our stories.

I have a deep gratitude for my friends who willingly waded through rough drafts before Grammarly cleaned them up.

John Oat is a talented artist and a dear friend. The cover he created is better than anything I could have imagined.

Thank you also to my editors, Elaine Bentley Baughn and Joan Sands because they made my manuscript the best it could be.

Finally, my heartfelt thanks to Mark McQuillan, writer and a friend for fifty years. I thought that if he could write a book, I could, too! Thanks, Muck, for the challenge and for making me laugh.

TABLE OF CONTENTS

CHAPTER 1	1
CHAPTER 2	15
CHAPTER 3	23
CHAPTER 4	31
CHAPTER 5	45
CHAPTER 6	53
CHAPTER 7	65
CHAPTER 8	79
CHAPTER 9	89
CHAPTER 11	115
CHAPTER 12	131
CHAPTER 13	145
CHAPTER 14	159

CHAPTER 15	175
CHAPTER 16	191
CHAPTER 17	211
CHAPTER 18	227
CHAPTER 19	241
CHAPTER 20	259
CHAPTER 21	277
CHAPTER 22	289

It's About Time

CHAPTER 1

A Glancing Blow

Bess

It's a blustery day in March on the Connecticut shoreline, and the wind chill is turning a balmy day frigid. Main Street, usually bustling with activity, is quiet. Even though the sun is shining, it's too raw for strolling or sitting on one of the benches that line the street. But I'm determined to go on a daily walk no matter what.

I catch a glimpse of my reflection in a storefront window as I trek up the street and note that I look pretty damn good for age fifty-three. I zip my L.L. Bean coat up to my chin against the cold. My graying blond hair blows around my face, sticking to my fresh lip balm. Hats are not my thing although, on a day like this, I concede to pulling the hood of my coat up over my head. New England Yankee blood runs deep in me, so I'm used to the weather's whims. It's all about proper clothing.

Leaning into the wind, I'm a woman on a mission and focused on getting to CVS. I'm not paying attention when suddenly I am knocked to the pavement by a couple of kids flying around the corner on skateboards. They are as shocked as I am, skidding to a halt and mumbling, "Sorry, lady." To their credit, they don't dash off but are clueless how to help.

I went down fast on all fours, before collapsing flat on my belly. That was not graceful. It felt like slow motion, but it only took a second. I pray no bones are broken. It takes me a second to catch my breath before attempting to get up off the sidewalk, awkward as a newborn foal. A shopkeeper magically appears, offering a hand to gently help me up. He waves the boys off, telling them he will take it from here. That's when the good Samaritan notices my torn tights and blood oozing from a scraped knee. My condo is close by, but I am shaky from the accident. Letting this man take me into his shop gives me time to pull myself together.

Inside the shop, I am instructed to sit on an antique-looking chair next to a huge teak worktable covered with tools, parts, and clocks in various states of disassembly. The distinctive scent of 3-IN-ONE oil lingers, reminding me of when I hung out in my grandfather's workshop while he got my bike ready for spring.

"I have a first aid kit in the back. Hang on while I go get it. Are you okay? Not going to faint or anything, are you?"

I assure the man that I will do my best not to faint and watch him rush off to the back of the shop. He is not a stunningly handsome man but has comfortable good looks. Probably in his late fifties with a sturdy six-foot frame, he has a full head of shaggy ginger hair shot with strands of gray. His wild hair contrasts starkly with a close, perfectly trimmed beard. He dresses like a practical man in jeans, a black tee shirt, and a tweed sport coat. His shoes are Merrell hiking boots. Casual, yet neat.

While I wait, I scan the shop sandwiched between The Framery Art Gallery and Hill O'Beans Coffee Shoppe. The front door, original to the historic building, is made of rough dark wood with a glass window where "It's About Time, J. Ogilvie Proprietor" is stenciled in gold letters. Natural light filters

It's About Time

through a large storefront window that has a display of clocks lined up on an antique library table. Shelves along one interior wall hold an assortment of clocks with tags attached. Nothing fancy, the store is long and narrow, functional and masculine. Being here is like going back in time which, since it's a clock shop, strikes me as funny. Soft ticking comes from everywhere. The proprietor hurries back with a first aid kit, a bottle of Talisker ten-year-old malt Scotch, and two shot glasses. He uses his forearm to clear a space on the work table and carefully sets everything down.

"Which one is the first aid kit?" I joke.

"First things first. I don't know if you need this or not, but I highly recommend it. And since witnessing your fall was traumatic for me, too, I'll join you." The wheeled leather desk chair makes a squishing sound as he plops himself down and glides closer. He proceeds to pour two shots of golden amber liquid, offering me one for medicinal purposes. Raising his glass, he says Slàinte Mhath, which he explains is a traditional Gaelic toast to good health. He swallows the shot of whiskey. I take a small sip of the liquid that smells like wood smoke.

"Seeing you fall scared the shit out of me. Nothing like a shot of whiskey to calm the nerves," the clock man explains.

"What is this stuff?" I grimace as I swallow the fiery liquid.

"First aid is first aid. In the old days, they would have doused your wounds with it. But despite your first impression, this stuff is too good for that. I was introduced to Talisker on one of my trips to Scotland, and we bonded. It's made on the Isle of Skye and has been in my private inventory ever since. By the way, my name is James. I own this place. And you are?"

"Bess. I live in town." I was tempted to babble on about who I was but held back. I don't know who this guy is and my trust issues are on alert.

"Nice to meet you, Bess, from town. Now, let me get a look at your wounds."

My wounds, as James refers to them, include torn tights exposing a skinned knee and some nasty road rash on the palms of my hands.

"It happened so fast I couldn't believe my eyes. I caught sight of the whole thing just as it happened. Man, you went down hard. I thought I would have to do CPR or call 911."

"Fortunately, L.L. Bean padded me enough to prevent bouncing my head off the pavement. That definitely would have been a 911 call," I remark. James cleans the abrasions and sticks a Band-Aid on my knee. For a large man, he is surprisingly gentle.

"I think I am getting used to this stuff," I tell James as I sip the whiskey. "Thank you for the rescue. It would be embarrassing if I had to crawl home bleeding. I can picture the story in The Post Road Review: 'Local Therapist Run Over on Main Street.' That would cause a stir."

"Oh, you're a therapist. What kind?" James asks.

"I'm a marriage and family therapist. I teach what I need to learn, I guess." That is enough to share. I already feel overexposed.

It's About Time

"I had some days I could have used an appointment." James says with a sheepish smile.
"I have an office down the street in the back of the Yoga Studio if you are in need." I hand James one of my cards and carefully stand up. "Well, I'm heading home. No sense in pushing my luck today. Besides, I might be the tiniest bit drunk," I giggle.

"Do you want a ride? Can I walk you home?" James asks eagerly. "I'll put the closed sign on the door, not that I am swamped with customers at the moment."

"Thank you for the offer but I can manage. I live close by." I take inventory of my limbs. Everything seems to be in working order and capable of getting me the few blocks to my condo. "Betcha I'll be sore tomorrow," I say as I limp for the door.

"Here, let me get that." James beats me to the door and holds it open as I hobble out to the street.

That was almost a year ago, but it seems like yesterday. Ever since that fateful encounter, I would walk down Main Street hoping to run into James. At first, we waved hello to each other. Sometimes, James would come outside to say hi, check on my wounds, and chat for a few minutes. Then, one day we went for coffee which turned into an hour of animated conversation. He's a delightful man with a quick sense of humor. His full name is James Andrew Ogilvie. His ancestors immigrated from Scotland to North Carolina in the 1700s, and that explains the ginger hair and the love of Scotch whiskey. Gradually, family members moved north and west. James's branch of the family tree ended up in New England.

Hillary Gauvreau Oat

If I don't run into James on Main Street, I'm disappointed. If his shop is unexpectedly closed, I wonder if he is okay. One day, James suggested we share cell phone numbers so we could stay in touch. Gradually, we spend more time together and I like it. We text each other several times a day, and James usually calls on his way home from the shop. Friendship with James is my little secret, however. I don't want the town busybodies gossiping about us although that ship has probably sailed. Days pass into months and, as the seasons change, James and I become close but with a respectful distance.

James and I talk about everything. I tell him about Prince Charming, aka Chad Winthrop, my second and final marriage. When I met Chad, I felt that irresistible tingle of attraction. I was ecstatic and thought the universe had answered my prayer, delivering the perfect match when I least expected it. Don't people say that is exactly how true love happens? It's also called being blindsided.

The universe is a mindless entity that doesn't care about any of us. We make all that kismet stuff up and, if you ask me, it's all bullshit. Sadly, Chad didn't care about anyone but himself. After enduring repeated humiliation, rejection, and extended punishing silences, I left him and moved into a sweet little condo on the beach. I decided that romantic chemistry is not to be trusted and promised myself to never recycle that Prince Charming-Cinderella-story ever again. I made it clear to James that I embrace the single life and focus on work, family, and friends. Period. No more romance for me.

James has similar feelings. Without going into gruesome detail, he shared that his marriage to Caroline was difficult. His wife succumbed to lung cancer eight years ago after a painful estrangement and an aborted divorce. James is a retired high

It's About Time

school chemistry teacher turned shopkeeper. His love of clocks and the talent for repairing them makes him happy and successful. I shifted from laboratory research to helping people as a psychotherapist. Not much difference, really, between clocks and people. James and I are both good at figuring out what makes them tick.

My friendship with James grows easily without drama. James is attractive, and his temperament is appealing. It would be easy for me to slip into a romance, but I will not let that happen. The plan is to keep expectations low and maintain some distance. I have never invited James to my home, which might seem weird, but he hasn't questioned it. Neither of us is looking to tempt fate with romantic impulses we would later regret.

On another beautiful early spring day, too nice to stay inside, I walk over to It's About Time to see if James wants to go to lunch. I push the door open and hear the familiar tinkle of the bell letting him know someone is entering the shop. He ducks his head out from the back room, clutching an oily rag. When he sees me, he smiles.

"Hey! What's up?" James calls. "Give me a minute to wash up." I can hear water running and drawers opening and closing. He dries his hands on a clean towel as he ambles the length of the shop toward me.

"You got time for lunch? My afternoon client rescheduled, so I don't have to get back to work. Want to play hooky?" I ask.

"Ah, how you tempt me, woman! I have a lot of work to do before the end of the week. However, a man has to eat and lunch sounds good."

"Great! Pizza or deli?"

"What do you think?" James laughs.
"Ok. Pizza it is."

James grabs his tweed jacket off the hook, and we walk out and around the corner to Sal's Pizza Palace. When we open the door, we are welcomed by the rich scents of yeasty dough, pungent cheese, and tomato sauce. There are plenty of tables so after placing our order, we settle into one by the front window. Main Street merchants are regulars, and Sal, the owner, knows everyone.

"Buongiorno! How are you guys doing today?" Sal greets us warmly as he places the fragrant margherita pie on the table with a flourish.

"We're good. How about you?" James manages to say before filling his mouth with crispy crust, earthy olive oil, garlic, and ripe tomatoes. Pizza is his favorite food, and he could eat it every day if his arteries allowed. Sal gives us a thumbs up and dashes off to pull another pie out of the wood-fired oven. Between mouthfuls, James asks me what I am doing after work.

"Well, for me, this is after work, and I am going to walk on the beach," I tease. "After that, not much, really. Probably read or check out TV. Why?"

It's About Time

James tells me he roasted a turkey and is sick of eating leftovers. "Want to come to my house and help me turn it into a culinary delight? We can use our science skills."

Normally, I would jump at the chance to spend time with James but this time I am oddly quiet. Painful memories bubble to the surface. I married Pete at twenty-four because he was responsible, motivated and, most importantly, he wanted me. From a very young age, I feared no one would ever want me, so a proposal was something I could not pass up.

I had everything I wanted—a husband, two children, and a home. But something wasn't right because I was deeply depressed. There were days when I could barely get out of bed, dreading another endless day. Pete never noticed. The relationship I thought I would have didn't materialize. The marriage was always about him and never about us. After twenty-one years of trying everything, I gave up and divorced Pete.

After that, I made a determined, but seriously misguided, effort to find a mate through the internet. It was exciting at first, flirting and meeting prospects, but it got old fast. Auditioning on dating sites was frustrating and just plain sad. The process is the equivalent of running through a gauntlet. The highs are Everest high, and the lows hit the bottom of the Mariana Trench, often on the same day. I wasn't pretty enough, sexy enough, or young enough. Not ever enough. Nevertheless, I pursued dating like a hungry lion chasing down a gazelle. They say you can't make a silk purse out of a sow's ear, but I tried. I wanted emotional security and someone to love who would care about me. I never found what I was looking for, so I accepted being single and gave it all up. That's when Chad showed up.

"So, sue me, but I am not interested in dating," I mutter under my breath.

"What?" James presses. "Where did you go? Are you ok?"

"Yeah, I'm fine. So, listen, that's a sweet offer and, as much as I love leftovers . . ." I make a yucky face and laugh, "I can't come . . . to dinner . . . at your house." There is an opening to explain what seems like irrational craziness, but I don't take it. James looks disappointed and confused. After almost a year, this is the first time going to his house has come up and it's freaking me out.

"Okay. I'm obviously crushed and stuck with that bird for another night." James fakes a sob.

I smile and say nothing. We walk out of Sal's Pizza Palace, and James heads back to his shop. I watch him, feeling my stomach tighten.

Around 6:00 p.m., like clockwork, no pun intended, my phone rings. It's James and I let it go to voicemail, something I never do. I'm not ready to talk. Then he texts me a picture of the turkey carcass with a big red bow on top. It's cute, so I text back a laughing emoji. James has to be picking up on the vibe that something is off, but he says nothing. I text that I will see him tomorrow.

The sun is going down, and it's getting dark in my condo. I stretch out in the recliner wrapped in a blanket that is like a soothing adult swaddle. I need to explain myself to James without looking like a complete jerk. He knows some of my

It's About Time

story, but this feels like a deeper level of vulnerability. It's best to tell the truth, but how much truth?

I hear the familiar ping of a text message. It's James telling me there's a surprise outside my door. My eyes open wide and I freeze. Is he lurking outside my door? The condo is my safe place, my holy sanctuary, and the outside world is not welcome unless I say so. I tiptoe over to the door in my fluffy rainbow-striped socks, catching a glimpse of myself in the hall mirror. Hair standing on end, no makeup, oversized sweatshirt, and wrapped in a blanket. What a sight. I am completely unprepared for company, especially James. I peek through the peephole and I'm relieved no one is peeking back at me. Cautiously, I open the door a crack. There, on my porch displayed in all its glory, is a picked-over turkey carcass on a platter wearing a red bow. Sticking out of a wing is a sign that says, "This turkey is sorry." I can't help but laugh. That's when James cautiously steps out of the shadows, trying not to scare the pants off me.

"Surprise." James says softly and smiles.

If my appearance is a reciprocal surprise, James gives no indication. He holds out a Tupperware container like a peace offering asking if he can come in.

"Are you serious? Look at me! I'm sorry, but no. As much as I appreciate your cute surprise, I am obviously not prepared for company." I hate saying no. "How do you know where I live?" An edge of irritation creeps into my voice, even though I am trying hard to sound friendly.

"I went up and down the street knocking on doors until I found you." James grins until he sees my look of horror. "Seriously, Bess, it's the twenty-first century. You can find out anything on this thing called the internet. Unless you are in the witness protection program, which you are not, because . . . voila . . . I found you." James looks thoughtful for a minute, carefully choosing his words. "What's the deal, Bess? I've done something to upset you. Will you tell me what I did, please?"

I accept the Tupperware container. "Thank you for this. What is it?"

"It's just leftovers . . . a little turkey, sweet potato, but no gravy because I ate that. Basically, it's an excuse sealed in Tupperware to come see what's going on." His kindness touches me, and I know I need to explain myself, but I'm not ready.

"Yes, something is going on. But it's about me, not you." *Oh, man, did I say that? God, that is so cliche.* "I need some time to think so I can explain clearly. I promise we will talk tomorrow. Okay? Can you give me a little space?"

James nods yes. "Of course. But ya know, Bess, talking with me doesn't have to be like presenting a legal brief, tied up in a neat bow with a summary and conclusions. I am a mess, too, and willing to sit with you while you unload whatever crap is going on and we can sort it out together. If you want to kill me, just shut me out." James pleads his case. No one has ever made me an offer like that before.

"James, you are so good to me." I reach out and touch his hand. "It's tempting for me to let you in, but I can't. Look at me!" Am I afraid to let James into my condo—or my life?

It's About Time

"You look fine to me." James shrugs acceptance and hugs me—blanket, fuzzy socks, and all. I almost cave because he is so kind and smells good, like wool and soap. I gently move away, say good night, and close the door. I can sense him standing on the porch, trying to figure out what the hell is going on. When I hear his footsteps walking away, I cry.

I stomp around the dark condo and shout, "Goddammit, I need some time. Is that too much to ask for?" It's the perfect setup for time. The guy loves clocks. Jeez.

I collapse into the recliner, blow my nose, sip wine, and think. What if I really want to get close to James? There is so much about him that I love. He is funny, smart, and he listens. I love the manly scent of him when he hugs me and his unruly auburn hair. Goddammit, I don't want those feelings. But they don't seem to care what I want.

Despite my efforts to hold it back, my affection for James is growing. I promised myself I would not do this love stuff ever again. Men are not invited into my holy sanctuary unless we're related or they're fixing the plumbing. I can't believe I'm questioning my solemn promise. But what if this man is different? *God, Bess, if you had a dollar for every time you thought that, you'd be rich.* Am I happy alone? Easy answer. Alone is safe and being happy is irrelevant. However, bungee cord jumps aren't safe, but people do them for the thrill. Am I missing the thrill of falling in love? Is being safe enough for me? What if James turns out to be a disappointing asshole? I suppose I would be no worse off than I am right now.

I turn on a Netflix movie as a distraction from my circular, getting nowhere thinking. I select a fluffy romantic comedy, probably a mistake, but whatever. When it ends, Peter and Debbie, after one hookup twenty years earlier and a lasting friendship, finally admit they've always loved each other and live happily ever after. I knew that was coming. I'm not cynical, mind you, just realistic. As much as I might want it, real life is not a romantic comedy. I turn the TV off and my eyes adjust to the dark. Outside the French doors, a full moon rises in the night sky.

James. There is no escaping thinking about him. Despite everything I have been through, that stupid movie makes me want a fairy tale. Now I am annoyed. Have I learned nothing? Am I talking myself into or out of something? I don't even know. This is why I need time.

It's About Time

CHAPTER 2

Wing Man

James

I walk away from Bess's front door, zipping my windbreaker up against the chill that wasn't just in the weather. I did my best to warm things up with Bess and thought the turkey was a cute touch. But Bess was not having it. One thing we have in common is a stubborn streak. I like that about her as long as we don't go head-to-head too often. I put the picked-over bird on the hood of my truck as I dig into my pocket for the keys.

Ever since I scooped Bess up off the sidewalk, I have enjoyed her company. Actually, no, it's more than that. Enjoying her company sounds like something I would say about my Auntie Flora. My Auntie is a wonderful woman, but the way I feel about Bess is more than that. Bess is amazing. Beautiful, intelligent, and funny. When I hug her, I feel happy, and I haven't felt happy in a long time. Content, yes, but not happy. I even wonder what it would be like if our friendship became something more. Would I want to marry again? I haven't met anyone who made me think about that since my wife, Caroline, died eight years ago. But every signal I get from Bess puts those thoughts on hold. It doesn't erase them, just presses the pause button. I know she has been through a lot of shit with the men in her life and I won't minimize that for one second. I don't want to be the next asshole on the list.

I secure the turkey in the passenger seat, get in the truck, and start her up. Before I back out of the parking spot, I wonder if I should try to talk to Bess again. My phone is sitting on the seat, taunting me. I am disappointed there are no texts from her. Calling would probably piss her off. Maybe a goodnight text would be okay.

"Good night. Talk tomorrow. J" My finger is poised over the phone as I debate the wisdom of hitting send. *Oh, what the fuck. Just send the goddamn thing.* Jesus, I have never felt so uncertain. I am picking through an emotional minefield, hoping not to get blown up again. I pull out of the parking area and head home. The turkey sits on the seat next to me looking sad and rejected. Bess kept the leftovers, but shut me and the bird out. As a wingman, the turkey left a lot to be desired.

"Sorry, old pal. It's been nice knowing you, but you go in the trash when we get home."

When I met Bess, I was not looking for a woman in my life. God no. But now? It's been almost a year, and I think I'm falling for her. We talk every day. I miss her if she doesn't poke her head in my shop. Once in a while, something gets under her skin and she goes silent. It dries me crazy because I've experienced punishing silences in the past. I need communication even if it is just to fuck off. I would rather be punched in the face than shut out. Seriously. It feels that bad. I need to tell Bess that and hope she cares. Sometimes, she may not be ready to talk, and that probably has nothing to do with me. So, as much as I hate it, I don't bug her while she takes the time she needs. I won't, however, let our disagreement rot on the vine. If the space becomes a chasm, I will assert myself. But man, this is hard. Patience isn't a skill I come by naturally.

Now that I think about it, it's interesting that Bess and I haven't been to each other's houses or met any family or friends. We keep each other secure in a bubble that the outside world cannot ruin. With each other, we only go so far before throwing

It's About Time

up the shields. We keep it light and safely shallow. I think I want more. But will she? I guess we have a lot to talk about, and the thought of rocking our little boat scares the crap out of me. I know that sounds weird for a brawny Scotsman to say. We get scared, but don't like to let it show. Any guy who goes commando in a skirt knows fear. Trust me.

I drive past the Black Sheep Irish Pub and consider stopping in for a pint and some laughs but decide against it. It's almost 9:00 and I have a lot of work at the shop tomorrow. Besides, I want to call my sister, Mary, and talk this situation over with her.

I pull into my driveway, lock up the truck, and toss the turkey in the trash. That's when I hear the text message ping. It's Bess saying good night. She's watching a movie. "Talk tomorrow." I smile. We're making progress.

I go into the house with my mood lifted and toss the keys on the kitchen counter and my jacket over a chair. I would love to make a fire in the wood stove, but I'd better call Mary now before it gets too late. Mary is my older sister and a font of wisdom. She also tells it like it is which I appreciate even when it's hard to hear.

"Mary? How are you? How are things in North Carolina? Got a minute to talk? Or are you and Graeme getting ready for a hot roll in the hay?" I laugh. Brotherly love, it's called.

"Funny, James. Wouldn't you be surprised if we were!" Mary scolds.

"Knowing you both, nope, not really. Nothing surprises me. So, I want to talk to you about something. Get your take on it. You know, a woman's perspective."

"Okay, sure."

"It's about Bess." Mary and I talk to each other frequently, so she is familiar with the story of Bess getting dropped to her knees in front of my shop. She is not aware of my growing feelings.

"Ah, I knew this was coming!" Mary laughs.

"What do you mean? I haven't told you anything yet?"

"James, I have known you your whole life. You haven't stopped talking about Bess since you met her. That means you're interested."

"That's not true. Is it? Jeez. Here I thought I was so smooth."

"About as smooth as our grandmother's scrub brush! But we love you that way."

I fill Mary in on the situation. How close we seem, yet not close enough to be risky, and now the turkey tragedy. "Everything was fine. We had just eaten lunch. The minute I asked her over for dinner, the curtain came down and she got quiet. It makes no sense to me. We spend a lot of time together. We eat together a few times a week, so eating doesn't seem to be the issue. You know me, Mary, I'm a charmer."

I can hear Mary snorting at that last comment. "No, stop laughing. Listen. I wanted to break the ice and get her to talk with me. So, I dressed up the turkey with a bow and a little sign and put it at her front door. I thought it was cute and would get me inside to talk. That's charming, yeah? But nope. She kicked me and the turkey out. She did take my leftovers, though."

It's About Time

"Oh, my God." Mary is laughing hard. "I'm starting to like this woman. What did the sign say?"

"It said 'This turkey is sorry'. Clever, huh?"

"Which turkey was sorry?" Mary can barely control her laughter. "You *are* a charmer, James. I'll hand you that. I take it she wasn't buying, huh? It sounds to me like she didn't want to go to your house. Have you ever asked her over before?"

"No. But why would that be a problem? By now she should know I'm not dangerous."

"I don't know. You have to ask her. Tell me, how do you feel about her?"

"Aargh. I knew you would ask me that. I like her. I enjoy her company." There was that phrase again.

"Really? You enjoy her company? That sounds like a seriously watered-down version if you ask me."

"Okay. God, nothing gets past you. Honestly? I'm falling for her. But I'm worried that she will never want to be in a relationship again in her life. She's had a rough time of it and seems determined to stay friends. Period. But the part that chaps my butt is when she withdraws. You know me. If you want to kill me, don't talk to me."

"I am very happy for you, James! It's about time you found someone you can get this worked up about. My advice, Mr. Talker, is to talk with her. What else can you do? You have to tell her how you feel. Otherwise, what's the point? Are you just going to sit on your hands and pretend you don't care? I can't see you pulling that off. In the meantime, get real. All of this playing-it-safe bullshit is stupid. In matters of the heart, none of us are safe, and it can't be any other way. Talk to her. If you want her to go deep, you have to go deep. And you damn well better be straight with her. Don't push her, you big brute. Find that sweet spot between push and indifference. I don't know what else to tell ya."

Mary is right. As long as I hold back, I have no business expecting anything different from Bess.

I change out of work clothes into cozy flannel pants and a well-worn UMass tee shirt. I stretch out on the sunroom couch with a glass of wine and the new Grisham novel from the library. After the first couple of pages, I give up. My mind keeps wandering back to Bess and the conversation with Mary. Not Grisham's fault. What *is* going on with Bess and the turkey tragedy? Mary is right. It looks like Bess didn't want to come to my house. But why? I have to talk with her. Be direct. I want to text her one more time but decide against it. I drain the wine, shut off the lights, and go to bed.

In the morning, fresh and rested, I am no clearer about the path forward with Bess. But it's not a one-man show. I can't have all the answers, and the only thing I am good at fixing is clocks.

Keep your feet on the ground, James, I tell myself. I wait until I am fully caffeinated before I text Bess that I want to talk, and I ask if I can come over after work. I promise to bring Talisker to help the conversation flow. I wait. And wait. My mother said a watched pot doesn't boil. This seems to be true for texts as well. Just as I am ready to leave for the shop, I hear the familiar ping. I lunge for the phone. It's the dentist reminding me of an appointment. *Shit. Really? Patience, James.* Mary said not to push. Bess will get back to me. She always does. No point in

It's About Time

getting neurotic about this. I grab my keys from the counter and head to work.

About an hour later, I am engrossed in repairing an antique clock. It ran but didn't keep good time. I promised to evaluate the problem and provide an estimate. In the middle of gears and springs, I get a text from Bess. Hallelujah! She said yes to talking, no to her place, and please leave the whiskey at home. Well, okay then. The woman knows her mind. Several texts later we decide on meeting at my shop after work. Perfect. So, now the question is, what do I say?

Hillary Gauvreau Oat

CHAPTER 3

Fog

Bess

The beach is fogged in, and the breeze brings rolling swirls of mist off the water. I like fog because it feels mystical and mysterious. Today I would like to walk into the mist and disappear. James and I agreed to have a conversation about turning down his dinner invitation. He suggested my place with the bottle of whiskey, thinking it would ease the flow of conversation. I was afraid my resolve to keep some distance might dissolve in alcohol and said no to both ideas. James honestly thought those were good ideas, and I can't fault him for that. In another universe, it might have been perfect. But I need to be clear-headed and sober while I try to explain myself. We compromised, agreeing to meet at his shop after hours. In the meantime, I have been thinking and driving myself crazy. Lost in a fog of thoughts, I stumble over a piece of driftwood.

"Dammit," I curse the wood and give it a kick. I will be happy when this conversation is over. It's giving me a headache. And now my foot hurts.

As I walk the half-mile length of the beach, I remember all the other times I've had serious conversations. A shiver goes through me. The four words I dread the most are, "We need to talk." It never means anything good. James was right when he said I don't have to prepare a legal brief, but it's what I do.

Hillary Gauvreau Oat

High-stakes conversations rattle me, and my mind goes blank. Later, I think of all the things I should've said. If I prepare a script, it's easier to get my thoughts out. I wish I could be spontaneous but haven't dared. The conversation with James needs to be clear and organized. Right now, I have no clue what to say.

There are piles of rocks and boulders where the beach meets the base of the bluff. I pick a rock I can sit on even though I'm getting cold. The waves lap gently against the sandy shore, and a seagull screams at me from overhead. Sorry buddy, no snacks for you today. How will I present my case to James? Maybe I have nothing to worry about. Maybe he will be calm and reasonable, and we will exchange our thoughts and come to an agreeable solution. He will understand my position and respect me for it. He, like me, has no intention of getting romantically involved. We will laugh at the silly misunderstanding and then go to dinner. That could happen. I'm probably making a bigger deal out of this than it is. He merely asked me to eat leftovers, for God's sake. The real problem is that I'm at odds with myself. I'm holding back feelings, and the thought of revealing them scares the shit out of me.

The sun is starting to warm the air and burn off the fog. I lift myself off the rock, stuff my hands in my pockets, and start back along the beach to my condo. I need a distraction. I call my friend, Virginia. At a time like this, she is just what I need.

"Virginia! Hey, what's up? Want to meet me for lunch?"

"Bess! Perfect timing. I'm starving. Now?" Virginia lives in town and I've known her my whole life. She is wise, and fun, and will certainly help me burn off some fog.

It's About Time

"I am ready when you are. We will call it brunch! How about Charlie's in fifteen minutes?"

"You got it. See you soon." Virginia disconnects, and I step up my pace, ducking into the condo for cash and car keys. I park in Charlie's lot and check for messages before going inside. Nothing new from James. I feel better already. Virginia pulls in as I get out of my car. I wave and we walk to the entrance together.

Charlie's is a large space with a lunch counter and two separate rooms with booths and tables. The aroma of strong coffee permeates the air at all times. We slide into a booth and order Charlie's delicious all-day breakfast special. Virginia is a few years younger than I am which puts her in the forty-nine to fifty range. Her long auburn curly hair is pulled back into a messy bun. Freckles dot her nose, and her cheeks are flushed pink. An extrovert extraordinaire, she is always up for adventure and any kind of social gathering. Her husband, Bob, is a great guy, and that shows there are some of those around. They have been married for almost thirty years, brought up two kids, and are now expecting their first grandchild.

"How exciting!" I say, "I remember when my first grandchild was on the way. We could hardly wait to see that little guy. Do you know if it's pink or blue?"

"No, we don't want to know. Two more months, and then I will fly out to Tucson to be with Gabe for the birth. So far, everything is looking good. But, dear friend, what about you? You have a glimmer in your eye." Virginia lowers her red-framed glasses, scrutinizing me.

"You read me like a book," I laugh.

Hillary Gauvreau Oat

"True. So, spill!"

"Well . . ." I start slowly "There is this guy."
"I knew it! You have that look about you. Who is he?" Virginia leans toward me to get all the juicy details.

"Before you get all excited, it's not what you think. We're just friends. So, here is what happened." I fill Virginia in on the dinner invitation, turkey, and my freaked-out reaction.

"Oh, my God!" Virginia howls with laughter. "He put the turkey at your feet with a little sign? That's adorable. What did the sign say? Did you let him in?"

"It said, 'This turkey is sorry.' And no, I did not!" I feel my cheeks get hot.

"You're blushing. Oh my, someone has a crush," Virginia teases.

"I do not. I have sworn off dating and romance and everything that goes along with it. Not that we are doing that, but I'm afraid, if I go to his house, one thing will lead to another and another and another. You know how that story goes. I do not need or want a romance."

"Who is he? Do I know him?"

"Maybe you do. But you have to promise to keep this quiet. Please?"

"Cross my heart! I solemnly swear and all that shit. Come on? Who?"

It's About Time

Our food comes, and I tell the story between bites. I start with the crash and burn on the sidewalk and the knight-in-shining-armor rescue.

"How long ago was that?" Virginia demands. "How come this is the first I am hearing about this guy?"

"Hmmm, maybe a year or so. I kept him under wraps because I don't want people asking questions. Virginia!" I flash a stern look. "Even though we hang out, and it's fun, it's friends only. Until this whole issue about going to his house came up. Honestly, Virginia, I freaked out. Tonight, we are talking about it. I have no idea what I am going to say. I don't want to come off like some nut job."

"If he's been hanging with you for this long, he already knows you're a nut job." Virginia laughs while I feign outrage. "But only of the nicest variety. Seriously, you tell him what you just told me. You freaked out. The conversation should flow from there if he is at all interested in knowing why."

"You're right, of course. Keep it simple. What scares me is how easy it would be to slip into a romance. I don't trust myself."

"You like him!" Virginia grins.

"Yes, I will admit that. I do like him. A little. It would be awful if he doesn't think of me . . . you know . . . in that way. What if he laughs? I might not want a relationship, but I want him to want one. See? I don't know what I'm doing. I'm tied in knots."

"*Who* is he? Tell me!"

"You know the clock shop?" I ask.
"James Ogilvie?" Virginia asks, her blue eyes lighting up.

I nod yes. "He seems like a nice man. Relatively normal, whatever that is. He's smart, communicates well, is funny and considerate. So, do you know him? Any red flags you're aware of?"

Virginia finishes the last bite of pancake, pushes her plate aside, and looks me in the eye. "As far as I know, he is everything you just said. He is kind of cute in an Old Spice-tweedy way. I don't know him personally because I never got knocked down in front of his shop." She smiles. "But wait a sec . . . you have sworn off love? For the rest of your life? Are you serious?" She is incredulous. The waitress comes to take our plates and refill our coffee with a slight smile on her face. She must have overheard that last bit.

"Are you seriously asking me that after my last marriage fiasco? Relationships haven't worked out for me. I'm done. If James and I get romantically involved, it could ruin a beautiful friendship."

"It could also be the best thing that has ever happened. For both of you. Seriously, have you considered that? Why must we always go to the dark side?" Virginia and I get our checks, slide out of the booth, and pay for our meals. In the parking lot, we linger by my car talking.

"The bottom line, Virginia, is that I am scared. What if I blow it? What if James is normal but I'm not? What if he just seems nice and, then, when I am hooked, he turns into a narcissistic asshole? What if it screws up my life? *Again*! I just started feeling comfortable and happy."

It's About Time

"Honey, we're all scared. And nothing is guaranteed. So, do you want to play it safe and be alone or take a chance on love? Your choice, and you know I will love you no matter what. Aren't you just a tiny bit curious about what it would be like, especially with what you learned from the last go around? I can tell you are attracted to this guy. But, be that as it may, for now just talk with him like you talk to me. Take the pressure off yourself to do it right or perfectly or whatever it is you're trying to do. Do you want me to send Bob to check him out? We must have an old clock around the house to use as a decoy. Bob has good Spidey sense. You know that sixth sense Spiderman has?"

"Maybe it would be good to get Bob's take on him. Let me see how tonight goes and I'll let you know if there is any point in sending Spiderman in. Think about me, okay? I will let you know what happens."

"You better let me know! I want a full report!" We hug each other, and Virginia walks to her car. When the car starts, she rolls down her window and yells, "I think you should go for it! Just my opinion."

"You don't even know him!" I yell back and laugh. My first client is due in an hour so I drive to my office to get my head in the right professional place. This day is lasting forever.

Hillary Gauvreau Oat

It's About Time

CHAPTER 4

The Talk

Bess

Focusing on my work is a break from thinking about James but, after the last client, my nerves return. I guess it's true that we teach what we need to learn. Almost every client today was struggling with an anxiety issue. I might as well take the advice I dish out and face it directly. Even though I'm early, I go straight to James's shop. Let's get this over with. The late afternoon sky is gray and threatening rain. I hope that as soon as I see James I will relax, the sky will clear, and everything will be okay. Fingers crossed.

I arrive at It's About Time, take a deep breath, and turn the doorknob. The door is locked. I am ready to sprint, and now I'm stuck at the starting line. Crap. Lights are on, but I don't see James. No text messages. I knock but get no response. My stress is redlining, and I don't need more, so I text him.

Text to JO: "At IAT. Locked. Should I call paramedics? Wink emoji." Send.

I wait for a few seconds, and it seems like an hour. PING. James is on his way and asks me not to leave. Fortunately, the entryway is recessed and large enough for me to tuck myself inside out of a sudden burst of rain. This is the first time I'm going into a serious conversation feeling unclear and unprepared. I'm not sure if that's progress or a potential disaster. Where is James? Suddenly, he appears, loping around the corner wearing his bright yellow slicker and carrying a pizza box. I'm happy to see his face and the pizza. I move aside as he unlocks the door, and we go in. James hangs our wet coats on a coat tree and fires up the space heater.

"Hey. Glad you're here. I thought you might be hungry, so I ran around the corner to pick up a pizza. You're early. I'm sorry you had to wait in the rain." James bustles around grabbing napkins, paper plates, bottles of spring water, and the ever-present whiskey. I settle into the now familiar antique chair, shivering from the raw weather and nerves. James pours two shots of whiskey and sets one in front of me.

"I know you said no whiskey but, after being out in the rain, this might be welcome. Your decision." James holds up the shot glass offering his usual toast, and downs the shot. He seems upbeat while serving the pizza, without a care in the world.

Am I making this drama up in my head? This meeting certainly doesn't seem to bother him, and that is disappointing. I would like to think it is serious enough for him to get a little stressed out. Despite my vow to stay sober and clear-headed, I sip the whiskey, hoping it will help me relax and warm up. It is still as smoky as I remember and burns going down my throat. Between the pizza, the whiskey, and the heater, I relax a little. After we shove the leftover pizza aside, James rolls closer in his desk chair and opens the conversation.

"Bess, I have a feeling that I've offended you. What's up? Let me have it. I can take it like a man, whatever that means." James smiles and waits.

It's About Time

I take a deep breath and slowly exhale, my heart pounding. I remember Virginia's advice and start there because I have nothing better. "The truth is I freaked out. I was scared to go to your house." There is a lot more to be said, but that is an honest, vulnerable, and simple opening. I am shivering.

"Okay. Why?" James asks, his brow furrowed in concern.

"I mean it isn't because I think you're dangerous or anything. I'm afraid it means our friendship is changing into something I'm not ready for. Explaining why that's scary is complicated."

James wheels a little closer, listening intently. My mother's voice in my head admonishes me not to bother anyone, so I try to make my story brief.

"I value our friendship. A lot! I pumped the brakes to maintain the status quo, friendly and casual."

"Casual? Is that what you think we are?" James looks hurt.

"Oh, jeez. That didn't come out right. Not casual at all, and that is what I am afraid of. Okay, that doesn't sound much better, does it?"

"I'm not sure. Keep going and I will let you know." James suggests.

"I was trying to protect the friendship we have. My plan was for us to keep some distance, you know, boundaries. I had this idea in my head that if I didn't go to your house, it would keep us out of trouble. I'm sorry I never actually verbalized any of that. It must have left you guessing."

Hillary Gauvreau Oat

"Trouble? What kind of trouble?"

"Romantic trouble. In all the time I have known you this never came up so I thought you felt the same way. I should have checked that out, huh? When you asked me to come over for dinner I freaked. Remember, I said I couldn't let you in?" James nods yes and winces slightly. "I was afraid to let you into my condo but, more than that, I am afraid of getting closer. And now, I feel really stupid because I could be way off and imagining all of it." I take a sip of whiskey for courage.

James pours himself another shot. "Well, I know you're not stupid, and I completely understand a fear like that. I don't want to risk what we have, either, unless we can have something even better. You did leave me guessing, but now it makes sense. Remember, I said I was a mess, too, and that you could dump your crap and we would sort it out together?" My turn to nod, yes. "I meant it. I still mean it. Thank you for talking to me about this. I never would have figured this out on my own. You have no idea what was going through my mind, all the possible scenarios."

"Tell me about it! I thought about some pretty crazy scenarios, too. James, I have been seduced into opening myself up to some pretty terrible people. It makes me very careful. Too careful maybe. After my divorce from Chad, I vowed to never be that vulnerable again. And yet, here I am. Vulnerable and drinking scotch." I roll my eyes. James is quiet.

"I have been through some awful shit too, so I get where you're coming from. *And* I need you to know that shutting me out is the most painful thing you can do to me. I get that you need space to think. I will try to be patient with that but, no matter what you are thinking or feeling, I need to hear about it. Okay?"

It's About Time

James smiles, stands up, and pulls me out of the chair, wrapping his arms around me. He's warm and smells slightly of wood smoke. His heartbeat is strong against my chest. He holds me for a long time until I finally stop shivering. He didn't run away, tell me to buck up, or try to fix anything. When I sit back down James smiles at me and starts cleaning up.

"Are we done?" I ask.

"Not by a long shot. We just got started. Bess, can we please go to my house?" James holds up his hands to signal he understands the problem. "I know that is what started this. I get it, and I won't pressure you. I'm wondering if maybe talking about it has changed your mind. I want to sit by my woodstove and warm up. Take a minute to consider the idea before you dismiss it, okay? I'll start a fire, we can sip some tea, and spend as much time as we need getting this sorted out. I promise, no romance." James waits for me to respond.

"Tea? What, no whiskey?" I tease.

"I have whatever is your pleasure. Cow's milk, oat milk, coffee, tea, whiskey, water, seltzer, margaritas. I run a full-service establishment!"

"Okay." Deep breath in and out. "Yes, I will go home with you."

Not giving me time to change my mind, James grabs our coats, flips off the heater and the lights, and we head out into the rain. He opens the passenger door of his Ford F-150 and, after only a slight hesitation, I climb in. The truck starts smoothly, and the mellow voice of Tony Bennett comes through the speakers. We are quiet on the way to his house which is a short drive outside of town. His cottage, situated on the shore of a pond, is covered in weathered gray cedar shingles. The shutters and front door are painted the color of a tropical ocean. He pulls into the driveway, shuts off the truck, opens his door, and looks at me.

"Sure you're okay with this?"

I nod yes, but I'm honestly not sure. It's a short walk to the back deck and the kitchen door. The lights come on automatically, and I notice James has a security camera. Once inside, we are in a cozy sunroom that leads into the kitchen. He tosses his jacket over a white wicker chair, and I do the same. The room is spacious with a wood stove in the corner, just as he said. Matching upholstered furniture is grouped near the stove. A view of the lake is framed by large windows and the silhouettes of trees. This is a holy sanctuary, for sure. I make use of the guest bathroom and, when I come out, James is busy in the kitchen boiling water for tea and arranging biscuits on a University of North Carolina Tar Heels plate.

"You were serious about tea!"

"Yes, I was. Unless you want something else? I didn't ask, but I thought you were pretty clear about whiskey."

"Tea is great, thanks. I guess I never thought of you as a tea drinker. That plate is pretty manly. What's the connection to UNC?" I ask.

"My sister lives in North Carolina, and she thinks everyone is a Tar Heels fan." James rolls his eyes.

The updated kitchen has a beachy feel with white cabinetry and blue-green granite countertops that remind me of the sea.

It's About Time

An island in the middle of the room has four tall chairs lined up along one side. I carry the plate of cookies and follow James into the sunroom. He puts mugs of steaming tea on the coffee table within our reach. I nibble on shortbread cookies while he makes a fire in the wood stove. Once we feel the heat, we get comfortable on opposite ends of the couch. The spicy aroma of chai fills the air as we sit in the glow of firelight. If I didn't know better, this could be pretty damn romantic. James breaks the silence first.

"What you said about fear and trust is all familiar territory to me, too." James begins telling his story. He met his wife, Caroline, when they were at UMass grad school. He acquired a teaching certificate, and she got an MFA in music composition. "Caroline was brilliant and magical in her creativity. I was mesmerized by her and, when she agreed to go out with me, I was overjoyed. Within a year, I proposed and she said, yes."

James describes their first years together as fun and exciting. Caroline was making connections in the music industry and had several of her songs picked up by well-known producers. "I was content to be teaching at a private school in Hartford with quiet nights at home. Caroline was ambitious, traveling and meeting some pretty accomplished music people. Then we got pregnant with our son, Andrew. He was a surprise but a very welcome one. A new baby, no sleep, and work demands created a lot of stress. Our relationship grew tense, but I knew we would get through it. Then when Andy was two, we were expecting again. Another boy that we named Thomas. Caroline wasn't thrilled about it because she was eager to get on with her career. I did everything I could to take care of things at home because I wanted her to be happy. After a few years, her personality changed. I didn't understand what was going on. She was self-absorbed, angry, and blaming me for everything. Once Thomas was old enough for kindergarten, Caroline resumed her career, traveling more and more. She was rarely home, often in the house just long enough to make plans for her next trip. I missed the woman I fell in love with but, each time she left, the tension lifted and I was relieved. Then guilty for feeling relieved. You know? We drifted along like that for years. One day, she came home from a trip and blasted me, calling me a stupid, lazy loser."

"Ouch."

"No shit. But that wasn't the worst of it." Anger flushes James's face crimson, and his hands curl into fists as he tells his story. "She said she had other men in her life. Men that had way more to offer than I did. I offered her freedom, love, a steady income, and two beautiful children that I took care of. What was more than that? I told her to go live with them because I was done. In that moment, I wanted the earth to open up and swallow her so I would never have to look at her face again. Needless to say, we got into a huge fight, and I filed for divorce not long after. The pain was excruciating. So, I understand hurt and rage." James pauses to collect his thoughts. "I couldn't feel that amount of pain every day. I became depressed. I needed to do something to keep myself together for the boys. A teacher at school said he was worried about me. I must have looked pretty bad. He gave me the name of a psychotherapist who saved my life, believe me."

James tells me he hired a lawyer, but neither of them was pushing for the divorce. Then, when Andrew was in his senior year of high school, Caroline came home after a long absence. She looked like a rack of bones. "Turned out to be stage four lung cancer. We started the rounds of doctors and treatments.

It's About Time

The prognosis wasn't good and within one horrible year, she was gone. I stayed by her. I loved her. What else could I do?" James looks at me, pain written all over his face. "When we knew this was the end of her life, I hoped we could find our way back to the love we started with. But it didn't happen." He bends over, holding his face in his hands. I slide over to sit beside him, resting my hand on his shoulder.

"I am so sorry, James. I had no idea." I grab my bag and rummage for tissues.

"No one does. People think of me as the poor widower who lost his loving wife and best friend. Honestly, I felt enormous relief when she died, quickly followed by more guilt." I hand James a tissue, and he dabs at his eyes. "That was eight years ago. So, now you know that you are not the only one who is scared. I dated off and on, but it never went anywhere. Like you, I don't know that I want another relationship. What I do know is that I enjoy our time together. Hanging out with you, talking, and laughing feels comforting. I like it and don't want to mess that up."

By now it's dark outside, and the fire in the wood stove is glowing embers. James pokes at it and throws a log on before coming back to sit next to me on the couch.

"Your turn. I want to know your story." James waits. I try to think about what and how to share. "Bess, you don't have to if you don't want to. I don't mean to make it sound like I am keeping score."

"No, it's okay. I'll tell you about Chad, my most recent divorce and last straw."

Hillary Gauvreau Oat

"I was swept off my feet by Chad and I loved it! In hindsight, there were red flags but I wanted the fairy tale love story so I overlooked them. I thought we had it all . . . love, fun, and common interests. He told me all the single women he knew would be jealous of me, and I bought it. Now, I'm embarrassed to admit that I was an easy target. He made me feel special which was something I wanted my whole life." I described getting engaged and our gorgeous wedding that was literally like a fairy tale.

"That made what followed very confusing. Looking back, I never felt comfortable around Chad but thought it was my anxiety issue. I am really angry at the people who knew who he was and didn't warn me about him. But I was in love and probably wouldn't have listened anyway. My prince arrived in a golden carriage after I had survived the heroine's journey of single life. It was so perfect. When Chad stopped doing thoughtful things for me, I figured we were settling into real life. But, as time went on, it became clear that wasn't it. The man I married never existed. It was all a game to him. With Chad, my pain was about what he didn't do, which is very hard to explain. People asked me why I left him. I felt like such a jerk when I couldn't clearly point to A, B and C that were deal breakers. The biggest betrayal was discovering he never loved me. Actually, I don't think he is capable of love at all. He didn't talk to me, leaving me guessing constantly. He was cold and distant. He was really good at dropping hints that made me feel insecure. I thought I was too sensitive. I got into therapy because I was suffering and didn't know how to put words to any of it. Thank God I had a terrific therapist who helped me understand what was going on. I knew I couldn't stay in the marriage and survive. So, I left. Maybe someday you will know all my history. This is enough for now."

It's About Time

James takes my hand, and I hold it tight. "I'm so sorry, Bess. I understand how awful that is."

"Do you really get it? I'm used to defending myself because people who have not experienced this kind of thing really can't imagine it. People think Chad is a great guy because that is what he wants them to think. I thought that too, so I get it. It's only behind closed doors that the demon comes out. And, if I have to hear one more person tell me that he was always nice to them and they aren't taking sides, I will fucking scream."

"I hear ya, Bess. My situation was not the same, but I also had to deal with insensitive assholes. It hurts a lot. That's why I kept my mouth shut."

"Yes, it does. I'm relieved you understand. I am not willing to put up with bullshit anymore."

"I'm with you there." James smiles at me. "Back at the shop, you said you were afraid our relationship was changing. It sounded like you wondered if that was your imagination and how I felt about that."

"Yes. That's true. I was afraid you were going to hit on me. I'm embarrassed to admit that." I laugh. "It seems silly now saying that after having this conversation. It shows you the kind of men I have known."

"It's been a while since I've been accused of that. However, after tonight I do think our friendship is changing. We took off our armor and revealed more of ourselves." James says, "There is more to friendship than a few laughs and a pizza. Am I right? Can I hear an amen?"

"Amen, brother," I say, and we high-five.

"Tonight, we got to know each other better. Trust each other a little bit more. My respect and affection for you, Bess Parker, is growing." In the glow of the fire, James takes my hand in his and looks at me. "Taking our time getting to know each other is a good thing. I'm on board with that. However, going full-stop will not work for me. My heart has been hermetically sealed long enough. You're going to know my feelings, like it or not. I want our relationship to evolve into whatever it will be. No holds barred! Is ours a happily ever after love story, or a forever friendship? I don't know. But, please, let's not hold back—and just see what happens. Am I freaking you out?"

"Okay. Freaked out, yes, but in a good way. What do we do now? People are already whispering about us."

James grins. "I think we keep 'em guessing. That'll be fun."

James and I lean back into the couch cushions, holding hands, and that feels natural in this moment. The flames flicker and cast light and shadow around the room. I feel a huge burden lifted off of me.

"You know, I didn't sleep last night thinking about this conversation. You're right about me presenting a legal brief. It's a habit. This time, I had nothing." I smile. "Turned out to be a pretty interesting experience. My affection for you is growing, too. Not romance, mind you. Affection."

"Yup. I can hear the movie announcer's voiceover saying, 'How brave can James and Bess be in a relationship?'" I laugh at his dramatic impression. "We will avoid all traditional roles and let nature take its course. We should probably have some

It's About Time

guidelines, like no making out." James laughs a full belly laugh. "Or not. What do you think?" he asks with a twinkle in his eye.

"I agree. No making out unless it's CPR!" It's a relief to laugh. "And we can go to each other's houses, but no sleepovers! And never say we are dating. No dating."

"Dating? Horrors." James laughs again. "Okay, it's getting late. I probably should get you home before people really talk." We stand and, without speaking a word, hold each other. "Good night, moon," James says, referring to the sweet children's story by Margaret Wise Brown. I lean back to see his face and ask where that came from.

"It just popped into my head." James pulls me back against him, and I respond with, "Good night room. I was going to go with Seuss but decided not to break the thread."

"I appreciate that. Good literature should not be messed with."

After James drops me off at my condo, I text Virginia to let her know I'm home. She calls immediately, wanting to know every detail. Am I okay? Did it go well? Are we still dating?

"We are not dating, never were, and still not. Let's get that straight. It's a long story, and I promise to fill you in completely after I get a good night's sleep. For now, I will say that, yes, it went well, and we are still friends. Close friends."

"I am so relieved. Proud of you Bess. Love always finds a way."

"Thanks, Virginia. Don't scare me with the L word. Talk tomorrow."

Hillary Gauvreau Oat

It's About Time

CHAPTER 5

Mac and Cheese

Bess

Light is filtering around the edges of the window shade, so I know it's early morning. A dream about driving on a desolate, icy, unpaved trail woke me up. The trail was steep, an uphill climb, that was covered in frozen packed snow with dark patches of ground showing through. There was a drop-off on my left with no guardrail. The mountains were towering and jagged like the Alps. The trail clung to the wall of a sheer cliff on my right. Small loose rocks tumbled down and landed harmlessly in front of me. A section high up was coming loose and I knew it was a potential avalanche, but it didn't fall. When I got to the top of the incline, the road seemed to disappear. It could be an optical illusion. I walked up to the edge to check it out. The crest was a razor-sharp ridge of rock, too sharp and narrow to stand on. The height was dizzying with an abyss on the other side. There was nowhere to go, so I slowly and carefully went back down the way I came. During this perilous adventure, I was cautious but not afraid which I thought was odd because I don't like heights or driving on icy snow.

I prop myself up in bed to write down what I remember. Maybe it's simply a reminder of my fear of heights. Or a warning that I am in a potentially perilous situation? That feels more accurate. I'm not in a physically dangerous situation that I know of but, emotionally, it feels dangerous. I can't help but connect the dream to James and being at the edge of my comfort zone with him.

This dream reminds me of how scary and out-of-control getting close to James feels. A sense of foreboding is hanging on. I hope it isn't a premonition. I swing my legs out from under the covers and sit on the edge of the bed. Today is Friday, and I have things to do. James and I reserve Friday nights for dinner at his place or mine. We eat and talk, sharing as deeply as we can. It's an attempt to stay ahead of unresolved issues that can poison a friendship. After that, we get to enjoy the rest of the evening however we like. It has been a month since we decided to let our friendship evolve without holding ourselves back. We are letting nature take its course, albeit slowly and cautiously. Tonight's dinner is at my place.

After work and a quick trip to the grocery store, I get home and change my clothes, pulling on jeans and a sweater. It's getting close to 5:00, so James will be arriving soon. I turn on the gas fireplace, light candles, and open the French doors a crack to let a whiff of sea air in. Normally, I like to have everything ready when guests arrive but James feels less like company these days and more like he belongs. While I study the mac and cheese recipe, I hear the door open and James steps into the foyer holding two bottles of wine.

"Hi Bess. TGIF! I didn't know if we would want red or white tonight, so I brought both," James says.

"Wonderful. White is the winner. We are celebrating with lobster mac and cheese tonight."

James gets a couple of wine glasses and works on opening the bottle of cold Pinot Grigio. "So, what are we celebrating?" he asks.

It's About Time

"It's been a month since our agreement, and so far, so good. I'm always up for a celebration."
James hands me my wine, and we get down to the business of prepping ingredients and cooking dinner. He grates the cheese, and I boil water for the pasta and start the sauce. Side by side, we cook and sip wine until the dish finally goes in the oven. While the mac and cheese bakes, we set the table and sit down.

"I am starving. How long does that stuff take? How was your day?" James inquires.

"You're always starving. I don't know where you put all that pizza you eat. I would be big as a house. It takes about half an hour. My day was good. It went by fast. I had a weird dream this morning, though." I fill him in on the precarious snowy climb up the mountain. "What do you think it means?" I ask.

"Search me. I don't pay attention to dreams. Mostly, I think it's just the brain resetting."

"Well, aren't you the pragmatic one? Sure, dreams can be a reset, but they can also be messages from the subconscious. The challenge is figuring out what the message is." I shake my head. "I can see by your glazed-over expression that you are not interested. Did you have a tough day?"

"Sorry, I guess I went elsewhere. Got some things on my mind." James shakes his head like a dog shaking off water. "I am back!"

An antique dealer asked James to get a bunch of clocks running and keeping proper time so they could be sold. If it works out James will have a regular gig with the guy. "It's a good contract but takes a lot of time," he chuckles. "Get it? Takes a lot of time."

I roll my eyes. "I get it. Is that what's on your mind? Work? Anything I can help with?"

"Nah. I can handle it. It's just stuff."

The oven timer interrupts the conversation. I lift the casserole out of the oven and set it on top of the stove. We fill our plates in the kitchen and carry them and a green salad to the table.

"Oh my God, this is amazing, Bess. It will be a hard act to follow at Chez James next Friday."

"Not that we are competing! I hate it when dinners start simple and gradually escalate until we are scouring *Bon Appetit* for new recipes with exotic ingredients. It takes all the fun out of it. As long as you don't serve pizza, I'll be happy. This dinner probably has a month's worth of calories and cholesterol in it so it will hold me for a while. Don't expect to see it again any time soon."

James and I chat amiably through dinner about work, kids, and the latest gossip on Main Street. Whatever is on his mind has been set it aside for now. After dinner, we refill our wine glasses and plop down on the couch in front of the fireplace. James cues up relaxing smooth jazz on his phone that comes through my Bluetooth speaker. I lean back into the couch cushions, put my feet up and let the soft, bluesy voice of Norah Jones wash over me.

"So? Got anything you want to discuss tonight?" James asks. "Since we are celebrating, I am kinda hoping you say no. I

It's About Time

know how important this time is to you, but I would just like to enjoy tonight."

"Well, I do have something to talk about, but it's no big deal, so you can relax. I am wondering how you feel about coming out of the closet and socializing with friends. Remember my friend, Virginia? You met her at the grocery store a while ago. She is dying of curiosity and would love to have us over for dinner. She and her husband, Bob, are great people and I think you will like them."

"Sure. Let's do it. Sounds like fun."

"Okay, great. I will let them know. It does put some pressure on us, though."

"Pressure? How so?" James asks.

"Well, it's couples stuff. One couple invites another couple over for dinner. Know what I mean? I keep telling them we are just friends, but I'm not sure they buy it. Knowing them, you will be gently interrogated because they think there is more going on than we admit to. You may want to prepare some snappy answers."

"It doesn't bother me a bit. Bring it on. I will bring my resume and references just in case."

"Very funny. Resume not required, but references? Hmmm . . . maybe," I tease. "I guess I'm just a little nervous about it even though they are really easy, close friends," I tell James.

"I can understand that. They are important to you, so what they think is important, too. I promise to behave myself."

"Wonderful. I will keep you posted about the plans. So, what about you? Do you have friends you want us to hang out with?" I ask.
James gets serious and carefully selects his words. "There is someone you may meet, but we won't be hanging out."

"Ok. But why? Who is he?"

"It's not a he. It's a she named Maura.

"A woman?" I ask, the pitch of my voice rising slightly.

"Yes, a woman. I have known her since college but haven't seen her in over a year. She texted me today that she is coming to visit." James is agitated and looks away.

"Okay, sure. I'm willing to meet her. How come I haven't heard about her before this?" I'm trying not to sound prickly but James kept this person under wraps for a year. That surprises me. What's up with that? He has a right to all the women he wants in his life, but why hasn't he mentioned her? Our enjoyable evening is taking a downward turn.

James looks at me quizzically. "Why does it feel like you're slamming down the storm shutters?"

"Huh? Oh. Sorry. Just thinking." I'm not letting my fondness for James blind me to sketchy behavior, if I can help it. "We agreed to be completely honest, yes? No matter how messy? Dump it out, you said." James's eyes narrow. "To be completely honest, I'm surprised to find out now, after all this time, about a significant woman in your life." My voice is a lot

It's About Time

calmer than I'm feeling. The recording in my head tells me that I'm too sensitive and insecure, nothing is going on, blah blah blah. In other words, don't look at the man behind the curtain. Bullshit. Something is going on. I can smell it. "It seems strange she wasn't mentioned in all the stories you told about UMass. It makes me curious. Why haven't you ever mentioned her?" I squeeze words out of my constricting throat. James is pensive while I wait nervously for him to say something. Suddenly, he throws his hands down, slapping his thighs, and launches up off the couch.

"This is exactly why I didn't bring up Maura. I don't need to explain myself and deal with a jealous woman. Maura and I are friends. That's it. There is nothing else to say."

"Whoa, now look who's throwing down the storm shutters." I stand and face James. "You never *need* to explain yourself, but we are friends, so talking is part of the deal. You're dealing with a jealous woman? Ouch. Where did that come from?"

"That's how you're acting! You can't tell me what to do and who to be friends with."

I watch James angrily stride around the room.

"Wow. Really? I call bullshit." I watch James pace. "Where in this conversation did I tell you who you could be friends with? Huh? Whether I like her or not, I would never tell you not to be friends with Maura. That is totally up to you. You know my story, and how important trust is to me. Why not mention a woman who has been in your life since college? Why keep her a secret?" The volume of my voice is rising. "Can we talk about this or are you just going to ride around on your high horse?

Level with me, James. Don't blame me for whatever is going on with you." James huffs, still not looking at me. "You don't want me to shut you out, so don't shut me out, either."

"I don't want to talk about it. Jeez, Bess. I'm not shutting you out. It's no big deal. Let it go." James glares at me.

"You don't want to talk about it, but you're not shutting me out?" I shake my head. James is hiding something. Since we are only friends, do I have a right to ask questions and feel these feelings? Am I supposed to keep quiet like a good girl while he makes proclamations and keeps secrets? That's old familiar territory to me and not the kind of friendship I want to have. I am so fucking tired of making sure everyone is comfortable while I twist in the wind. If I am not allowed to ask questions and share how I feel, then what the fuck are we doing together? No more twisting.

"I call bullshit again. The way you're acting, it seems like a *very* big deal." I take a deep breath and turn down my volume. "James, I trust you have your reasons for not talking about Maura. I hope, once you calm down, that you will tell me what they are. There is more to this story than what you're telling me. I have never seen you like this. If we are going to stay friends, we have to be honest with each other. Take time to think about it, but I can't let it slide."

"Bullshit to your bullshit," James shouts. "I don't need to calm down. This is insane. I'm not going to be interrogated by you." He grabs his coat and leaves, slamming the door.

It's About Time

CHAPTER 6

Trouble

James

I run out of Bess's condo like I am fleeing a demon. I am. A demon from my past named Maura. Sprinting to the truck, I mutter repeatedly that I'm sorry. The list of things I am sorry for is long. I hate how I acted with Bess but couldn't help it. When Bess brought up adding friends to our circle it was the perfect time to mention Maura. But then she started asking questions and I didn't want to talk about Maura. Bess wouldn't let it go so I took the coward's way out, pushed her away with a ridiculous display of manly outrage, and ran. I get in the driver's seat of my truck and lock the doors, breathing hard. *Shit. Fuck. Shit. Shit. Shit.* I curse pounding the steering wheel with my fists. I reach for the door handle ready to go back in to apologize and talk this over. That is the sensible thing to do but I stop myself. I have to know what Maura is up to first. I lean back against the headrest and close my eyes. Bess is right. Unless you have gone through something like this no one understands. She might be the one person who gets it but instead of giving her a chance, I ran away. What the fuck is wrong with me?

Maura's text message says she is already waiting at my house, so I don't want to go there. Putting that reunion off is the best I can hope for. I got used to a peaceful, easy life in the year of Maura's absence. Knowing Bess drove Maura right out of my mind. Denial, I suspect, because the woman has been like gum on my shoe for years. People who have never been fucked over by a crazy person ask why I don't just tell her to go away. Just ignore her, they say. Easier said than done, my friend. For now, all I can do is pretend everything is status quo, keep her far away from Bess, and get her to leave soon.

My breathing is returning to normal and my brain is starting to function again after losing my mind for a time. I can't let Maura find out about Bess. The damage she did to me and Caroline was unforgivable. Maura's idea of relationship is control, manipulation, and extortion. It started when we were in college. Maura was, and is, gorgeous and sexy. I was stupid and horny and still paying for that. Once we started sleeping together Maura's grip tightened. She inserted herself into every aspect of my life. She accused me of stupid shit and never left me alone. At first, I tolerated it because I could not in my wildest imaginings know what Maura was capable of. Yeah, she was annoying and possessive but the sex was fun and before long we would graduate and it would be over. I remember counting the days.

After graduation, Maura moved to New York City and I fell hard for her friend Caroline. I assumed Maura would move on but discovering how much I loved Caroline enraged her. How dare I love someone else! On the surface she was happy for us, she and Caroline stayed friends, but underneath there was a streak of cold, punishing cruelty. Her vendetta knew no limits. She was going to make me pay for not loving her until the end of my days. When Bess told me about her ex-husband's behavior, I knew exactly what she was talking about. If I can get through the next few days, it will be okay. Then I can explain everything to Bess and hope she understands.

I start the truck and pull out of the parking lot heading to the Irish pub because I can't face going home. It's early so the bar is mostly empty. I take a stool at the bar and order a beer. Then another beer. People start coming in and filling the bar with talk

It's About Time

and laughter. I am getting a buzz so I order another beer to keep that going. There are a few Main Street people at the end of the bar that I met at a business meeting. I wave wondering if they remember me. They wave back so I move down to join them. What follows are several more rounds of drinks. We are getting pretty drunk and extra friendly. We play darts and in our condition it's fortunate no one loses an eye. The beer is doing its job and pushing all concerns from my mind. A lovely lass flirts shamelessly and with no inhibitions left I flirt back until I start feeling queasy. The lobster in my stomach is protesting the beer.

I untangle myself from the woman and head to the back parking lot for some air. I make it just in time to throw dinner up all over the pavement. It was more appetizing going down than coming up. Considering my condition, it seems prudent to head home. Amazingly I locate my truck and the keys. I get in and try to focus on my phone. Two texts from Maura wondering where I am. Fuck her. Delete. I'll call my sister, Mary. She will know what to do.

"Mary, Mary, Mary."

"James? Are you okay? Where are you? Have you been drinking?" Nothing gets past my sister.

"Maybe a teeny tiny little bit. Hold on." I open the truck's door and throw up again. "Okay. I'm back. How are ya, Mary?"

"James, what the fuck is going on. Tell me where you are?" Mary is worried.

"Okay. I'm in my truck." I laugh hysterically.

"Oh, my God. You are scaring the crap out of me, James. Keep talking. Do not drive. You understand me?"

"Yep. Gotcha. Okay." I start to cry, huge deep sobs like only a drunk person can pull off.

"James, what is it? Talk to me."

"Mary, I lied to Bess. Maura is at my house. I made out with some woman in the bar and I threw up." That covers the highlights. "I love Bess, Mary. I do. I can't let Maura fuck this up for me. Not again." More sobbing.

"I hear you, honey. It's going to be okay, James. Right now, you just need to get home. Can someone pick you up?" Mary doesn't want me driving and I'm not sure I can.

"Yeah. I'll call Bess. She'll pick me up. Good idea Mary." I hang up and call Bess but she doesn't answer. I don't blame her. I wouldn't talk to me either. I have no choice but to drive very slowly and carefully home. No wait! I'll get an Uber. The way this night is going I don't need a DUI adding to my troubles. Fortunately, I already have the app on my phone because I am incapable of doing anything complex in my condition. I hope I don't throw up again. Uber drivers don't appreciate that.

The driver, I think it was a he, picked me up but I don't remember much about that except I got home. I couldn't see straight to figure out the tip so gave him all the cash I had in my wallet. Score for him. Probably happens a lot when they pick up drunks. I stagger to the back door and let myself in. Maura sits in the sunroom, arms crossed looking furious. Fuck her. I text Mary to let her know I got home okay.

It's About Time

"Where have you been? I have been waiting for hours. What kind of welcome home is this?" she spits out. "Who are you texting?"

Whoa, too many questions. The room is spinning. "Maura, honey, it's great to see you." That sounds feeble. I run to the bathroom in time to empty my stomach again. She follows me and tells me to get in the shower because I stink. I'm sure I do. I comply willingly. The shower feels good. I wish it would dissolve me and send me down the drain. Maura pounds on the door telling me to hurry up. In the condition I am in I can't argue. I get out, towel off, drop the towel on the floor, walk to the bedroom, and slide under the sheets. Maybe going to the pub wasn't such a good idea. Maura gets in bed just as I pass out.

In the morning, I am still alive but wishing I was dead. I have an excruciating headache and my breath reeks. Maura already made coffee and I pour myself a cup. After washing down several Advil tablets, I recline on the couch in the sunroom with a cold compress on my forehead, waiting for the pain to stop. Maura walks into the room, hands me a glass of water, and tells me to drink it. I learned a long time ago that I save myself a lot of grief if I do what she tells me. I take the glass and sip it slowly not wanting my stomach to eject it or the coffee.

"You're probably dehydrated after that bender you were on last night." She looks at me like I am the most disgusting example of a human she has ever seen.

"Who's Bess?" Maura demands.
"What? Why?"

Hillary Gauvreau Oat

"In your drunken state last night, you called me 'Bess'. I didn't appreciate it." I avoid commenting and shrug. I take another sip of coffee and rub my aching head.

"Why are you here, Maura?"

"You know why! Can't stay away," she says pinching my cheek. "You are my one true love. My husband finally passed away after a long and tedious illness. Once I got loose ends tied, I headed straight back here." Maura manages to seductively slide in next to me on the couch.

"Stop. Okay? Get off me." I push her away and she lands with a soft thud on the floor. "Maura my head is pounding and I feel sick. Please, just leave me alone. Okay?" She picks herself up and gives me the finger.

"Okay. Fine. But you better be ready to play tonight, my love." She walks off into the kitchen pouring herself another cup of coffee.

Most of the day I spend in recovery but late in the afternoon I perk up. Maura drives me to the pub to get my truck. When we get home, I'm hungry so we drive to Sal's Pizza Palace. Maybe not the best choice for my sensitive stomach, but pizza always sounds good to me.

We walk in and I wave to Sal who comes right over. Maura is a stunning woman who makes heads turn wherever she goes. Shoulder-length shining blond hair perfectly styled, slender five-foot-five frame, and high-end designer clothes make her fifty-five years look more like forty-five. I introduce Sal and in true Maura fashion, she turns on the charm. Nobody has flirted with Sal since 1982 so he eats it up. While she chats, she calls me honey and reaches across the table to pat my hand. Sal is taken in by her because after the pizza he brings us cannoli on

It's About Time

the house. In all the years I have known him that has never happened.

Driving home she sits as close to me as my truck will allow, her hand resting on the inside of my thigh. She babbles on about Barcelona, her dead husband, and plans for the future.

"How long will you be here Maura?" I try to sound nonchalant praying she will leave tomorrow.

"Oh, I'm not sure. Maybe a week. Could be longer. I have to wait for the house in Greenwich to be ready. Why? You want me to stay longer?" She strokes my leg. There hasn't been anyone significant in my life since Caroline died. I endured Maura's visits because they didn't disrupt my life. Now it's different because I have Bess to consider. I suggest she might want to supervise the work on her house but she says it isn't necessary. There's no way I can avoid Bess for a week. I have to find time to talk to her. That is when my phone pings a message. Maura grabs it from the console to see who it is. I hold my breath. It's Mary checking on me.

"Your sister wants to know how you're doing."

"Just leave it. I'll talk to her later," I say.

"No. I will text her. I don't want your sister interrupting us tonight." Maura sends a text that says I'm fine and not to bother checking in again.

"That's rude, don't you think?" I ask Maura.

"Who cares? She'll be fine."

Hillary Gauvreau Oat

"I care, Maura. I care. She's my sister."

When we get home, we put on a movie. It's hard for me to pay attention because all I can think about is finding a private moment to talk to Bess.

"I'm getting water, you want anything?" I ask. Maura, engrossed in the film, shakes her head no. I go into the kitchen, pop open a can of seltzer, and quietly step out on the deck to call Bess. I will have to make this quick. Before Bess can answer Maura grabs my phone.

"Who are you calling?" she demands.

"Mary. I want to tell her how I am and apologize for your rude text."

"Not now. Come on back. You're missing the best part."

My spirits sag. I feel like a fucking hostage in my own house. Maura is still holding my phone when it rings. Bess, calling me back. Shit.

"Who is Bess? Want me to answer it?"

"She's a friend. Give me my phone."

"She must be a pretty good friend. I thought you said you were calling your sister?"

"Yeah, well I lied. Something you're familiar with." I grab my phone away from her and put it in my pocket.

"My goodness. You are cranky. Still hungover? I know what you need." Maura gets the bottle of Talisker and a couple of glasses. She pours and hands me a glass. "Down the hatch.

It's About Time

Hair of the dog." I accept the glass and set it on the coffee table. "Tsk tsk tsk. You aren't going to make me drink alone, are you?" She moves closer to me.

"My stomach is still a little queasy. I'll pass." I'm squirming because I know what's coming and want no part of it.

"It will make you feel better, I promise." She coos, and hands me the glass again. There is no point in fighting her. I take a sip and then swallow it all down.

"Better?" She smiles. "You know how much I care about you. I hate to see you grumpy." She runs her fingers through my hair.

When the movie ends Maura stands up. "Come on, let's go to bed. I've missed you. I like that you're conscious tonight." She grabs my hand and pulls to get me up.

"No. The guest room is made up. You can sleep there. I'm not sleeping with you."

"Excuse me? Did you say no? Have you forgotten who you're talking to? We have a lot of history, remember? I bet your boys would love to hear all about that."

"Would you do that Maura? Would you really hurt my kids? You've known them since they were babies. Don't you care about anyone?"

"Hmm. Let me think." Maura taps her perfectly manicured finger on her chin and looks pensive. "Of course, I care, silly. Come on. Don't be a spoilsport. Relax. Have some fun with me. I know you want to." She yanks my arm. I reluctantly lift myself off the couch and trail after her. Maura leads the way down the hall to the bedrooms. I hesitate and at that crucial moment, I decide not to follow her. Bess and I are building something good, and I can't risk that just to keep the peace with Maura. She might make good on her threat to tell my boys stuff I'd rather they not know. It's a scary thought but I can't keep living like this.

"I said no and I mean it. You can have my room. I'll sleep in the guest room. Good night."

"What? Are you serious? I don't ever recall James Ogilvie turning down sex." She looks at me like I have sprouted wings.

I stand braced against the door jam, as Maura unbuttons her blouse and lets it slip off her shoulders. She smirks as she slowly unzips her skirt and slides it down past her hips, letting it drop to the floor and gracefully stepping out of it. She is gorgeous, clad only in black lace bra and panties. This is exactly what got me in trouble all those years ago. She kneels in front of me, peeking coyly up at me through mascara-laminated lashes, unzipping my jeans. She is like a desperate caricature of herself. I can't help but laugh. Fire flares in her eyes that is anger, not passion. I step back and zip up. Instead of being aroused, I feel sad.

"I said no. Good night." I turn and walk to the guest room shutting the door. She pounds on it while hurling threats at me.

"Boy, this Bess sure has you pussy whipped! So sad. Maybe she would like to hear about who you really are." I ignore her and lock the bedroom door.

Finally alone, I text Bess "I'm sorry. I miss you. Talk soon." There will be hell to pay tomorrow, but tonight I will sleep well.

In the morning, I feel clear. No matter how awful it might get, how much Maura will try to hurt me and my family, I will not let

It's About Time

her hold me hostage anymore. I trust that things will work out one way or another. I text Mary that I'm turning my phone off and will check in later. Then I lock the phone in my truck to keep it away from Maura. Rain is pounding on the roof and it's raw outside. I get a pot of coffee going and a fire in the wood stove. That's when Maura makes her entrance. She pours coffee for both of us and joins me on the couch in front of the fire.

"James, are you okay? I'm sorry I got pushy last night. I was just so surprised you didn't sleep with me. I've been looking forward to our reunion and thought you would be too." Maura is acting demure and contrite. Acting is the operative word. When I first met Maura that tactic worked. Now, I know not to trust anything she does or says.

"Good morning, Maura. I feel great, thanks. Did you sleep well?" I accept the steaming mug of coffee.

She smiles. "Want breakfast? I could make us some eggs?"

Wow, this was an interesting turnaround. "Sure. Make mine over easy with two slices of toast." Let's see how far she will take this act before the demon returns. I continue reading the news on my iPad, occasionally raising my eyes discreetly to see how she is doing. I see a quick flash of anger reminding me I am in dangerous territory. While I am enjoying this power shift, I have to be careful how far I push her. No point in asking for trouble.

After breakfast, Maura mentions she has some errands to run. She asks if I need anything.

"Nope, I'm good. Thanks" It is still pouring rain, but to keep the charade going I offer to get my umbrella and walk her to the car.

"That is so nice of you James." I open the umbrella out on the deck and she crowds under it with me, arm around my waist, beaming her 1000-watt smile. She is being so sweet it makes my teeth hurt. We get to her BMW and before I can open the door, she motions for me to come closer. I think she wants to tell me something but instead, she kisses me.

"There's more where that came from." She tosses her blonde hair and laughs. I open the car door and she slides in. "See you later." I shut her door without comment.

It's About Time

CHAPTER 7

Trust But Verify

Bess

Rain pelts against the windows hard. I put on my son's old Cooper Union sweatshirt and unplug the iPad from the charger. Today is Sunday and it feels like ages since our volatile Friday supper. One short text, one weird hang-up call, nothing else. I usually wake up to two or three text messages because James stays up later than I do. Something is definitely going on. This has never happened before so I'm not sure what to do, if anything. I text Virginia asking if she could meet me for brunch at Charlie's. She texts right back asking what time. I can always count on her. We agree to meet at 11:00.

I pick out a sweater, retrieve my jeans from the bedroom chair, and head to the shower. I can't stop thinking about James. I usually have a sense of what's going on but this time I have no idea. The man has never flipped out and gone dark before.

I make a stop at the grocery store before meeting Virginia. Running into the store, I get a cart, and start down the bread aisle. That's when I bump into Sal, the pizza man.

"Hey, Sal! Nice to see you." We hug and take a minute to chat. He tells me he was delighted to meet James's lady friend last night and that they were pretty chummy over a red veggie pizza. The air is knocked out of me and I don't know what to say. Sal doesn't normally pick up on social cues and this time was no exception. He chats on until I excuse myself to run away. I pick up the few things I need and dash through the checkout. Running, I splash through puddles to the car, throwing my bags in the back seat. Even though I am early I head straight to Charlie's hoping maybe Virginia is early too. I get the last available table and order coffee. The server asks how I am as he wipes the table down. I want to blurt out that I am crushed, demolished, and destroyed but instead, I tell him I am fine. For future reference, 'fine' is one of those words that never means 'fine'. I text Virginia that I have a table and tell her to take her time but hurry.

It seems to take Virginia forever to get here, but finally, I see her blow in on a gust of rain-soaked wind. She sees me wave and heads to the table.

"I am so glad to see you! I'm really upset." Virginia takes off her coat and drapes it over the chair next to her. She uses a napkin to wipe the rain off her glasses and looks at me.

"What's going on? You look like you have seen a murder or something."

"Yeah, well not yet, but that could be next," I say sarcastically. "I ran into Sal at the Stop & Shop a little while ago. James and a woman, whom I assume is Maura, had a very chummy pizza last night. No wonder I didn't hear from him. He was *busy*!" I continue to rant for a bit before finally telling Virginia I need her cool head and calm advice about what to do. Do I confront or give him space?

"Wait, who is Maura? Back up, I think I'm missing some pieces." Virginia rips open a sugar packet and empties it into her milky coffee.

It's About Time

"She is an old friend that James doesn't want to introduce me to. He met her at UMass years ago." Virginia listens as I fill her in on everything I know, which isn't much. I describe Friday's dinner and how I asked James about getting together with friends. "Then I asked if he had friends he wanted to socialize with. That's when Maura was brought up and he got weird. The lovely evening we were having turned ugly. All I wanted was information, but that never came because he left, slamming the door on his way out. He's never done that before. I figured he would cool off and we would talk about it. *That* didn't happen. Saturday, I got a call from him but he hung up before I could answer. When I called him back, he didn't pick up. Then last night I got a text saying he's sorry, he misses me and we will talk soon. That's it. It's weird." I shrug.

Virginia thinks and finally says "Well at least you know he's alive. You're right, it's weird. So, this is the first you heard about this mystery woman. Then James storms out and disappears. What do you think is going on?"

"I haven't a clue. He has talked a lot about his UMass days but she was never mentioned. Maybe he was, or is, in some sort of a relationship with her. But why hide it? He said I could trust him, and how about all that bullshit about caring and honesty?" I roll my eyes. "I believed him, and now I wonder if that was a mistake"

"You believe him because that is what trusting, honest people do, Bess. It's not the easiest road to travel but it's the best one. And not to dismiss the distress you're in, but right now we don't know what's going on. But we will find out! Finish your coffee. We're going for a ride." We gulp the last bit of coffee and get out of there.

"Where are we going?" I ask as we hustle through the rain to her car.
"We are going to do some reconnaissance. Where does James live?"

"Oh my God. Really? This is like stalking the cute guy in high school. I love it! He's on Lonely Hollow Road, by the lake. Know where it is?" Whether wise or foolish, whatever Virginia has in mind, I am all in. I look at Virginia's determined face as we drive through the rain, windshield wipers slapping rhythmically back and forth. Friends are there for each other, no matter what.

"Bess, I am going to ask you something and don't get pissed, okay?" I nod in agreement. "Is it possible that you have deeper feelings for James than friendship? Just wondering."

"You must have read my mind because I'm wondering the same thing. Would I feel upset if a friend lied and kept secrets? Yes, of course. But this feels different. Deeper. More disappointing. Maybe I'm kidding myself about just being friends."

"Maybe. What if he feels the same way and wants to resolve the Maura issue before he gets more involved with you? Might that explain his behavior?"

"Possibly. But why wouldn't he talk about it? We talk about everything. At least I thought we did." Lonely Hollow Road, where James lives, is the next right turn. We drive slowly up the road for about half a mile.

"Slow down. It's the next driveway on the left, past those trees." When we get close to the driveway, I can see James's

It's About Time

truck parked in the usual spot and right behind it is a late-model black BMW sedan.

"Oh shit," says Virginia. "James is coming out of the house with a woman." They are under a big black umbrella and I can see what Sal referred to as chummy behavior. She has her arm around him, tossing her blonde hair as she laughs. We move up the street a bit and adjust the car mirrors to try to see what is happening. They get to the BMW, James leans down and they kiss. Not a little peck on the cheek but a sock-it-to-me kiss. In the rain! Jesus, could it get any more Gene Kelly romantic than that?

"So much for our theories and giving the man a chance. Maybe he is just an asshole. Get us out of here Virginia. No. Wait. Can you turn around and pull over somewhere where they won't see us?" We drive a little farther up the road to turn around, hoping the neighbors don't notice and call the cops. There is only one way in and out of this road so we know which way she will go. "Let's see if she leaves alone." After turning the car around we pull over by some bushes and watch the BMW back out of the driveway and a solitary driver take off down the road.

"Go to his house, Virginia. I'm talking to James right now." Virginia looks at me.

"Are you sure about this?"

"No. But I have to get this over with." Virginia puts the car in gear and we head the short distance down the road, turning into the gravel driveway.

Hillary Gauvreau Oat

We get out of the car and dash through the rain to the back door. It's pouring but I don't even notice. Virginia comes with me for moral support and to keep me from doing anything I would regret later. I march up the stairs and onto the deck knocking loudly on the door. James is surprised to see us and opens the door.
"Bess! Come in, come in." Once inside James grabs me in a tight hug like he is clinging for life. "What are you doing here? Hi, Virginia." He invites us into the sunroom where a cheery fire is crackling in the wood stove and a couple of used coffee mugs sit on the table. How cozy, I think cynically. James is toweling off his wet hair. He asks if we want coffee. We probably look like drowned cats but I don't care. Virginia and I sit on the couch next to each other. I turn down coffee because I am fully caffeinated at the moment and don't need any extra stimulation. Virginia shakes her head no and looks back and forth between James and me, wondering what will happen next. James seats himself in an overstuffed chair, towel in his lap, his hair damp and spiky. I plunge right in.

"I apologize for barging in on you like this, but I am just a tad upset by the most recent course of events. Actually, no, that's not true. I am very upset. First, you go ballistic and storm out of my condo, then I don't hear from you and now I see you in the driveway with a woman I assume is Maura, but who knows who she is? We agreed to be honest and this is not it. And whether I am jealous or not is beside the point, so don't even go there."

At that moment the heavens open up and sheets of rain pound the roof, emulating my mood. Virginia, sits next to me, ready to assist. I can count on her to protect, defend, and tell the truth as she sees it.

It's About Time

"James, seeing you kiss her, whoever she is, hurt me," I confess. "I don't think men and women can be friends. I have been trying to protect myself by insisting we are just friends but you are more than that to me. This is a helluva way to find that out. Please tell me what's going on before I regret ever meeting you." I take a deep breath and wait.
James stares at the dying fire as he apologizes for running out on me Friday night. "I felt backed into a corner." He turns and looks at us. "When you asked about friends it was the perfect opening to bring up Maura. I didn't mentioned her before because I hadn't seen her in over a year. Okay, that is only half the story. I also don't like to talk about her for other complicated reasons. Friday, she texted that she was on her way here. When I mentioned her, you asked a lot of questions. Legitimate questions. I just couldn't talk about her. I should have said that but instead, I got defensive and ran. I'm sorry. I wanted to explain, but with Maura here I couldn't." James picked up the towel in both hands and rubbed his face before throwing it on the floor next to him.

"Maura is staying here? With you?" I want to ask if they are sleeping together but I'm afraid of the answer. "You couldn't talk to me? Why? I don't get it. Oh my God, are you married?" James winces.

"No, of course not. But while Maura is here my privacy is limited. I'm working on that and I know there is a lot I need to explain. You're right, Bess, you and I are more than just friends. I feel that too. I'm afraid Maura will screw that up before we have a chance. I'm stressed out of my mind trying to handle her and protect you. Us. I want her to go away so we won't ever have to deal with her again. But I have to figure that out."

Hillary Gauvreau Oat

"I agree, you have a lot of explaining to do. You are trying to handle her and protect me? What makes you think that is your job? I'm confused and hurt but I want us to have a chance too. This is not the best way to start that though." That is when I notice luggage stashed in the corner of the kitchen and ask if she is coming or going. James looks down at his hands, then up at me. That is when Virginia speaks up.
"Look, you have things to sort out and I know you will when you can. But for now, this is the situation you're stuck with. What do you think about coming for dinner tonight? It isn't going to fix anything but maybe it will help us get to know each other and understand better what's going on. Or maybe I'm just nosey and want to check out this Maura person. What do you think?"

"I would love to come to dinner. It sure beats staying home and ruminating." It will give Bob a chance to use his Spidey sense too. We look at James waiting for his reply. After what seems like an eternity, he says yes, he will be there. Virginia gives James the address. We stand to leave and James tries to hug me but this time I resist.

"Please be patient Bess. Trust me. I know that's asking a lot."

* * *

I arrive at Virginia's around six greeted by the delicious aroma of chili and freshly baked cornbread. It's the perfect menu for a raw, rainy day. Thirty or so years ago Bob and Virginia bought their old farmhouse on ten acres of land. During the summer the grounds are lush with gardens of fragrant herbs, flowers, and vegetables. The expansive deck is where they grill and hang out in the summer. Most of the first floor is a great room, both in size and appeal. There is the original massive fieldstone

It's About Time

fireplace at one end of the room and the updated gleaming kitchen at the other. In the center of the room is a long oak table paired with twelve beautifully mismatched antique oak chairs. Bob takes my coat and Virginia hugs me and tells me not to worry.

"It's going to be okay," she whispers. "He cares about you!" I smile but feel uncertain of anything.

"Put me to work" I encourage. They point me to the salad. As soon as I start tossing there is a knock on the door, and I see through the wet panes a sheepish-looking James standing next to a radiant woman. Bob opens the door and graciously welcomes them into the warm kitchen.

"You must be James. I've heard wonderful things about you." Bob extends his hand and James shakes it firmly, looking happy to see us. Then Bob turns to Maura and reaches out to shake her hand as well. "And you must be James's friend Maura. It is nice to meet you." Maura takes his hand, smiles, and says how happy she is to be invited. She adds it is a pleasure to meet people James cares about and hands Bob a bottle wrapped in gold paper held tight by a red wax seal. Pretty fancy and no doubt expensive. Bob cracks the seal and slides the bottle of Vega Sicilia Unico 2009 from the wrapper. I don't know a lot about wine, other than what I like, but this bottle impresses Bob.

"Oh my, this is an extraordinary bottle of red, Maura. Thank you so much!" He cannot resist hugging Maura and she is looking pretty smug. Bob looks at Virginia and asks her if they should save it for a special occasion. Maura interjects, gently placing a hand on his arm, encouraging him to open it because wine is best when shared with friends. Maura is working hard to win us over although I have my eye on James who looks uncomfortable. Bob takes their coats, hanging them on the long line of wall hooks, by the door.

"Come in. Come in and make yourselves comfortable." Bob is grinning from ear to ear. The wine made the intended impression. James catches my eye in the kitchen where I continue to toss the heck out of that salad. My head is spinning with all kinds of divergent thoughts, good, bad, and ugly. My pulse is racing. Maybe this dinner isn't such a good idea. Maura is stunning perfection. Her lithe body shows off skinny black Prada jeans, a tailored white silk blouse, and short Jimmy Choo stiletto boots. Her makeup is understated, and her shining blond hair looks like it has never seen a moment of frizz even in this rain. I suddenly feel like an underachiever. Do I really need to see this? Can I make a run for the door without anyone noticing? Maybe I can lock myself in the bathroom and climb out the window.

Virginia places stemware on the table for the "incredible" wine, smiles at James and heads over to Maura to welcome her to their home. I feel like I am in some alternate reality. Bob gets the corkscrew and cradles the bottle of wine like a newborn babe, making a big production out of opening it. He pours a small amount into a glass and swirls it around, appreciating the color and bouquet, before finally sipping. Eyes closed he has a look of rapture on his face.

"Come on, Bob! Enough with the big production, after seeing your winegasm we all want to try it." Virginia teases. We laugh and hold out our glasses ready to receive the precious liquid. Curiously, James refuses a glass of "incredible" wine so Bob offers him a beer. James follows Bob into the butler's pantry to make a selection. Before long the two of them emerge

It's About Time

talking animatedly about craft beer and microbrews. When we have our drinks, Maura offers a toast to friends. The wine is delicious.

Virginia asks if Maura and I will help set the table, handing us napkins, salad plates, and silverware. Bowls are waiting by the chili pot ready to be filled. I asked Maura to help me bring dishes of chili toppings to the table. She willingly pitches in and is so warm and friendly that it is hard not to like her.

Virginia takes warm cornbread from the oven and as she heads to the table, she calls for everyone to come fill their chili bowls. Animated chatter fills the kitchen as we line up at the chili pot. Bob sits at the head of the table with Virginia on his left. I take the chair next to her. To Bob's right sits James with Maura next to him.

The food is delicious, and I am so grateful for what Bob and Virginia have done on short notice. Virginia was right. This is a perfect icebreaker. It is nice to see Bob and James getting to know each other. I am pleasantly surprised by Maura but reserving judgment because James is not looking at all comfortable. People can seem lovely in social situations but be brutal behind closed doors. I know that from experience. As the eating slows, the conversation picks up covering a wide range of topics. We discussed plans to tear down a section of Main Street and erect a superstructure. People aren't happy about it but zoning leaves little to do except complain. James expresses concerns about parking for his shop and even the future of his location if this trend continues. Maura comments that the clock shop building is decrepit and he could do much better elsewhere. We don't know what to say to that. Then she tells us about similar projects in Barcelona, something none of us know anything about, but we listen and nod politely. James is unusually quiet.

"So, Maura, tell us a little about yourself. How long will you be staying?" Virginia cut right to the chase. Maura isn't shy when talking about herself. She has just flown in from Barcelona where she has a villa and usually spends half the year. Because her husband, a financial tycoon, had gotten seriously ill while they were there, she had no choice but to stay until he died. She sighed like that was a huge burden. This last husband's estate adds to the fortune Maura is accruing from dead husbands, which at last count was three. She has known James since college and he isn't on the "richest men alive" list, so I don't think she is after him, but I can't be sure.

She informs us she is staying with 'Jay-Jay' while waiting for her house in Greenwich to be ready. It's been closed up for over a year and needs cleaning and maintenance. She describes the Tudor-inspired manor house in detail including the 7 bedrooms and 11 bathrooms on four acres. I drift off halfway through the story watching James and wondering what is going on in his mind. Maura likes being the center of attention. If that is her worst fault we can deal with it, but from the look of James, I doubt it is. She complains that her Greenwich house requires too much upkeep, and is so exhausting, not like her villa in Spain that has a full staff. Then she regales us with how she and 'Jay-Jay' were inseparable in college until Caroline came on the scene. According to Maura the three of them continued to be close friends, but she confesses her heart was broken.

The hair on the back of my neck stands up and I have chills. I wonder if 'Jay-Jay' agrees with her version of the story. He isn't saying a word. As she talks, she strokes his shoulder, takes his hand, and makes references to private jokes between

It's About Time

them which is super irritating. It is obvious to anyone with eyes that even through smiles, she is giving us the pointed message that James belongs to her. James on the other hand looks like someone enduring a bad case of cramps. As the conversation winds down, Virginia asks if anyone wants coffee. None of us do except for Maura who asks for a half-caf iced cappuccino with whipped soy milk. I saw Virginia's eyebrows go up.

"Sadly, we don't have a barista in the house. How about regular coffee?" Virginia suggests. Maura declines. Virginia sees me roll my eyes and bites her lip to keep from laughing.

I've had enough for one day and want to go home. I push back my chair and ask if Virginia wants help cleaning up. She asks me to give her a hand clearing the table then she and Bob will take care of the rest. It's an excuse for us to bump elbows and exchange knowing glances. As I scoop leftover chili into a container, Virginia asks me quietly what I think. I shrug and can't wait to debrief with her later.

"Okay, you guys, I have to get going," I announce. Without conferring with James, Maura stands saying they need to go as well. James silently complies. We make the rounds of goodbyes. I hug Bob and then Virginia. I smile at James, wanting badly to hug him but holding back. Maura performs the grand gesture of European-style cheek kisses all around.

The three of us head out into the damp evening, not saying anything to each other as we climb into our vehicles. The polite distance between James and me tonight makes me miss my friend. His truck is parked behind me in the circular drive, and, as I adjust my mirrors I can see Maura gesticulating. She doesn't look happy. Then I see her slap his face, hard. What could have possibly set her off? James hardly said a word all night. I have the urge to leap to his defense, but I don't want to embarrass him. I put my car in gear and head home feeling sad. No big deal, he said. Really? There seems to be more going on than a reunion between old college friends.

It's About Time

CHAPTER 8

Debriefing

Bess

Early Monday morning, Virginia calls. "Took ya long enough!" I say, laughing, because I know she is as eager to talk about last night as I am.

"I was going to call you at 7:00, but Bob made me wait. Get your butt over here. No way we can do this on the phone. Bob says he will get bagels from The Bagel Baron if you're coming."

"I want a bagel. I will be there ASAP. See ya." I throw on yesterday's clothes piled on the bedroom chair, brush my teeth, and run a comb through my hair. At a little past 8:30, I pull into their driveway. It is still unseasonably cool, but the sun is shining for a change which improves my mood considerably. I bound up the steps and through the kitchen door.

"I'm here!" I announce, taking off my jacket and hanging it on a hook. Virginia and Bob welcome me with a mug of strong coffee, cream, no sugar, the way I like it.

"What?!? No half-caf iced cappuccino with whipped soy milk?" I tease. Virginia gives me a playful shove, and we giggle at our Maura inside joke. I help myself to a bagel from the bag next to the toaster. Bob and Virginia patiently wait for me to join them at the table. Without delay, we start to debrief our meet and greet with Maura.

"So, do we like her? All in favor raise your hand." Virginia asks. Bob and I shake our heads, no.

"Okay, at first, she wasn't all that bad. Annoying, yes. Self-absorbed, for sure. But she does have good taste in wine. Right, Bob? And she is freaking gorgeous! I hate that about her." I wrinkle my nose and bite into my bagel.

"True. All true," agrees Bob. "That's why it's hard to understand why I felt so uncomfortable around her. I felt like I was being evaluated and coming up short."

"That's your Spidey sense, Bob. Virginia told me about it. Seriously, I think we need to pay attention to that."

Virginia agrees and adds that she isn't sure if it was Maura making her uncomfortable, or seeing how she was with James that made her squirm.

"James was so quiet. Maura was bubbly, charming, and all over James. It was weird."

"It was pretty squirm-worthy," I say. "So, this might also make you squirm. After dinner, the three of us walked out together. Remember? James's truck was parked behind me so when I was checking my mirrors, I could see them. It looked like Maura was dishing out a ration of shit to James. She was pointing at him, her mouth was going, and then she hauled off and slapped him hard. I obviously couldn't hear what they were saying but I was shocked. Did you guys notice anything that would set her off like that?" Both Bob and Virginia shake their heads and look surprised.

"What did James do?" Bob asks.

It's About Time

"Nothing as far as I could tell. He didn't hit her back, which I thought showed remarkable restraint. I wanted to spare him the embarrassment of having a witness to the spectacle, so I drove away. I haven't heard from him since but didn't expect to. Remember he's not allowed to talk to anyone when Maura is in the house." I roll my eyes.

"Huh. I can't imagine what would have brought that on." Virginia says, looking at Bob and then back at me. "I thought everything went pretty well, considering what we were working with. Maura went out of her way to impress us but I think she tried too hard. That wine, while you loved it, Bob, was way over the top for people she doesn't even know. And, did you notice she wasn't interested in knowing us at all?"

"I did notice that! It was like we were extras on her movie set. She kept James on a short leash too. I have never known him to be so quiet." I add.

"I felt pretty irrelevant in my own house!" Bob says. "James seems like a warm and honest guy. When we went to get his beer, he was friendly and relaxed. The minute we came back to the group he clammed up. Did you see that?"

"Yup. But the meal could have been a lot more awkward than it was, so I'm grateful for small blessings. Now we know who she is firsthand. Something is going on with those two and I hope James can handle it." Virginia acknowledges.

"I hope I can handle it too. None of this makes sense. Why would he never mention Maura in all of his stories about UMass, his happy place? It's weird how defensive he got Friday night. Considering all that, I was ready to dislike her. But she brought that incredible wine and was so friendly I thought I would give her a chance. Now I don't know what to think."

"You're right, Bess. I was pulled in right away," said Bob. "Do you know that bottle of wine goes for almost $500? If you can even get it. Quite the hostess gift! She must have the kind of money where a gift like that is no biggie. She couldn't possibly know that I would recognize the vintage. Most people, unless you're a wine snob like me, wouldn't know the difference between a bottle of Josh and a Vega Sicilia Unico."

"That's true. I certainly don't. So maybe she wasn't trying to impress us. Maybe she had it in her suitcase and saved herself a trip to the package store." I joke. "But what would be the point if no one knew what a precious gift it was?"

"I hate to be the Grinch here, but from what I saw she probably would have told us what it cost if you hadn't surprised her, Bob. Maybe her dead husband had a case of the stuff in the basement and like you said, no biggie." Virginia suggests.

"Yeah. You could be right. Where do you think she finds those rich old husbands, by the way?" I ask. "I could use a villa in Spain."

"She probably hangs out on Wall Street or exclusive country clubs." We laugh and then Bob gets serious. "If you ask me something feels off about her. There is nothing obvious, I just feel wary. I don't like thinking badly of James's friend, but I don't want to spend time with her. Know what I mean?" We nod in agreement. "And this is Vegas. What's said in Vegas, stays in Vegas. Agree?" Virginia and I cross our hearts and swear to keep whatever Bob shares confidential.

"My first impression was, wow, this woman knows how to make an entrance. The outfit, the gift, and the appropriately nice words, all impressed me like it was supposed to. After a while,

It's About Time

she revealed who she really is. When she asked if we liked the wine she barely listened to the answer. She plays a good game, but it doesn't ring true to me. Those poor dead husbands probably didn't have a clue what they were getting into. She dazzles with her looks, and, while men are blinded by the light, she goes in for the kill. Metaphorically, I hope. I bet James knows who she is, probably better than any of us. I have worked with people like her in the construction business and needed to tread carefully. Piss them off, and they would not hesitate to destroy my business. With someone like Maura, it's impossible to know what she is capable of. Being self-absorbed and manipulative is bad enough behavior, I hope she isn't also dangerous in other ways. Let's hope her husbands all died of natural causes without help from her. Does that sound too dramatic?" Bob asks.

Virginia and I look at Bob wide-eyed.

"Wow. That is serious stuff and way more ominous than what I was expecting, Bob," says Virginia.

'I think Bob is right. We need to be careful. We cross paths with dangerous people all the time without knowing it. It isn't something normal people ever expect so we are not looking for it. But when they come to dinner, we need to pay attention. It's unanimous. No more dinners with Maura." I say. "I wasn't sure if I was the only wary person, but seems I'm not. Thanks for the confirmation, Bob. Your Spidey sense is working."

"Well, ladies, that's all I have. Now I am going to work." Bob pushes away from the table, kisses Virginia, and is out the door. I'm happy he made time to be with us this morning. Virginia and I put our coffee mugs in the kitchen sink then wander to the fireplace and sit on the couch.

"You're preoccupied. What are you thinking about? Like I can't guess." Virginia asks.
"I'm thinking about James, of course. And everything Bob just said. Trying to figure out what's going on. With my background, I can guess what Maura's problem is. I'm relieved we all saw the same thing, and that it's not just me being insecure. Although I am a little jealous." Marigold, their sweet yellow tabby cat, jumps up on the couch lobbying for attention. I pet her and she curls up next to Virginia, purring.

"You? Insecure? Give me a break. You are anything but insecure at this stage of your life. You had to work for that and I want you to know I see it." Virginia tells me.

"Thanks for the vote of confidence. Yes, worked for it and have the scars to prove it. James has battle scars too. It's obvious he is uncomfortable around Maura. They have known each other for a long time so the hold she has on him could be anything."

"She reminds me of a siren of the sea. You know, the mythological woman who lured sailors to destruction with her sweet song? It's easy to get charmed by her. Don't you think? You saw how Bob responded. Maybe it only works on men." Virginia observes.

"Yes, she is a siren! At least Bob was able to come around and not be dashed on the rocks. Charmed is an understatement. Seduced and manipulated feels more accurate. Whatever we call it, she's good at it. Does Bob know the story of James and Caroline?" Virginia shakes her head, no, she doesn't think so.

"Feel free to tell him if you want. It's not confidential information. I suspect the common denominator in James' marriage trouble

It's About Time

is Maura. It sounds like she was pretty attached to James and didn't take the breakup all that well despite what she says."

"Was attached and still is," Virginia adds.

"True. If she wants to make James pay for loving Caroline, what better way than to destroy his marriage and hold him hostage for eternity? I doubt ethics would stand in her way. It always surprises me how long someone like her is willing to hold a grudge."

"If that's true, and she isn't done punishing James, where does that leave you, Bess? Remember he said he needs to protect you from her. You need to listen to him." Virginia is one step ahead of me.

"You're right. It puts me smack in the middle of a long-term feud. I wish I had known about all this before I got close to James. I've had enough drama in my life. He has to take care of this mess himself if we're going to have any kind of relationship."

"When you talk to James, Bess, ask him what's going on, and what he is willing to do about it. Let's hope he's aware and candid." I agree, that is exactly what I will ask him.

"If he can't be candid and disconnect from Maura I don't see much of a future for us in any capacity. I like him. I hope he can stand up to her. I'm not interested in a threesome. Know what I mean?"

"Don't all guys want a threesome?" Virginia cracks herself up.

"Yup, but probably not this kind of threesome." I agree. "I believe he's a good man, but he's been tangled up with Maura for a long time. If he can't resolve this mess I will have to back away, and that makes me so sad."

"You're right. Makes me sad too," agrees Virginia.

"I wish I could be there with you when you talk to him. For support, of course, but also because I'm dying of curiosity. I have an idea! Why don't you record the conversation on your phone so I can listen to it later? Oops, I mean so you can listen later." Virginia smiles.

"That is not a bad idea. Along the lines of covert recordings, I thought about doing a background check on Maura. Maybe I can find out more about what's going on."

"Bess, wouldn't you love to know if she knocked off one or two of those old husbands?" Virginia's face lights up.

"I would! I wouldn't put it past her. However, the reason I feel good today is because I realize Maura is not my problem. If I start digging, and help too much, I am afraid I will get tangled up in trying to fix things. This is his business, and, while I am happy to play a supporting role, he is the one who has to figure this out and take care of it. I have no desire to be in any kind of relationship with Maura. Even at a distance."

"Maybe you should do a background check on James. How do you know you can trust him if you don't have objective information? Has blindly trusting worked out in the past, Bess? Maybe they both need background checks." Virginia makes a good point.

"Besides, these days people do background checks all the time. I have a friend who uses internet dating sites and I swear she keeps background check companies in business. One time she discovered a man she was dating was arrested for sexual assault. Not that I believe for one second that James is a predator. Maura on the other hand…" Virginia raises her eyebrows posing the possibility. "But really, it's easy to do and then you know. Bob does background checks all the time on his clients and employees. He could run them for you if you decide to do it."

"Maybe. I'll think about it. I should get out of here before it's time for lunch. I still need to shower." I snagged a bagel for the road. This morning gave me a lot to think about. In the car, I text James that I want to talk.

Hillary Gauvreau Oat

CHAPTER 9

Lies and Threats

Bess

When I get home from work, I have way too much time on my hands. James is occupied with Maura and I try not to think about what's going on over there but it's a lost cause. I imagine them having passionate sex and laughing about poor clueless Bess. I can't help it. It's an artifact from my time living with a covert narcissist. He thought it was fun to insinuate there were other women and smirk while he watched me react. Then he would blame me for being insecure. Insult to injury. Sweet guy. James hasn't said a word since dinner last Sunday, and, it's now Thursday. My plan to stay independent and unattached has failed miserably because I miss him.

I change out of work clothes and put on leggings and a cozy sweatshirt. After pouring a glass of wine, I sink into the recliner. I'm hungry but have no energy to cook or pick up takeout. If James were here, I am certain there would be a pizza on the table. That thought makes me sad. Just as I put my feet up there is a knock at the door. Probably a delivery. Let them leave it on the porch because I am not getting up. Then I hear a second, more insistent knock. Annoyed, I quietly tiptoe to the door and look through the peephole. Maura. Shit. What is she doing here? I debate quickly whether I can pretend not to be home, but my curiosity gets the best of me, and I open the door.

"Maura. What a surprise. What can I do for you?" I ask cautiously. Maura smiles and extends a large brown takeout bag toward me that smells heavenly.

"I brought Chinese. I hope you don't mind me dropping in on you like this." she purrs. Before I can respond she slides past me into my condo. She has been here all of ten seconds and already I'm annoyed.

"We haven't had much time to talk, and I want to get to know you better." She wears designer jeans, a light blue linen shirt, large diamond stud earrings, and a sparkling diamond pendant necklace that brings attention to her perfect cleavage. I wonder who bought those breasts for her. Her well-practiced disarming smile would work on me if I didn't know better. She scans my condo in a way that feels like she is taking critical inventory. I feel self-conscious as she looks me up and down and smiles in an 'aren't you cute' condescending kind of way. I imagine she would not be caught dead in a sweatshirt.

"I love your condo! It's so…cozy." She oozes. That feels patronizing. I quickly glance around to see how messy my place is, happy that I did the dishes.

"Where should I put this?" She holds out the takeout bag, and I show her to the table.

"Can I have one of those too?" she asks, pointing to my glass of wine. "Sorry, I didn't think to bring wine with me. I am glad you have some open." I pour her a glass and sit at the table while she unpacks containers of fried rice, spring rolls, steamed dumplings, edamame, Moo Goo Gai Pan, sweet and sour pork, and Pad Thai.

It's About Time

"Maura, this is enough food to feed an army." It smells delicious so I decide I can eat and still keep my guard up. There is no point in wasting good food.

"Well, I wasn't sure what you liked so I got a little of everything." Once again, she smiles. Caroline comes into my mind, and I wonder if she was seduced by Maura's charm. Although I never met Caroline, I feel a sympathetic kinship with her. I bring plates and napkins from the kitchen to the table, open a set of chopsticks, and scoop a little of everything onto my plate. I eat with relish while Maura picks.

"So, how long have you known James?" Maura asks as she pokes her Pad Thai with a chopstick. Ah, here it comes, she is bribing me with Chinese food to get information.

"About a year. Why?"

"I am just curious how well you know him. He seems to be doing better than he was."

Leading statements like that irk me. I'm tempted to ignore Maura's I-know-something-you-don't-know hook, but I'm curious, so I bite.

"Better?"

"Yes, better. More relaxed. Happier. He seems quite fond of you." She sips her wine.
"So, James tells me you're his therapist. How did you get into that profession?" She is trying to show interest in me, but it feels more like data mining. I focus on the food and keep information to a minimum.

"Yes, I am a therapist. To be clear, I am not *his* therapist. Did he tell you that?"

"Oh, no. When he said you were a therapist I simply assumed."

"I see. Well, you know what they say about assuming. What about you? What's your profession?" Fleecing sick old men comes to mind, but I keep my mouth shut for a change.

"Oh, me? Hmmm. Well, I graduated with a liberal arts education which prepared me for absolutely nothing and at the same time, everything." She laughs. "Caroline helped me make connections in publishing. I worked as an editor for a prominent magazine in New York. Then I met my first husband and there was no time for a job, what with travel and charity work." I notice how she never offers specific information like which prominent magazine she worked for. I suspect she is either padding her resume or, for all I know, making it up completely. Maybe a background check is a good idea to fill in the blanks and sort fact from fiction. I continue asking her questions, to keep her from prying into my life.

"It was generous of you to bring that wine on Sunday. Bob was thrilled. Where did you ever find it?" Maura brightens at the compliment telling me she had several bottles shipped from Spain to James's house. It is a favorite of hers in Barcelona. She pronounces Barcelona with a lisping *-th* sound to let me know how savvy she is.

"But, this bottle of red you have, isn't too bad." Maura takes another sip and slightly wrinkles her nose. Her distaste for California wine doesn't seem to prevent her from drinking it.

It's About Time

"Thanks. It's a Bourbon Barrel Cabernet. Twenty bucks a bottle. But it's worth it." I know I'm being bitchy, but I can't help it. I don't want to parry with her all night, though. Let's move this conversation along and find out why she is here.

"Maura, you said James was better. Was he ill?" I innocently inquire.

"You don't know?!?" Maura feigns wide-eyed surprise. One-upmanship again. "After Caroline died there was an investigation because of the domestic abuse charges. That was why Caroline stayed away so much. James has mental health issues that can make him pretty volatile. She was sick with worry about those boys but unless she went to court her hands were tied. If she sued for custody, he would have made her pay dearly in a lot of ways. I thought you knew all that, as a good friend and all."

Ouch. That's a passive-aggressive punch in the gut. That's not the story James told me. I'll listen and sort out the facts later. If James had any domestic abuse charges against him, they should be easy to find with a background check. As Maura continues telling me about their past, I get a text message notification on my phone. I excuse myself, saying it might be a client. It's James telling me Maura is leaving tomorrow. That's a relief so I send a celebration emoji. Holding the phone in my hand I remember Virginia suggesting I record my talk with James. It takes less than a second to decide I want a recording of this conversation. The phone is already in my hand so no suspicions are aroused when I open voice memos, hit record, and place the phone face down on the table.

"That was James, wasn't it?" Maura asks. I have to hand it to her. She doesn't miss much. Not wanting to complicate whatever is going on with lies, I say yes, it was.

"I figured the minute I left him alone he would reach out to you."

"Really? I don't understand why he can't reach out when you're around. Do you know why that is?"

"Who knows?" Maura shrugs her shoulders. "He's very secretive. Not that I care about what he's up to." I don't believe that for one minute.

"So, you would be okay if he talked with friends while you are visiting? It would be great if you would let him know that." She looks surprised by my suggestion and smoothly shifts the conversation.

"I came to see you because you need to know who he is, for your own sake. I'd hate to see you get hurt." She is back to making James the bad guy. "Please don't tell him I was here. He thinks I'm out running errands to get ready to leave tomorrow. He would be furious if he knew."

"He would? Why?"

"My goodness, you sound just like a therapist with all these questions!" she clucks.

"Do I?" I smile, knowing I'm getting under her skin.

"Obviously, he doesn't want you and me to talk because he is afraid you will find out the truth." I have my doubts about that. Truth seems pretty flexible for Maura and reminds me of Jack

It's About Time

Nicholson telling Diane Keaton a "version of the truth" in the movie *Something's Gotta Give.* This is Maura's version. She asks me to please keep her visit and our conversation confidential. "I know therapists are good at that." She beams another enchanting smile expecting me to nod and comply.

"Since this isn't a therapy session, I won't promise not to tell James you came to see me. James and I don't keep secrets."

"That's what Caroline said too. Until she discovered how many secrets he kept." Behind Maura's pleasant demeanor, there is a flash of anger. She doesn't like it when people don't do what she tells them.

"What are you talking about?" I ask. Up until this moment, I felt confident I knew what was going on. James is the good guy. Maura is the toxic manipulator. What if I'm wrong? What if James has seduced me into believing he is the victim and Maura is honestly trying to help me? Maura sighs in frustration.

"I tried to tell Caroline but she thought she knew him better than I did. She was stubborn. Maybe you are too." She softens and attempts to bring me into her confidence. "I did everything I could to convince her, but after a while, I had to let go, and she did what she wanted. You know how that turned out." This woman is like a chameleon. I feel sure of who she is, then she finds a way to make me doubt what I know. What if I'm wrong about James? She is pushing to get me to agree with her story, telling me how heartbreaking it was to watch Caroline suffer because she cared about her. I'm not convinced but she has poked around enough to find a chink in my armor. I am beginning to question the story I heard from James. After all, he did omit Maura and keep her a secret. Does he not want me to hear the truth from her? I'm getting pulled down Maura's rabbit hole and unsure what to believe.

"Caroline and I were friends first and I was the one who introduced her to James. I regret that. We would get together sometimes when she was on her work trips and she would tell me what was going on at home. She described how controlling and angry he was all the time. I was shocked. That wasn't the James I knew. I encouraged her to leave him, but she was afraid. When she was away on trips I would help James with the kids. One night after the kids went to bed, he pulled out the bottle of whiskey and…well…let's just say he seduced me. We had a passionate sexual relationship in college, but it had been years since I thought of him that way. Then he demanded we sleep together whenever I visited or he would tell Caroline about it and blame me. I was so confused. My feelings for James were real, but I cared about Caroline too. I was trapped. I would have just stayed away but I was close to the boys and knew they needed someone to care about them. Caroline was powerless to do anything because she was afraid he would turn the boys against her. Then when she got sick, he took total control over her life and death. Caroline didn't have the energy to fight him. After she died, he told everyone he was the victim. Such bullshit." Maura confided.

Maura's story made my head spin. None of that sounds like James. She continues talking while I pour wine, and turn on some lights. As I putter around, she makes it a point to tell me firmly that James is not to be trusted. According to Maura, he is a liar and a cheat. I don't know what to think anymore. Is she throwing her shit on James hoping it will stick? I have learned through painful experiences not to believe everything people tell me. Trust but verify is my motto. If James is the one lying, I will be disappointed, but better to know now than to get blindsided later.

It's About Time

"Maura, I appreciate the warning and will certainly be careful in my dealings with James from now on. But I am confused. It seems you and James have been close for years. If he is so awful, why are you still friends? Why are you here in town, at his house? Especially considering what he did to your friend Caroline? I would think you would want a lot of distance." Maura pours herself more wine and looks directly at me.
"I know this might be hard for you to believe but he was, and is, my first love. I fell hard for him in college and was devastated when he married Caroline. I couldn't imagine not having him in my life, in some capacity. Even though it was painful, I stayed close. I guess I hoped he would see the light, and discover I am his one true love. When he started to unravel…drinking, cheating, getting in fights, and neglecting the boys…I couldn't abandon him. He needed me." If James unraveled, I can picture Maura pulling the threads. In my kindest, most empathetic therapist's voice, I challenge her.

"Maura, I am so sorry. That must have been heartbreaking. What do you want from him now? You had to lie and sneak over here because he would be furious if he knew. Why bother with all that drama? If he isn't interested in you and has so many issues, why not move on?" She dug this hole, making her case against James. Let's see how comfortable she is lying in it.

"I did not sneak over here!" She snaps at me. "And you have no business telling me what to do." It seems I hit a nerve.

"Wow, that got a reaction! It was an obvious question for me to ask. I'm sorry it upset you." I need a clearer idea of who Maura is. She glares at me like she is sizing up an adversary.

"I don't mean to piss you off, but honestly, why are you here? I don't get it." I dig a little more.

"I don't have to answer any of your questions. Why I'm here is none of your goddamn business." She spits out.

"Ok. Fair enough." I back off a little, sipping my wine. This is more like the Maura I was expecting and my confusion is clearing up. There is one last thing I want to ask her about. "I'm trying to figure out how what you're telling me lines up with what I saw when we left Virginia's Sunday. You're telling me James is untrustworthy and hinting he's possibly dangerous. But that isn't what I observed in the truck when we were leaving. It looked to me like you were the aggressor. What did he do to trigger that, Maura?" I can see the muscles in Maura's jaw clenching.

"What happened in the truck is between me and James. But if you really must know he deserves that and more. I saw him looking at you. I wouldn't have been surprised if you two were playing footsies under the table. I was mortified. This week he has been impossible for me to deal with. Our whole relationship has been destroyed because of *you*. You're like Caroline all over again. If he suffers and pays for hurting me then bravo! Maybe he will finally come around to know I am the one who really loves him." That is a bizarre kind of logic but sounds like the unvarnished truth.

"So, years ago he dumped you and chose Caroline. You punished him by ruining his marriage and hope he will see how much you love him. Have I got the story straight?" If looks could kill, I would be dead.

It's About Time

Her beautifully manicured hands are clenched, and her face is flushed with anger. She doesn't confirm or deny my accusation, which gives me my answer by default. I've had enough. Before the conversation can turn explosive, I bring dishes into the kitchen and pack up leftovers. Maura knows I am beginning to see through her facade, and that makes me an enemy. The sooner I get her out of my house the better.

"Maura, do you want to take leftovers back to James's? There's still a lot of food here." She shakes her head no, and tells me to keep it. Her eyes follow me as I clean up, boring a hole in my back. After a few silent, brooding minutes, she gulps down the last of her wine, neatly tucks away her outrage, and sweet Maura is back.

"I'm sorry we have gotten off on such a sour note. I leave for Greenwich tomorrow," she informs me. "But I promise to stay in touch. Hopefully, as we get to know each other we can resolve our differences." I walk to the table but don't sit down because her time is up.

"Sounds good," I say. "It's getting late and I had a long day. I hope you don't mind me throwing you out." I smile but I'm not kidding. She takes her sweet ass time but finally gets up to leave. She clamps me in an unexpected hug that's like being crushed by a boa constrictor. She whispers that she worries about me and hopes I will be safe. That is ominously creepy. Safe from what I wonder? I peel her off me and reassure her I will be fine as I steer her to the door.

Once she is out, I shut the door and lock the dead bolt. Then I remember my phone is still recording. I hit stop and since Maura has just left, I have a small window to text James before he goes dark again. I text him that I want to see him tomorrow after Maura leaves, adding 'WE NEED TO TALK'.

Then I text Virginia to tell her about Maura's surprise visit and that she is leaving tomorrow. I am probably being overly cautious but tell her I am sending her an audio file of our conversation asking her to keep it safe. She texts me right back asking if she can listen to it. I give her permission, and email the file to her, knowing it will flip her out.

I thought I was tired before but now I am exhausted. Dealing with Maura put me over the top. At least my stomach is full. Overall, I'm satisfied with how that went. I still don't know how much of what she said is true and will have a come-to-Jesus talk with James as soon as possible. I plop down in the recliner and crack open a fortune cookie forgotten in the bottom of the takeout bag. It says, "Expect the unexpected". No shit!

It's About Time

Chapter 10

Truth

Bess

It's Friday afternoon. I wait impatiently to hear that Maura is on the road. Around supper time, James finally walks in the door.

"Thank God! I have been waiting all day. Come on in. We have a lot to talk about. What the fuck, James? A whole week with hardly a word from you? I considered having the cops do a wellness check." James looks like he has been dragged through a knothole sideways. "Are you okay? You look like shit."

"This was a hard week, Bess. Got anything to drink? Can we just sit for a bit before you rake me over the coals?"

"Sure. You want a glass of wine or something stronger?" I ask.

"Stronger if you have it." James sinks down onto the couch with a groan. I bring him a glass and the bottle of Talisker. He pours a hefty amount and swallows it down fast.

In light of James's haggard condition, I suggest relaxing on the beach before we talk. He agrees. With sweatshirts and beach chairs under our arms, we walk to the water's edge. The late April sun and the gently rolling waves soothe body, mind, and spirit. I sit down with a sigh.

"You do look like shit, you know. What happened to you this week?" I poke him gently in the ribs trying to get a reaction. He opens one eye to peek at me from behind sunglasses. The sun brightens the coppery color of his hair and illuminates a few additional strands of gray that I'm sure have Maura's name on them. So far, he has said little, but dark circles under his eyes and new lines etched into his face speak volumes. The week with Maura sucked about ten years out of him. I'm not sure what will happen now, but I know I'm not happy about the way this situation went down. We sit without talking.

"Are you hungry?" I ask James. "I have a lot of leftover Chinese food if that appeals to you, or we can pick up something else. I'm not prepared to cook tonight." If he isn't hungry, I know something is very wrong. The man is usually a bottomless pit.

"Whatever you want to do is fine. I don't want to go out. It's so peaceful here right now. Is it okay with you if we stay out here for a while longer?" he reaches for my hand lacing his fingers in mine.

"Of course. Are you okay James? I'm worried about you."

"Yeah, I'm okay. I'm exhausted and dreading getting into the discussion I know is coming."

"I can understand that. Nothing like getting ripped a new one when you're down. I promise to be gentle. We'll take our time. No rush unless she is coming back tomorrow. She isn't, is she?" I ask startled by the thought. He frowns and says he hopes not. Looking at him makes it hard for me to believe what Maura said about him. But I often overlook red flags when I like someone. And I like James. A lot. I have to navigate this swamp of contradicting stories to get to the truth. Maura is making him the bad guy, but it doesn't mean he's completely innocent. Or guilty, for that matter.

It's About Time

Half an hour later I'm starving and have to get food in me. We carry the chairs back to the patio. Inside, James turns on the television and parks himself on the couch in front of it. That's a first. The news anchor drones on about war and inflation while I get food ready. I open a bottle of wine and pour a glass. James has not moved.

"Okay, I think we're ready." I tap James on the shoulder to get his attention. "Come eat." I turn off the news channel and pour James a glass of wine. "Get a plate and help yourself." As we eat, James eventually asks why I have so much Chinese food.

"Maura."

"What did you say?" James's eyes get big.

"If you're asking which Chinese restaurant this came from, I don't know, because Maura brought it. She surprised me yesterday and came over with takeout. From the look on your face, I see you had no idea. I wanted to tell you when you got here but you looked like you needed some time."

"She was here when I texted you?"

"Yup. And, bless her heart, she knew it was you." James grits his teeth, gets up, and without a word dumps the contents of his plate into the trash like it's poison. He throws each carton into the garbage with repeated thuds. I lose my appetite and hand him my plate. Once all the remnants of Maura's food are in the trash, James ties up the trash bag and determinedly marches it out to the dumpster. If only getting rid of Maura was that easy. When he comes back, I hand him a pint of ice cream.

"House rules are that halfway down your pint, we switch because pistachio and Cherry Garcia are both my favorites. My house. My rules." I smile hoping he will too. He doesn't. James accepts the ice cream without comment, and we sit on the couch by the fireplace. He is really in a funk.

"That was a strong reaction to Chinese food. Or is it a reaction to Maura coming here? Are you going to talk to me?" I ask gently.

"I'm not mad at you. None of this is your fault." James turns and looks at me. "Why did she come here?"

"She said she wanted to get to know me. But her real motive was to scare me away from you under the guise of protecting me. Do you want to tell me what this is all about? I'm not too happy about any of this."

"I'm so sorry, Bess. I didn't want you to have to deal with Maura. I should have known she would show up because she is like gum on my fucking shoe. But I hoped I had seen the last of her. When she texted me that she was coming, there was no time to prepare myself, or you. I acted like a jerk on Friday. I'm sorry."

"Yeah, I noticed the jerk part. Who is she? What's going on? A whole week without hearing from you is weird. I missed you. If we are going to have any kind of relationship you need to find a better way to deal with this. Whatever it is."

"I missed you too. You're right. This whole week I have been trying to figure out how to get rid of her for good. I don't mean that the way it sounds."

"I know."

It's About Time

"I felt like I was being held hostage. Everything was about what Maura wanted. All my energy was spent pushing her away and trying not to piss her off. There is so much I need to explain. After what you've gone through, I knew you would understand. But I couldn't get away from Maura long enough to explain. It's such a long and involved story. I should have stayed on Friday and talked with you. Instead, I doubled down on being a jerk and got drunk. I need help with this, Bess."

"Sounds like she has you by the balls. Not a comfortable place to be. I got Maura's version of the story and now I want to hear your side."

"Yeah. What did she tell you? Oh God, I can only imagine."

"Well, it started with a knock on my door and I was annoyed. You know how I am about surprise visits. But then, I thought it might be you. Needless to say, it wasn't. I was curious what she wanted so I let her in. Her visit was interesting. She pumped me for information but didn't get much. The story she told made you the bad guy. You, she said, are a liar, a cheat, violent, and have mental health issues. Were you charged with domestic abuse?"

"WHAT?!? She said WHAT?" James launches up off the couch. "The only mental health issue I had was depression caused by my failing marriage. Domestic abuse? Never! That's insane." His hands are shaking as he sits back down.

"She also said you seduced her and threatened to tell Caroline if she didn't sleep with you."

"Oh my God. That is a total lie. *She* was the one who threatened *me*!" James pulls his hands through his hair in frustration.

"I asked why she stays friends with you if you are so despicable. She told me she cares about you."

"She sure has a fucked-up way of showing that,"

"I saw what happened in your truck when we were leaving Virginia's on Sunday. When I asked what triggered her, she said the reason was none of my business."

"Damn it. You saw that? I'll tell you what it was about. She thought I looked at you too much. She thought we were exchanging "knowing glances" at her expense. The woman is a lunatic. I argued with her but it was a waste of time. She screamed at me to stop being an asshole and you saw the rest." James bowed his head in shame.

"Wow. Knowing glances?" I laugh. "Well, she told me she wanted to make you pay for everything you did to her. I guess getting bitch slapped is part of that. Do you want to hear what she said? I recorded it."

There is a text notification ping on my phone and I don't recognize the number.

 "Holy shit!" I pass the phone to James. It's a text from Maura letting me know how much she enjoyed our time together and that she got home safely. She added a heart emoji like she is my best and most caring friend.

"That manipulative bitch." James blasts. "You see what she's doing, don't you?"

"I think so but maybe you can fill me in. Should I text her back?" James tells me he will take care of it.

It's About Time

"How? How are you going to take care of it? Let's think about this before you do anything. Okay? Please?" James agrees but I can tell he isn't happy about it. Neither am I. The last thing I need is to be stalked by a crazy woman. James asks me to play the recording.

"I may as well know everything. Did she know you did that?" he asks.

"No. After you texted me, I opened voice memos and laid the phone on the table." I press play and James listens while pacing around the room. When the recording ends, he looks confused.

"I can't believe it. Does she think that's what happened or is she just telling you a story to manipulate you?" James asks.

"I don't know. I'm hoping you can answer that question."

"Well, a lot of what she said is true, but the roles were different. This is so fucked up."

The sun was getting low in the sky and I suggested a walk on the beach to help us clear our minds. As we walk toward the bluff to sit on the rocks, we're quiet, thinking.

"Okay, I've thought about it. I want you to block her number. Please?" James tells me. Let's figure out how to deal with Maura. Together. I will not let her come between us. The only way to defeat her is to keep talking. No secrets. There is a lot of backstory you don't know, but I promise to tell you everything."

"Interesting. She also mentioned secrets being kept. She told Caroline about your secrets. I imagine that created a rupture in your marriage. James?" I stop walking and look at his face, "There can't be any secrets between us. Confidences, sure. Privacy, okay. But secrets? No way. If you got 'em, I want to hear about them."

It is probably going to be a long night. When we get back, we sit on the couch, James on one end, and me on the other. Before we start, I block Maura's number.
"Okay, I blocked her." James takes a resolute breath and begins his story at UMass Amherst in the 1980's.

"I majored in chemistry at UMass. It was great and I loved everything about that place. As a senior, I lived in an apartment off campus with a couple of guys. I was taking a throwaway class in film, just for a couple of easy credits. That's where I met Maura. We were assigned a project and needed a partner. She asked if I would like to work with her, and I said, sure. Man, do I regret that decision. Well, one thing led to another and we started hanging out. She was beautiful, and I couldn't believe she wanted to be with me, a science nerd in grungy blue jeans. After we slept together, she was at my apartment night and day, but I accepted it. I was in my twenties with an abundance of testosterone, and the sex was good so I let it be. I had no idea what I was setting myself up for. After graduation, I wanted to get a Master's in Education at UMass so I could teach chemistry to high school kids and inspire them to love science like I do.

"I was accepted and Maura wasn't happy about that. Her friend Caroline hooked her up with a job at some teen magazine in New York City and she was chomping at the bit to go. She was pressuring me to go to school there, to get engaged and make plans for the future with her. But I wasn't sure about her, or getting married, and I wanted to stay at UMass. Not doing what she wants is a big problem.

It's About Time

"Maura was super possessive, and, if I said hi to a girl walking across campus Maura would be all over me asking me who she was, how I knew her, and what was going on. It was annoying as hell. I couldn't wait for her to leave at the end of the year so I could have some space.

"One day Maura and I walked into the bookstore and ran into her friend Caroline. Oh, my God, it was like in the movies, music played, hearts appeared everywhere, and I was tongue-tied. I had never felt that way before. But with Maura attached to me, there was no way I could even talk to Caroline without getting nailed. So, I accepted my fate and counted the days until the semester was over."

"James, why did you put up with her? Was it the sex? Is that a guy thing?" I interjected.

"I don't know. The sex part is definitely a guy thing, at that age anyway. But there was more to it than that. Getting away from her wasn't easy. It seems ridiculous that this little girl could intimidate the shit out of a big guy like me. But that was the truth. I walked on eggshells all the time. I'm living proof brawn is not required to bully someone into submission. Maura dazzled me with her beauty and charm before going in for the kill. I never saw it coming. She gradually and insidiously eroded my confidence. I couldn't tell up from down."

"That sounds familiar to me. Go on with your story."

"The month before graduation Maura pressured me nonstop to go to New York with her but I refused. Man, she did not like that. I think she gave me the silent treatment for a week, but at least she wasn't screaming at me. Basically, over time, I learned it was easier to just go along with her. I was depressed and felt trapped. After we graduated, she reluctantly left for New York City. At least I had some physical distance, and I immersed myself in the Master's program. But I never forgot Caroline.

"That summer I got a campus job with the admissions office and stayed in my apartment with the guys, who were happy to see me without Maura tagging along like Yoko Ono.

"One day when I was leading a tour of prospective students, I saw Caroline walking across the quad. I almost left my group and ran over to her, thrilled to know she was still on campus. I had to figure out how to get in touch with her. Hoping to run into her on campus didn't seem very efficient. She was probably a grad student so when I got back to the admissions office, I did a search and found her. She was an MFA student in music. Her class schedule helped narrow things down. Focusing on science, I had little contact with the arts but I did know where the music building was. I figured she would eventually show up for class so I hung around when I could. It took a while but I was determined and finally saw her. My heart leaped, I was so nervous and excited. I tried to be cool walking up to her and nonchalantly asking if she remembered me. It was a stupid line, but I couldn't think of anything else. Surprisingly, she said she did and called me Maura's fiancé. I corrected that error immediately and asked if she would have coffee with me. She agreed and that was it. I knew she was the one.

"Once Maura got wind that Caroline and I were dating she was furious and accused me of cheating on her, which technically, I guess I was. From my perspective, our relationship was over when Maura left, but it wasn't spelled out exactly because I didn't want to deal with her shit. But shit came anyway, in spades. Maura has a way of seeming so kind and helpful with friends that it's hard for them to believe the hell she put me through. She continued to insinuate herself in my life with

It's About Time

Caroline under the guise of being happy for us and staying friends, but I didn't trust her. As time went on Maura got distracted by life in the big city and showed up less frequently, but she was never far away. After we got married and moved to Connecticut she would visit. She brought baby gifts when Andy was born. She would meet up with Caroline in New York and sometimes out in LA. Then she started coming to Connecticut to see the boys and hang out with me when Caroline was away. It seemed fine, so I started to relax believing maybe time heals all wounds, and we could be friends. But I was wrong. I missed Caroline because she was away from home a lot, and it put a strain on our marriage.

"One weekend in the summer Maura came to visit, and I am ashamed to say, we slept together. I should have known this would not end well. She was married, but it was rocky. He was much older, his health was bad and while there were a lot of perks, Maura wasn't getting the attention she demanded. Plus, she was as horny as I was. I figured we would have a fun weekend and that would be it. I was stupid, stupid, stupid. She was relentless, calling and texting constantly. Whenever Caroline left for a work trip, Maura was on my doorstep. I tried to end it, but she threatened to tell Caroline and ruin my marriage. She said it would be easy to pay off high school girls to swear I had sex with them. She threatened to get me fired from my job and to ruin my reputation. When she said I would lose the boys, I caved to her demands.

"Meanwhile, things were getting worse with Caroline. Do you remember I told you she seemed like a different person? I couldn't do anything right, and she looked at me with such contempt. But I wasn't feeling too happy with myself either. I was depressed. If it wasn't for the boys, I don't know what I would have done. That was when I filed for divorce. Maura zoomed right in to supposedly comfort me. Then when Caroline came home sick, there were so many mixed feelings. Love, anger, hurt, shame, and grief swirled inside me. But I never stopped loving Caroline so I committed myself to her care hoping we could fix what was broken before it was too late. During that time Maura mainly stayed away from us but she texted me and left voice messages every day. I knew she was also calling Caroline but I don't know what they talked about. Maura wanted me to ship Caroline off to her family under the guise of doing what was best for her. I refused."

"Interesting that when we had 'the talk', you told me about you and Caroline but omitted Maura. Why?"

"I was ashamed. I didn't want you to know how stupid I was. And I hoped that we would never have to deal with her."

"I see. That didn't work out too well." I shake my head. "From now on, the whole truth. Okay? Maura told me you kept family and friends from seeing Caroline, Is that true?" I find it hard to believe but have to ask. James's face contorts with pain as he remembers that awful time.

"Absolutely not! Why would I do such a thing? She stayed in touch with her musician friends, and some visited when she felt well enough. The family was always welcome. Her sister came frequently, and her mother practically lived with us during that time. When Hospice said to gather people to say goodbye, I let everyone know. There was a stream of people, food, and flowers coming through. I wasn't the only person who loved her, that was clear. Maura, who supposedly cared so much for Caroline was noticeably absent." James shook his head, trying to shake off bad memories. "You're a therapist. You know how people work. Does this make any sense to you?"

It's About Time

"Well, yes, it's starting to. I learned the hard way about personality disorders which seems to describe Maura. It doesn't make sense if you're a normal person expecting everyone else to be the same." I think James is telling the truth. For him to get away from Maura's clutches, he will need to understand what's going on and know it is not his fault no matter what Maura tells him. He is only responsible for whatever regrettable decisions he made along the way.

"I want to hear the rest of your story." I rest my hand on James's arm.

"After Caroline died, Maura thought we would get back together. By then, her decrepit husband had died. She raked in a good share of his estate and, in her mind, the widow and widower would live happily ever after. Let me tell you, she does not like hearing the word, no. I refused to participate in her plan. After that, she made it a point to barge in on my life whenever she wanted, just to fuck me over. That is what I fear she is doing now. To us. That's why I want to keep her away from you."

"I get it. I understand."

"Bess, Maura has been in and out of my life for a long time, and I am ashamed to say I have let her push me around. We've slept together off and on for years because I never had the guts, or energy, to say no. This week she wanted to pick right up where she left off. I said no and she threatened me. She said she would tell the kids stuff about me. It almost worked. But then I thought about you, us, and the trust we're building. I couldn't risk hurting you and fucking that up. I don't care what Maura threatens me with, I will handle it. It's time to come clean and get my life back. So, I refused to cooperate with her agenda and held my ground. That's why I look like shit. She was brutal, but I feel a tiny bit better about myself."

"James, that is such a relief for me to hear. I didn't know what was going on at your house and imagined all kinds of things. She is gorgeous and probably hard to resist."

"True. Until you get to know her."

"I know we are just friends at this point, but at your house last weekend we hinted there could be more. Remember?" I ask.

"Yes, of course I remember. Do you still think it's possible? Even after this past week?"

"Well, there's work to do, but I'm staying open to the possibility. One thing I know is I cannot co-exist with Maura. You have to handle this. I am willing to be supportive, but this is something you have to do. How's that for a definite maybe?"

I slide over next to James on the couch, my head on his shoulder. I pull a blanket around both of us. James rests his head on the back of the couch and closes his eyes.

"James? Are you awake?" I sit up, knowing it has to be late. He stirs and mumbles no. "It's late and you look exhausted. Want to crash in my spare room tonight?"

"I would like that. Thanks, Bess."

"Come on. Let's go to bed." I take his hand and show him the way.

"Goodnight, moon." James smiles and walks into the bedroom.

"Goodnight, James."

CHAPTER 11

Push Back

Bess

The enticing scent of freshly brewed coffee and pancakes wafts into my bedroom. I smile at the thought of James cooking in the kitchen. Yawning, I stretch, throw the covers off, and go into the bathroom. It's been a long time since I've had a man in my place cooking breakfast. I splash water on my face, scrub off smudged mascara, brush my teeth, and comb my hair. That's when I notice hushed voices in the kitchen. I listen, wondering if it's morning TV, but it doesn't sound like it. Maybe James is talking on the phone. Whatever it is, I can't stay in the bathroom much longer with the lure of pancakes in the kitchen. I exchange my pajamas for jeans and a sweatshirt to venture forth.

That's when I see Maura.

"Maura. What are you doing here? I thought you went home yesterday." My voice sounds horrified like I am witnessing a three-car pileup on I-95. Maybe I'm still asleep and having a nightmare. She glides over, gives me obnoxious cheek kisses, and says I look adorable in my sweatshirt. Nope, it's not a dream, this is real. I'm not happy and I glare at James accusingly. My home is being desecrated, and my pleasant mood evaporates like a whiff of Maura's expensive perfume. James sheepishly hands me a mug of hot coffee mouthing "I'm sorry."

Hillary Gauvreau Oat

"James, are we out of half-and-half?" I ask as I search the refrigerator. Before he can respond, Maura announces that she found a beautiful creamer in the cabinet and decided to use it.

"It's on the table. Come on over and have a seat." Maura says sweetly as she herds me to the table. How dare she make herself at home in my condo! After what James shared last night, I want her out of my house and my life. The woman has the absolute gall to make nice with a man that she threatened to destroy. She is either completely clueless or a sociopath. I'm leaning toward the second option. Supremely annoyed, I yank a chair out from the table and sit as far away from Maura as I can get. My mind sifts through options for getting her the fuck out of my house. James puts a stack of pancakes on the table that smell heavenly but I refuse to share a meal with that woman. Just the thought gives me the dry heaves. She continues chatting, oblivious to how she is ruining my morning. James brings warm maple syrup to the table and sits between us, which is interesting considering Maura's attempts at triangulation.

"Maura. What are you doing in my house?" I demand. She launches into a story about how the house in Greenwich was a shambles when she got there. The poor thing could hardly find a toothbrush.

"I couldn't possibly stay there. I gave the caretaker a piece of my mind! The house needs to be in order when I get back, or he will be looking for another job." She huffs. "I tolerated being there for the night but could not possibly stay under those conditions. Early this morning I jumped in my car and headed back to James's place. Isn't it great that we live so close to each other?" Maura pats James's hand. "And...this is the exciting part...as I was driving, I had the most amazing idea. I

It's About Time

am sick of that huge mausoleum in Greenwich. It belonged to my second husband and never was my style. With real estate prices so high I could make a bundle if I sell it. Then I can buy a beach house right here in Old Lyme and be close to both of you. Wouldn't that be great?" Maura grins with evil delight while the color drains from my face, and a shot of adrenaline surges through me. That is a terrible, horrible, no-good idea. Maura would be constantly messing in our lives, and threatening James on a full-time basis. She can live wherever she wants, I can't stop that, but she is not going to insert herself into my life. Not now, not ever. James looks stunned. Maura continues talking animatedly about her plans, ignoring our reactions.

"I was surprised when I got to James's house and he wasn't there. He's always home." She looks at him with sad eyes and an exaggerated frown, then brightens and says she decided to come to my place. "I figured you would know a good realtor, Bess, and I could wait here for James to get home. Imagine my surprise when James answered the door being all domestic and making breakfast. Hmm, I wonder what was going on here last night." She snickers and narrows her eyes. There is no reason for me to be pleasant with Maura. She has nothing on me, and I want her out.

"I want you to leave my house. Now," I say calmly, but firmly. James stiffens. Everything we talked about last night is going through my mind. Her lies, threats, and coercive control make her a mental health hazard that should be wrapped in yellow caution tape. Give this woman an inch and she will suck the life right out of us. I am not going to let that happen and I hope James will stand up to her too. I am sorry this is happening now before James and I have a chance to formulate a plan.

But when an opportunity presents itself it's best to take it. Maura's smile vanishes and I see rage like hot lava bubbling below the surface of her charm.

"How dare you talk to me like that! James, come on, let's go home." She stands up and grabs his arm to pull him along. I am holding my breath, saying a silent prayer that for once he will not let her push him around. If he follows her like a whipped puppy our friendship is over. I will not have my peaceful life upended with this crap. James stays seated at the table. He glances at me and I see a glimmer of the man I knew before Maura arrived on the scene. He turns to Maura and starts to speak.

"First, I am not going anywhere with you. Second, my home is not your home. You are not welcome there, or here. I'm going to change the locks this weekend. Do you understand? Now please sit down. I have some things to say." Maura is furious and refuses to sit. Instinctively I glance around the room for sharp objects. Thankfully, no obvious weapons are within reach. Still, under the right circumstances, anything can be a weapon, like a fork in the eye. I wince at the thought. That may sound like an overreaction, but I don't underestimate people like Maura. I'm not sure where James is going with this conversation but I'm thrilled with how he started it.

"Maura, for a long time you have made my life a living hell. I will not allow that anymore. You destroyed my marriage and have threatened me for years. No more. I'm done." He looks over at me, then back at Maura. "I want you to leave Bess alone. I want you to leave me alone. Is that clear?" James's voice is calm and steady but I suspect he has a lot going on inside. "If you refuse, trust me, there will be consequences. Bess has asked you to leave, so do us all a favor and just go." James stands, and moves toward me, protectively putting his

It's About Time

hand on my shoulder. I'm so relieved I don't know whether to laugh or cry.

"Consequences? There will be consequences," Maura mocks.

I feel James tense up like a coiled spring.

"Finally get some balls, did ya? You get 'em from your girlfriend here?" Maura angrily spits the words out.

"Fuck you, Maura!" James shouts, fists tight. "I'll show you who's got balls. Get the fuck out of this house. Now!" James takes a step toward Maura. I grab the back of his shirt, pulling to get his attention and prevent more trouble.

Maura sputters and fumes a bit more, but backs off. As a final act of defiance, she deliberately spills her coffee on my beautiful table.

"Oops." She sneers, turns on her heel, and leaves slamming the door behind her. James mops up the coffee while I lock the door. I sit at the table, take James's hand, and squeeze it tight.

"That was intense. What is she, four years old? I thought you were going to hurt her. Are you okay?"

"Yeah, well, I sincerely wanted to. I think I'm okay. Are you?" he asks.

"Yes, for now. The gall of that woman. I'm so happy you stood up to her. You were awesome. I think you scared her, James." I push away from the table and stand up. "Come here." I open my arms to him, and he moves into them, speaking softly.

"Bess, I had to get my self-respect back. What she said triggered the hell out of me because I suspect it's true. I have been afraid to stand up to her. But enough is enough." He takes a deep breath, moves away from me, and sits down. "I don't know what she will do now, but I can't worry about it."

"Everyone says that bullies back down when confronted. You proved it. She could not get out of here fast enough. Damn, I was shocked to see Maura in the kitchen. That's not how I imagined my morning going. And what the fuck, James, you let her in?"

"I didn't have a chance to. She just slithered past me."

"She did that to me too. You're changing the locks at your house? Can we find a locksmith on a Saturday?" I brought the stack of pancakes into the kitchen, inserting several into the toaster oven to warm.

"We don't need a locksmith, just Home Depot. I'll pick up some new deadbolts and install them. I want you to have a key Bess. Just in case."

"In case of what? You get locked out? Hopefully not because you expect something more gruesome." While I hate to think about anything bad happening, it makes sense to be prepared.

"In case of whatever. And while I am there, I will get you a chain lock. Let's make it a little harder for Maura to slither. I would feel safer if we set you up with a security camera too." That sounds good to me. My phone rings and we both jump. It's Virginia so I answer it.

"Hey. What's up?" Virginia asks.

It's About Time

"We are eating pancakes," I say.

"We, Kemosabe? You have company?" I could feel Virginia grinning through the phone. "And who might that be? Hmmm? Anyone I know?"

"Yup. James is here and making pancakes for breakfast. Isn't that nice?" I will fill her in later. She knows there is more to the story.

"You tell me. Is it nice?" She chuckles. "Listen, it's supposed to be a nice day and I wondered if you …and maybe your personal pancake maker…want to come over and cook out later?"

"That sounds great. Count me in. Hold on." I ask James if he wants to go and he nods his head yes. "We'll be there. We have some things to do this afternoon. What time do you want us? Can I bring anything?"

"Come on over when you get that stuff done. We're just working in the yard. Bring a salad and a six-pack."

"You got it. See you later. I'll text when we are on the way."

"James, do you think Maura has left the area? Gone back to Greenwich? I'm afraid she will jump out of the bushes at any moment. She keeps showing up when I least expect it." James is finishing his pancake and stops chewing when I ask about Maura.

"Oh, man. I was so relieved when she left your house it never dawned on me that she might not leave town. Keep your doors locked Bess. We will get the camera up tomorrow. I will make sure everything is secure here after the cookout."

"Sounds good." James finishes his breakfast and gets ready to leave. "Be careful out there. Text me if anything comes up, okay?" He agrees, leans in close, and kisses me, tasting like coffee and maple syrup.

"Kissing?" Even though we broke our sleepover rule last night, we haven't changed our original agreement. I wonder how long that will last the way things are going.

"You don't like it?"

"Oh no, I love it, just wondering what's going on."

"Nothing going on. I'm just feeling good. You love it! Good to know." He smiles and leaves for Home Depot. I head into the shower. Right now, the last thing on my mind is Maura, and that feels nice.

* * *

I make the salad with romaine, heirloom tomatoes that don't taste like cardboard, sweet onions, feta, and briny Kalamata olives. Then whip up a dressing of fresh lemon juice and olive oil. I haven't heard from James so I assume he is still busy with projects. I take the book that I got from the library and go out on the patio to read until James gets back. At about four o'clock I hear a knock on the door. It's James, locked out as promised.

He puts the Home Depot bag and an assortment of tools on the counter and sighs.

It's About Time

"You were right. She didn't leave. I'm not sure she is gone now, but I did my best."

"Come. Sit." I sit on the couch and pat the cushion next to me. "What happened?" I move a little closer. James tells me he went home to replace the locks. He was working on the old front door which needed adjustments for the new lock to fit.

"I was focused on what I was doing and never saw her until she marched up the front steps and into my face. She was mad as hell and screaming like a banshee. She demanded to know what was going on and blamed you for turning me against her." He shook his head in disbelief. "I told her to leave. She laughed. I had a hammer in my hand and was afraid I would lose control and hit her. That thought scared the crap out of me. I got it together and asked her to sit down so we could talk. I hoped that would calm things down even if she wasn't happy about what I was going to say."

"Oh wow. Did she sit? What did you say?"

"Yes, she did, thankfully. She calmed down because she expected I would apologize, and beg for forgiveness, as usual. That wasn't where I was going." I smile and give James a thumbs-up. "I told her to get out of my life. Period. There was no point in getting into a discussion about why. She's not stupid and knows exactly what has gone down all these years. She never thinks anything is her fault so asking her to take responsibility is a waste of breath. This time I didn't need her agreement and I didn't care if she understood. I calmly told her not to call, text, or show up at my house ever again. Bess, her reaction was freakin' weird. Her face was blank. She agreed and left. Honestly, the lack of response was completely unexpected and freaked me out. I am used to her threats and rages, but that cold, blank, stare was much scarier. There is something wrong with her. Somehow, I managed to finish the job on the door, locked up, and here I am."

"Wow. James, I'm happy you're standing up to her. I know how hard that is."

"It was a long time coming, Bess." He turns to look at me. "I was having flashbacks of feeling suffocated by Maura and I could feel depression creeping up on me. If we have a future, and I am not assuming anything, I will not let Maura ruin it for us." James presses a shiny new key in my hand.

"I am so relieved. I don't know what the future holds, but I didn't want Maura in it. Ever. At all. I am so happy you are holding the line with her. I will keep the key safe and get mine made for you. Just in case." I smile.

When we get to Virginia's they are relaxing on the deck. New green leaves cast shade, and birds crowd around the birdfeeder flapping and chirping. The air is filled with the scent of freshly mowed grass and cultivated rich dark earth. We step up onto the deck and remark on all the work they have done in the yard.

"Hey, your gardens look ready to go. Doesn't it feel good to get your hands in the dirt? That is one thing I miss about condo living." I say, as I hug Virginia and Bob.

"Thanks," says Bob. "Digging in the dirt is our therapy. Come on by and help whenever. We can always use the company."

"Hey, you have music playing. You wouldn't happen to have *One Moment in Time* by Whitney Houston on your play list,

It's About Time

would you?" I put the salad on the table and open beers while Bob scrolls through music on his iPad.

When I hear Whitney's opening notes, I tell them the song has been in my head all day. I whisper to Virginia that I think it's *our song*. "You know? Clocks? Time? No brainer."

"You have a song?" Virginia asks, raising an eyebrow. "Seems we have some catching up to do," she says quietly.

James and Bob drift over to the gas grill to start it for the burgers. Virginia and I troop back and forth to the kitchen gathering condiments, rolls, and sliced onion to be cooked on the grill.

"Hey do either of you dudes want a veggie burger?" Bob shakes his head no while James looks at Virginia like she has lost her mind. "I am just asking! Jeesh. For all I know you're a vegan, James."

"I'm a Highlander! There are no vegans in my family tree," he says with pseudo indignation. "No offense to vegans. I'm sure they are nice people." He smiles.

The next song up is "I Wanna Dance With Somebody", another great Whitney hit. Virginia dances over to Bob, grabs him and they spin out into the middle of the deck like a *Dancing with the Stars* audition.

"I didn't know you guys could dance like that! Wowzers! I'm impressed."

Hillary Gauvreau Oat

"That's what happens when you have been married as long as we have. After all the blood, sweat, tears, and child-raising, you get happy feet." And with that, Bob spins Virginia around one last time, kisses her, and heads back to the grill. Being with these people distracts me from how my day started. I'm still slightly on edge after so many Maura surprises and wonder if James is looking over his shoulder, too.

It's nice to see the guys cooking at the grill, chatting. Bob flips the burgers and James tends the onions on the side griddle.

"Isn't it sexy when a man cooks? They need matching barbeque aprons, dontcha think?" Virginia nudges me. We sit at the table sipping beer waiting for the food.

"I am going to cut to the chase and poke my nose in your business. Did you and the pancake man sleep together last night? Pancakes? Song? Come on, tell me!" She whispers. "Just nod yes or no." She nods her head yes while I laugh and shake my head no. Before I can comment further, the menfolk join us bearing a platter of perfectly grilled burgers.

After dinner, we linger at the table chatting and drinking beer. Virginia and Bob are going to Tucson at the end of next week for the baby vigil. Their son Gabe is a wreck trying to make sure everything is perfect. But Pam, his wife, seems relatively calm. During late-stage pregnancy, there isn't much else she can do. I remember those days when it finally dawned on me that there was no turning back. That other human being was going to have to get out of my body and into the world. Freaking out wasn't helpful so I just leaned back, put up my swollen feet, and surrendered to the inevitable. We share our stories of having babies. James mentions that his firstborn baby just got engaged to be married, and we remark on how fast time passes. He takes out his phone to share the

It's About Time

engagement picture and his smile fades. He recovers quickly, finds the picture, and passes it around to oohs and ahs. I give James a questioning look. He shakes his head, no, he doesn't want to get into it now so I let it go but feel his mood shift. That's when Virginia asks what we have been doing the last couple of days. I look at James.

"Do you want to get into it?" I ask him. He shrugs and says why not.

"Well, after that intriguing question, I think you have to fill us in! Come on. What's up? Inquiring minds want to know." Bob scoops the last bits of salad onto his plate, spears an olive, and waits for us to start.

"Ok, well Maura has become a bit of an issue," I tell them. James grunts saying that's the understatement of the year. I continue my story.

"You knew she came to see me Thursday night, right? She was set to leave for Greenwich the next day. James was going to come over after she left so we could talk. And that's what we did. We talked." I look intently at Virginia. "It got late and we were exhausted so James slept in the spare room. When I got up this morning James was making pancakes and guess who was in the kitchen?"

"Oh my God. No!" Virginia's jaw drops. "I thought she went back to Greenwich?"

"So did we. I am learning that Maura is unpredictable and not to assume anything. Right James?" He frowns and nods in agreement.

"Then what happened?" Both Bob and Virginia are eager for the details.

"I asked her what she was doing in my house. She rambled on about how her place was a shambles and she couldn't stay there, so she ended up in our lap. Then she said, get this, she wants to buy a beach house in Old Lyme! Can you believe that? I told her I wanted her out of my house. Period. End of story. She was insulted and tried to get James to leave with her like she owned him or something. James said no. It was a beautiful sight to behold." I smile at him. "Then she left in a huff."

"After all that excitement, James went to Home Depot to get new locks. You want to take it from there James?" Virginia and Bob are looking at us with their mouths open in disbelief.

"Wow? There's more to the story?" Virginia blurts out. "This is crazy!"

"Oh yeah. Crazy for sure. But we are handling it." James says. "It isn't easy because nothing ever is with Maura, but I drew a line in the sand." He continues the story. "Maura has had a key to my place for years. Not knowing what she is up to, I wanted to change the locks today. While I was dealing with the front door she showed up, in my face, angry as hell." James tells the story, keeping it simple, ending by telling Maura to get out of his life. "That isn't exactly how I said it, but that's the gist."

"Holy crap. I'm speechless. Good for you James!"" says Virginia. "But I bet you haven't seen the last of her."

It's About Time

"You're probably right. I want Bess to have a security camera and keep her doors locked. I don't think Maura would physically hurt anyone, but she can be a terror in every other respect. And since she knows you guys too, it makes sense to be alert and careful. I'm sorry you're being dragged through my dung pile." Bob tells James not to worry because they need fertilizer for the garden. We all laugh a little nervously.

"Do you want us to keep an eye on your homestead while you are in Tucson?" I ask. Virginia thinks that is a good idea and wonders if they should also get a security camera.

"We could do that. Then we would be able to monitor the wildlife." Bob gets excited, and James offers to help with the installation. While the guys make plans, Virginia and I bring out the strawberry shortcake. Freshly baked biscuits. Juicy sliced strawberries from the farm. A can of sweet whipped cream that circulates until it sputters empty. Just as we finish dessert, the Edison string lights come on overhead. The guys take that as a cue to clean up, chatting the whole time about security cameras. Virginia and I get comfortable by the fire pit.

I smile at Virginia and pat her hand. "As you already know, because I can see it on your face, there is way more to the Maura and James story. Pancake man, as you call him, shared most of it with me last night. It's too much to get into now, but what I went through with Prince Charming is half of what Maura puts him through. James shows signs of post-traumatic stress and I can understand why. I wasn't sure if he could stand up to her, but he is. Having friends like us behind him helps, I think. Let's hope he can hold that line in the sand. We'll see. Maybe, just maybe, something good could come of this for us." Virginia puts her hands together in prayer. The guys join us, and start a fire in the fire pit. We chat and listen to music until the stars come out. A meteor shoots across the sky and I make a wish that Maura leaves us alone.

Driving home in James's truck I asked him about the mood shift when he looked at his phone. He tells me that Maura texted him. I was afraid of that.

"You want to see it?" He asks.

"No, not really. She's testing you ya know."

"Yeah, I figured that. I'll block her number if I have to. For now, I think I would like to know where she is and what she's up to. It's my keep your friends close, and your enemies close, strategy. I suspect she won't go away quietly." I agree. It's encouraging to see this side of James, but I worry that we are not finished with Maura.

CHAPTER 12

The Other Shoe Drops

Bess

The sticky, humid days of summer are punctuated by an occasional cooling thunderstorm. Tourists have discovered our quaint town and the streets are packed with cars, and people dodging them as they cross Main Street. Locals tend to grouse. We like stopping for an ice cream cone without having to line up and wait twenty minutes. But we also take pride in having a community people love to visit. My clients ebb and flow creating a balance of work and free time. Best of all there is peace. Maura has stayed away ever since James delivered his ultimatum and we are gradually starting to relax.

In July, James's son Thomas visited from Florida. Thomas seems to take after his mother in looks and musical talent. He is in a graduate program for music production at the University of Florida in Gainesville. He keeps himself solvent working sound gigs for local bands and as a teaching assistant. He is creative, sensitive, and a bit intense. I'm not quite sure what he thought about me. He was polite but that was the extent of it.

James and I spend lots of time together, but I still refer to him as my friend. Virginia is rooting for us to move forward, but I'm not quite ready. Besides, what we have is wonderful. The only element we are missing is sleeping together, and I know taking that step would change everything. My past romances have been disappointing, to say the least, and I don't want a repeat performance.

Andy, James's older son, recently sent a "save the date" card for his wedding. The family has been discussing wedding plans for weeks and decided on a small wedding in Montana's Glacier National Park next June. Spring will be blooming in Glacier Park and most likely the snow will be gone by then. We hope. Andy has a master's degree in forestry and environmental conservation and is a Park Ranger at Glacier. He has his heart set on marrying Emily in the majestic cathedral of mountains that he loves.

It's late Friday afternoon, and James's turn to make supper. I pull into his driveway and step out of the cool car into a wall of stifling heat. By the time I reach the back door, I am a frizzy-haired, ball of sweat. It's not an attractive look. I let myself in and thank God James and I are past the need to impress each other every minute of the day. When I had a stomach bug, he kindly held my hair back while I tossed the contents of my GI system into the toilet repeatedly. If that didn't send him running, a little frizz is no problem. I notice James is on a Zoom call with Andy and Emily at the kitchen island. He waves hello and calls me over, introducing me as a friend with a capital 'F'. I think he made that point a little too vigorously, but that is what we are, with a capital F. They are easy to talk to and I enjoy our chat. After a few minutes, I excuse myself so they can get back to planning. Andy is like his father in looks and disposition. He is a gentle, warm, nature boy with a full beard. His fiancé Emily seems like a smart, self-possessed pixie with sapphire blue eyes. Andy loves his father, but, as in any family, there have been disagreements. From what I can tell they haven't prevented a warm and loving relationship. I overhear Andy saying they're keeping the guest list to the immediate family because the location in the park has limited accessibility. The

It's About Time

reception will be casual in a Vrbo rental to be determined with enough space for everyone to stay together. This is the first time the family will be in Montana, and Andy wants to maximize that time. James asks if Thomas is coming and who else is on the guest list.

"Thomas is coming and already making plans. He will be on summer break and excited to see Montana." I hear Andy say. He laughs and tells his father that Thomas is more excited about being in Montana than at the wedding. He fills James in on the guest list and to my absolute horror, *Auntie Maura* is on the list. James covers his surprise pretty well but I know we both feel the impact. In his enthusiasm, Andy doesn't notice his father's reaction and quickly moves on to other details. He asks his father if he remembers a song his mother wrote called "Together". James says he certainly does remember it. He tells Andy it's perfect for the wedding and that his mother wrote the song when she was pregnant with him. He promises to dig out Caroline's old computer and will send him the file. When they close, James tells his son he loves him, offers whatever wedding help he needs, and promises to talk soon. He gently closes his laptop and stares out the kitchen window. I can see the conversation has stirred up something in James. Humans can hold such diverse feelings as love and sadness, anger and regret, all at the same time. His past with Caroline, the love and loss of so much, his love for the boys, and the horror of Maura, have to be weighing on him. After a while, he shakes it off, goes to the refrigerator, and pours two glasses of chilled white wine. He looks at them, both hands gripping the kitchen counter. I come up behind him and put my arms around his middle, resting my cheek on his shoulder.

"You ok?" I asked gently.

"Yeah. I don't know. I think so. Lots of memories." James turns and puts his arms around me. "I didn't realize the wedding would bring up so much. Did you hear he is inviting Maura?"

"Yup."

"That song is perfect for Andy to play at his wedding. Caroline and I were so happy when she wrote it." James shares as we move to the sunroom and sit down. "It's hard to understand how so much love could go so wrong. I regret allowing Maura into our lives, and now she is invited to a very small intimate family wedding. It is not okay, Bess. Not okay at all. But what do I do about it? It's Andy's wedding. He has a right to invite whoever he wants." James leans back into the couch cushions and sips his wine.

"Well, If Andy insists then there isn't much you can do except, pray she doesn't go. I can't imagine all of you being cozy in a house with her. That's some serious tension to deal with. Especially after drawing your line in the sand." Maura spent a lot of time with James and the kids when Caroline was away and then after she died. It wasn't what it seemed on the surface but the kids don't know that. She can be charming when she wants to be so I understand if Andy feels a connection to her. He has no idea what she has done to his father.

"There isn't enough whiskey on the planet to make that situation tolerable." James reaches for my hand. "I am happy they got to meet you, at least virtually. I didn't get to ask about bringing you to the wedding because the conversation took a turn."

"It's okay. Since it's only immediate family I'm out anyway, unless you adopt me," I tease. "So, the boys know nothing about what Maura did to you?"

It's About Time

"No, I don't think so. They may have noticed things over the years, but we never talked about it."

"Maybe it's time to talk about it. They're old enough to understand, and there's no need to go into gruesome detail. I hate the thought of Andy's big day being ruined by the presence of that manipulative, conniving you-know-what. If she was your ex-wife or your crabby Aunt Minnie, I could understand sucking it up and getting through the wedding for everyone's sake. But she's not. Time to shed light on this mess. At the very least, you could tell Andy you don't want her there. Would he want her there if he knew?" James sighs and shakes his head no.

"You're right. I don't know how he will react but I have to be honest with him."

* * *

Saturday morning, I get up early and meet Virginia for a walk at State Beach Park, then bagels at her house. The air is still heavy but it's a tiny bit cooler by the water. I tell Virginia about the wedding plans and Maura.

"Are you kidding me? I thought you were done with her." Virginia frowns.

"It's a process. Her tendrils go deep into this family. James is going to talk with Andy and tell him he doesn't want her invited. As far as he knows the boys have no idea what Maura has done."

"Good for him!"

"We don't know how much contact Maura has with the boys now, if any. Or the lies she may be telling them. I'm hoping their relationship with her is all past tense."
"Well, she is present tense enough for Andy to put her on the list," Virginia observes and she is right.

"Maybe he's doing it for his father because he thinks they're close. It's certainly useless to appeal to Maura to do the right thing. James will handle it."

"Maura wouldn't know the right thing if it bit her on the butt. Good thing you have that recording of her spewing venom. If you need proof for the boys, there it is." Virginia's face is red from heat and exertion. Time to get out of this heat and go home for coffee and cool air conditioning. When we get to her house, we make iced coffee and Virginia laughs.

"I can't look at iced coffee anymore without thinking of Maura and her iced half-caf bullshit." We laugh.

"I forgot about that recording, Virginia. I'm going to remind James about it. Airing the truth is like cleaning out a closet. It gets worse before it gets better. At least we have time to sort things out before the wedding. Those poor boys have no idea what ugly business was going on." I slip bagels in the toaster oven. Virginia gets cream cheese out of the refrigerator. When the bagels are ready, we bring our plates and a second iced coffee to the table. I tell her how teeny tiny the wedding is going to be. Small enough to fit into one large Vrbo rental. Too small to avoid Maura.

"So even though James wants me to go, I don't think I will be invited. This is an immediate family-only ceremony and I don't qualify. Plus, we are just friends and friends don't shack up at their kid's wedding."

It's About Time

"Well, maybe you will be shacking up by then." Virginia grins wickedly and pokes me.
"Do you realize how complicated everything would get if we slept together? It would change everything!"

Virginia raises an eyebrow and looks at me.

"What?" I demand.

"Complicated? Really? You two are like an old married couple. You finish each other's sentences for God's sake. But seriously, it is obvious, to me at least, how much you two love each other."

"You're right. We have a very sweet connection. But don't say the L word or you'll jinx me." I laugh and cover my ears. Virginia shakes her head at me.

"You know it is so hot and steamy when you two are around that Bob and I can't wait to get into the bedroom. Really. I'm serious. I don't know how you two can hold out." She crosses her heart. "That is the truth."

"Okay, I'll take that under advisement. I would hate to make you and Bob suffer needlessly." Chuckling, I put my dishes in the dishwasher, hug Virginia, and tell her I love her even if she is a pain in my ass.

Errands done. Groceries bought and put away. Laundry in the dryer. Clean sheets on both beds. I finally collapse on the couch with a glass of iced tea when my phone rings. It's James.

"Hey. What's up?" I hope nothing is up because I am considering curling up with a book and maybe taking a nap.

"Can you come over? Soon? Are you busy? I found something you have to see." Well, that piqued my curiosity.

"On my way." Groaning, I pull myself off the comfy couch. I slip my purse over my shoulder and pick the keys up from the counter. It takes me under ten minutes to get to his house and I let myself in the kitchen door.

"Hello? I am here? Where are you?" I don't see James, who is usually hanging out in the sunroom. "Marco?" I call hoping he will respond with "Polo", like the pool game. I guess he isn't playing. I see him walk through the living room toward the kitchen looking serious and without as much as a hello he tells me to come with him. I follow along into a spare room that he uses as an office. The computer screen is lit up. James pulls an extra chair over for me and we sit down.

I ask him what's going on, and notice he is clenching his jaw. He tells me he dug out Caroline's old computer looking for the song Andy wanted. He found a lot more than a song.

"I haven't looked at Caroline's computer since she died. It hurt too much and felt like an invasion of her privacy. Plus, I was afraid to see things I didn't want to know. That ship has sailed. I found the computer and booted it up. Caroline left a small notebook with passwords in it so I figured I could open what I needed. I saw a folder called 'journal' on the desktop. It went way back to the good times and then straight on through until she couldn't keep it up anymore. Now, I am so fucking outraged that if Maura was here, I'm afraid of what I would do. Remember when I said that Caroline acted like a different person? Yeah, well now I know why." James is so angry the veins at his temples are pulsing. I am afraid he will have a stroke if he doesn't calm down. He shows me an entry from way back when she first started going to LA for work. She talked about how much she loved her work, but she missed James. She poked

It's About Time

fun at him being such a homebody while she was off gallivanting but expressed gratitude for the relationship even if mystified how they ever found common ground. Then he moves forward in time to another entry. He reads it aloud to me.

"Maura came to visit me today at my hotel in Los Angeles. We had a great day. I showed her around the studio, and she met my compadres. Later we went to dinner at my favorite little bistro, just the two of us. That was when Maura got serious and said she hesitated to say anything because she didn't want me to be hurt, but figured I had to know the truth. James and she are close so this was almost as painful for her as for me. She struggled to tell me the most horrible stories about James. His drinking is out of control, his rages that are terrifying the boys, and his affairs. I could not eat after that so we left and went back to my hotel where I lost it. I wailed and sobbed and ranted into the wee hours of the morning until I was exhausted. Maura, bless her, is such a good friend. She stayed with me, offering comfort and support. I don't know what to do now. If it wasn't for the boys I would never go home to that bastard again. But I love the kids and I will have to figure out how to get through this. Where is the man I fell in love with? How could he have changed so much? I am supposed to go home next week, it's going to be hard for me to even look at him."

"Lies! Maura filled her head with *lies*. No wonder she was different." James slams the laptop shut and we look at each other. There is so much pain, betrayal, and heartbreak in that one entry that tears well up in my eyes. James is enraged. I can't blame him.

"There are more entries, hundreds of them that are all filled with the most outrageous bullshit I have ever heard. About how I got drunk and tried to rape Maura. Me? I leave the kids alone for long periods and beat them when I'm drunk. And while she is telling Caroline all that shit, she is coming to me to offer support and advice about my marriage. It's so fucked up." He pounds his fist down on the desk. "How could Caroline believe all those lies? I thought she loved me. Why didn't she talk to me? Question me? Scream at me? If she said something the house of lies Maura built would have fallen apart."

"James, Maura is good at manipulating people. She uses a dash of truth to make her lies believable. Then throws in fear to keep people from fact-checking. It's disappointing that Caroline didn't talk to you, but don't blame her. Look at how Maura has manipulated you."

"Maura is a fucking psycho. I don't want her near my kids." James gets up and angrily paces the room. "I have to talk to Andy. There is no way she can be at that wedding. Period!"

"James, do you have any idea what Maura has told the boys? I'm wondering how close they are. Andy thought enough of her to put her on the guest list."

"Jesus," James says it almost as a prayer of intercession. He runs his hands through his hair as is his habit when he's stressed. "I didn't even think of that. What has she told them? Has she fucked with them too? I wouldn't be surprised. It makes me wonder if she instigated some of the issues I had with Andy and Thomas over the years. Dear God, I wish I had known. This is all my fault. I am the one who didn't have the balls to dump Maura when she went to New York. But, Bess, I honestly didn't know. Never even suspected what she was doing. I saw the obvious stuff, of course. She was possessive and difficult to deal with, but this evil?? I never had a clue."

"Of course you didn't. How could you? This kind of behavior is not what any of us expect from people we know. So please, be angry, but don't blame yourself. Maura fools a lot of people including three dead husbands. I'm guessing that when you chose Caroline over her, you made an enemy for life." James's anger is calming down and now he looks befuddled.

"What a fucking mess." James bows his head. "It is hard to believe people like Maura are out there in the world fucking up people's lives for sport."

"What are you going to do now?" I ask.

"Will you go for a walk with me? I need to think."

"Of course. Come on." I take his hand and we go out into the humid heat to walk around the lake.

We walk mostly in silence accompanied by the summer sounds of cicadas and an occasional bullfrog. I can almost hear the wheels turning in James's head as he remembers things and starts to put pieces together. Pandora's box is open and he is firmly in reality now. What he thought was a difficult situation has turned into something much worse. Nothing, his marriage, Maura, his life, is what he thought it was. He and Caroline were played for fools by a bitter, disturbed woman, determined to destroy their happiness. When we get back to his house, he is calm and resolute. He says he has to call Andy. We pour some iced tea and talk.

"James, I know you want to rant about Maura, but that is probably not a good idea to do with Andy. Rant all you want with me. But keep it clean and simple with your kids. Know what I mean?"

"Yeah. I get it. It isn't their fight." James sits at the kitchen island.

"James, do you know what you're going to say?"

"I'm going to tell him not to invite Maura to the wedding for starters."

"Perfect! Maybe she's not important to him, and then you can let the rest go. Imagine you're peeling this conversation off in layers. With each layer, you'll know what and how much to tell him. Make sense?"

"Yep. Totally. What time is it?"

"It's around 5:30. I know you've got this! It's going to be okay."

James retrieves his laptop from the office and sets it up in the kitchen. He texts Andy asking if he can Zoom with him and sends him the link. He waits, staring at the Zoom screen. I stay out of the way, offering moral support from the sun room and saying silent prayers that this conversation goes well. Andy enters the meeting and is happy to see his Dad, remarking that talking two days in a row has got to be a record. James agrees.

Andy asks what's up and wonders if something is wrong because James looks serious. James starts by asking why Andy wants to invite Maura to the wedding. Andy tells him that she was around so much when he was younger that she felt like family and he thought his Dad would appreciate her being there. That's when James, without going into detail, says he prefers she not be invited. As simple as that. Good job James! He tells Andy they are not close anymore and it would be difficult being together at the wedding for reasons he doesn't want to get into. Andy has no problem with that saying they aren't close anymore either. He asks his Dad if there would be

It's About Time

a problem since they already sent a save-the-date card. James says no, just don't send an invitation. Andy comments that it works out better not to have an extra person because of the limited accommodations. He doesn't seem bothered by his dad's request at all. James is flooded with relief. He thanks Andy for understanding and tells him he found the song and will email the file to him. They end their call, and it's done. James closes his laptop breathing a huge sigh of relief. Then he smiles at me.

"I didn't have to get into it at all! I am so relieved." He comes over to me, pulls me off the couch, and spins me around.

"So now we are dancing?" I laugh. "I am so happy for you! Now all you have to do is enjoy the wedding. What's for dinner or is this going to be the second night in a row with no plan?" I tease and poke him in the ribs. He tries to tickle me but I get away running through the house with James chasing after me. We end up in a pillow fight. This exuberant release of energy feels exhilarating after so much tension. It's like shaking up a can of seltzer and popping the top. I laugh so much my cheeks hurt. We collapse on a pile of pillows and couch cushions giggling like children. Our arms and legs tangled up, and James's body is next to me. That's when it happens. The kiss. It is passionate and mutual. I feel like I am being swept away by a huge wave. Then I freak out. I remember what Virginia said earlier about the sexual tension between us. It would be so easy to surrender at this moment. But then what? I can't set myself up for another relationship disaster. My body tenses and I pull away from James.

"Hey, where are you going? I like that. Please come back?" He reaches for me from the pile of cushions. I like it, too, and that is the problem. I throw a pillow at him, trying to make light of the kiss saying I need something to eat. We are reaching a turning point, and we both feel it. James gets up off the floor telling me he's sorry. He knows he broke our carefully crafted rules. Seems we are doing that a lot lately.

"It just happened, Bess. I know I crossed a line, I'm sorry." I look up at him and smile.

"It's okay. You did nothing wrong. I liked it too. I'm the one who is sorry. Do you want to hear something funny? Virginia told me that when we are around there is so much sexual tension between us that she and Bob race to the bedroom when we leave."

"Really? Did she say that? Too much." We both laugh and put cushions and pillows back on the couch so we can sit down.

James looks at me. "Bess, I have a lot of feelings for you. I want to make this a real thing. You and me."

I stroke his face. "If you are trying to seduce me it's working." I yank gently on his beard. "I have feelings for you too. Can you be patient with me? I don't want to mess this up."

"Of course, I can be patient. As long as I know you're interested in the same thing I am, and we are working toward it. That's what counts." Indeed, it does.

"Oh, I'm interested, James. And that is what scares me." I kiss him softly.

"I hear ya." James pulls me close. "I think I have fallen for you, Bess. I am beyond help."

"Yup. We are definitely on the same page." I whisper into his ear.

It's About Time

CHAPTER 13

Fear and Longing in Connecticut

Bess

There is a saying that our greatest longing is our deepest fear. It's like stomping on the brake and the gas at the same time. Maura has been the focus of our attention, but that kiss brought me hurtling back to *us*. We have been dancing around the edges of that kiss for a while. Virginia could see it coming a mile away.

Getting to know James has been easy. We're comfortable together. He reminds me that good men exist in our jaded world. We're at a turning point. It's been over a year since he rescued me from the sidewalk so it's about time to get past my fear or I could miss my chance with James. I don't want to be that bitter old lady all alone in the nursing home filled with regret.

It's Friday night, and I look forward to seeing James at my condo for our usual dinner and debrief. What's the best way to bring up a relationship talk with James? Should I be cute and light-hearted or serious? Actually, it is serious and I want him to know how important this is to me. I feel a bit excited and a lot scared. What if he rejects me? Then being friends would never be the same. I take a deep breath and buckle myself in for the big moment.

I didn't plan anything fancy for dinner, just burgers and sweetcorn on the grill. It's after five o'clock so James will be here soon. I open a bottle of wine, pour a glass, and sit on the patio waiting for him. It's still hot and muggy but the ocean breeze makes it bearable. I'm wearing my bathing suit thinking it would be nice to swim before dinner. I get up and walk down to the shore, gingerly poking a toe into the cold water. I like to enter some things slowly and cautiously, the ocean and love for example. I don't like getting in over my head, preferring to have my feet touch the ground. Alas, I am already in over my head with James. I slide into the cool, salty waves, come up for air, and swim. Once I get past the initial chill the water feels exhilarating. As I wade out of the water, I see James wave from the patio. I wave back and run to greet him.

"How are you? Did you bring your suit? Swim or food?" My anxiety has dissolved in the salt water.

"Yes, please! First a swim and then food. Are we cooking out?" James calls over his shoulder as he goes inside to change.

"Yes, cooking out. Keeping it simple. We will make the fire, and cook when we get out of the water." James emerges from the bedroom tying swim shorts. A tee shirt is tossed casually over one shoulder. He is a fair-skinned man who will never bronze but has developed a light golden color this summer with a splash of freckles.

"What are you smiling about?" he teases.

"Oh, nothing. Just admiring your freckles…uh…tan." I tease. The grill is wheeled out onto the beach away from the building, and we get the charcoal started. Then we pick our way into the water. I would like to say that James swims with the grace of a dolphin but I can't. He admits to feeling awkward in the water and not much of a swimmer which makes us a match. I could save myself, if necessary, but I was never swim team material. We dunk our bodies in the salty water and pop-up smiling.

It's About Time

"Hungry?" I ask. He pulls me close and kisses me, tasting like salt.

"Yes, I am very hungry."

"For what?" I tease. "Race ya." I swim away, heading for the beach. On shore, James tends the grill and I go inside to get the food. It's a perfect summer evening.

Cooking out is not something I do often because it's a pain in the neck at the condo. But it's fun with James. He brings the grilled food to the patio and we chat while gnawing on corn cobs, picking kernels off our chins, and licking butter from our fingers. There is nothing better than summer sweetcorn.

"Do we have anything to talk about tonight?" James asks hesitantly as he makes short work of sliced ripe peaches with whipped cream.

"Yes, there is something," I say. Okay, here I go. Wish me luck.

James looks at me like he hates hearing that, but doesn't object. I light the citronella candle on the table, as James sits patiently waiting for me to speak. No need to rush. In my family, we were always rushed. I felt constant pressure to hurry up and not keep anyone waiting. It was another way Bess should not bother anyone.

"What do you want to talk about?" James asks.

"Don't worry. It's nothing bad. At least I don't think it's bad. Give me a minute. I'll be right back." I go inside and peel off my wet bathing suit pull on sexy lace panties and a soft pale blue tee-shirt dress. I run a comb through my hair and snag the bottle of wine on my way out to the patio. Talking in a bathing suit felt like I was auditioning for the Miss America pageant. This is more comfortable. I rejoin James at the table, smiling. Soft light flickers from the candle. A gentle breeze cools the air. Very romantic. I reach across the table and take his hand in mine.

"James, do you remember the other day when you kissed me and said you wanted more 'you and me'?"

"Nope. Are you sure that was me?" I must look horrified because he quickly adds, "Of course, I remember. Are you serious?"

"Jeez man, don't do that to me. You almost gave me a heart attack." I smack his arm and we both laugh nervously.

"Okay, just so there is no misunderstanding, tell me what you mean. What exactly do you want?" James was thoughtful for a moment, and then began to explain.

"Bess, I want to be with you without holding anything back. I have never known anyone like you. You were like a warrior goddess with Maura. No one, except my sister, has ever stood up for me like that before. Yet, you are also tender and willing to be vulnerable, like now. Being with you feels safe, even when I'm being a jerk. Not that I am a jerk very often." James chuckles and I nod yes, that is true. "Not only that, I am incredibly attracted to you. It's hard to stay in the friend lane, Bess. That no dating clause in our agreement needs to go!" He catches me smiling.

"Yes." That is the only word that comes into my mind. It's a good word.

"Yes?" James looks surprised. I'm surprised too.

It's About Time

"Yes. But . . ."

"But?"

"Settle down, let me finish. After everything that has happened to me, I don't trust easily. But I trust you enough to try this. I don't want to miss out on what we might have together because I'm afraid of getting hurt. If you're willing to give us a chance then so am I."

"Wait, you are? Really?"

"Yes, *really*."

"Okay then. Yes!" James is grinning. "That was way easier than I thought it would be."

"Calm down, I have to tell you about my but."

"Your butt? One T, or two?" James laughs.

"Ha. Ha. Very funny" I roll my eyes at him. "James, I need to go slow. That's my but."

"Are you kidding? I'll go any speed you want. I have never approached a relationship like this before. It was always hormones and chemistry that drove me forward. Not to say that I don't have some active chemistry going on, you understand?" He tells me.

"Yep, I can relate. I don't want to screw this up. One more heartbreak and I will end up in the cardiac intensive care unit. I *never* wanted to do this romance thing again. But you, James

Ogilvie, are a complete surprise to me. I never saw you coming in my wildest imaginings. Of course, I never saw the kids on skateboards either. I am so happy you showed up." I smile and squeeze his hand.

"So…I guess we go on record as a couple."

"Yes, I think so. Virginia and Bob will be relieved, I know that for sure. They saw this coming a long time ago and were frustrated with my snail's pace. Virginia will say it's about time." I look at him with surprise when those words pop out of my mouth.

"That's true. It is about time. No one can say we rushed into anything. Is there anything else you want to say before it's my turn?" James asks cautiously.

"Nope. That's all I've got. Your turn."

'This is all I've got." James stands in front of me and pulls me up. Looking into my eyes he says "I love you with all I have in me. I'm not perfect but promise to do the best I can." This time our kiss came as no surprise. James wraps me in his arms.

"I expect I will have a craving for pancakes in the morning. Can I talk you into staying tonight?" I ask.

"Are you kidding? You may never get rid of me." James says eagerly.

"James?" I snuggle against his chest and squeeze him tight. "I think I love you, too."

James kisses the top of my head. We blow out the candle, pick up our wine glasses, and go inside.

It's About Time

* * *

Saturday morning, I open my eyes to see James sleeping peacefully next to me. I guess it is about seven o'clock by the way the light comes through the shade. I could get up and make coffee, or I can stay here and watch James sleep for a little while longer. I can finally admit I love this man. I have no idea what comes next but I'm feeling hopeful.

"Are you staring at me?" James asks, eyes closed still half asleep.

"Yes. Yes, I am. How did you know that?" He opens one eye and says he can feel me looking at him. He asks what time it is.

"Probably around 7:00. Why? You got a date?" I giggle.

"Mmm, yes, I do with a woman I met on the street. Literally. Right down on the pavement." He smiles, opens his eyes, and kisses me good morning.

"James, I feel like I'm dreaming. Pinch me so I know I am awake." And he did. "Ow. Not that hard. I'm awake. Jeesh. Hey, you know what today is?"

"Saturday."

"Yes, and the first day I get to wake up and tell you I love you, James Ogilvie. Now what about those pancakes you promised?"

"Okay. In a minute. I want to feel you next to me for a little while longer." he burrows into my pillow and drapes his arm over my body.

"Mmm, that's nice. I could get used to this." I say as I snuggle against him.

"Let's stay in bed today," suggests James.
"That would be nice. But, right now I have to go to the bathroom. Be right back." I slip out from under his arm, pick up my dress from the floor, and go into the bathroom. After sprucing myself up and rinsing with mouthwash, I walk to the kitchen and start the coffee. Back in the bedroom, James has not moved. I slip back into bed, drape his arm over me, and curl up against him.

"Are you asleep?" I ask as I place a line of tiny kisses on his shoulder and upper arm, connecting the dots of his freckles. "You have a lot of freckles."

"I was asleep, but not anymore." James rolls toward me, kissing me deeply and all thoughts of pancakes fly out of my head.

Sometime later, the aroma of coffee drifts to the bedroom, and like love, it cannot be denied. We let each other go and climb reluctantly out of bed.

"You look cute in the morning Mr. Ogilvie." James is dressing in shorts and an old UMass tee shirt from last night. His hair is standing on end and I have never seen anyone more handsome. "Hold still, I want to take a picture in my mind."

James laughs and shakes his head at me, wrapping me in his arms. "At this rate, we may never get out of the bedroom," he tells me.

It's About Time

"Yeah. Maybe we can have food delivered. People will wonder if we have been abducted by aliens." I kiss him. "Speaking of food, I am getting hungry."

"Okay, I can take a hint. Bess? I love you."

"I love you, too." I can't help but grin.

We pour coffee and James busies himself making pancake batter.

"Do you have any plans today?" I ask James. "It might be nice to get together with Virginia and Bob to share our good news. Of course, they have probably already detected a disturbance in the force so it will come as no surprise." James likes that idea.

"Want to invite them over to Chez James?" He asks. "We could cook out again." I like the idea and think maybe grilling chicken and veggies would be nice. He agrees and we have a plan.

"I'll text Virginia after we eat."

While he cooks, I read him articles from the New York Times, avoiding any of the outrageous baloney politicians are up to. "It says that in Texas the heat can make you faint. Let's not go there. Oh, but here's an article about how to spend 36 hours in Paris. Let's do that." James is whisking pancake batter and heating the griddle.

"Sounds good." he says. "I also want to go back to Scotland. Check-in on the dead relatives." James flips the first batch of fluffy buttermilk pancakes onto plates. After eating our fill and talking non-stop, I text Virginia.

"Yes! What time? What can we bring?" says the text from Virginia. That was quick.

"They're coming, James. That clinches a trip to the grocery store." I text Virginia that we have a surprise and ask them to come around five o'clock. They will bring dessert.

We linger at the breakfast table until the mailman arrives. This morning together feels so magical I hate breaking the spell with real life. I leaf through the envelopes tossing the junk in the trash. There is a postcard invitation to a housewarming in Old Lyme. No name on it, only a phone number for RSVPs.

"Hey James, look at this. Odd that there is no name. Who do you think it's from? Do we know anyone who just moved there?" I hand him the card.

"Hmm. I can't think of anyone. Hold onto it. Maybe we'll figure it out later." James packs up his stuff to head home. On his way to the door, we linger over a kiss. "Later," James says. "Save more of that for later," he whispers in my ear. We separate and he is on his way.

*   *   *

I bring groceries into James's house and see the mysterious housewarming invitation sitting on the counter. James got one too.

"James, that is so odd. We will have to ask Virginia and Bob if they got one. Maybe it's a local business or a gallery or something."

"Maybe, but wouldn't they say so on the invitation? What's the point of marketing if you don't identify yourself?"

It's About Time

"Good point. Nothing is to be gained by being mysterious. Well, we may just have to show up, indulge ourselves with food and drink, and find out." I shake my head at the absurdity of it. Who sends an invitation unsigned? When prep work is done, we sit on the deck drinking seltzer, waiting for our friends to arrive.

Their car pulls into the driveway on the dot of five. Virginia jumps out waving and carrying contributions to our meal. We go inside to put things away while the guys discuss brands of grills and the benefits of charcoal over gas. I watch them, smiling.

"Guys!" I remark. "They're such simple folk." Virginia laughs and adds, except when they aren't. That cracks us up and the guys look at us wondering what's so funny. Virginia brought fixings for ice cream sundaes and a bottle of Pinot Grigio. After taking a poll it is decided that gin and tonic would it the spot. Virginia and I set about making them in tall glasses with fresh lime and Highclere Castle gin. That is when Virginia notices the invitation on the counter.

"Hey, James got one too? Do you know who it's from?" she asks, picking up the card and studying it. I shake my head no.

"But we wondered if you got one too. All of us are invited. We could make it a date!" I suggest. That perks Virginia up.

"A date?" she asks raising her eyebrows.

"Virginia, you and Bob will be happy to know that James and I are…well…we became a couple recently. This is our one-day anniversary." I grin. She whoops with joy and hugs me, jumping up and down.

"For freaking finally. Hey Bob? Guess what?" Virginia and I bring the drinks out to the guys who both turn from grill talk to look at us.

"You told her! Didn't you?" James admonishes, teasing. I walk over to James, take his arm, and say yes, I couldn't hold back. He kisses me a real juicy kiss while Virginia cheers. Bob slaps James on the back and we hold up our glasses in a toast to love and friends.

After dinner, the mysterious invitation is the topic of conversation.

"You got one, too?" asks Bob.

"Yes, it seems we all did. I wonder if everyone in town got an invitation?" I ask.

"Well, one way to find out." Bob texts a guy he works with who has a tile business. The tile guy texts Bob back right away with a negative.

"Hmm, what about Sal? He knows everyone from his pizza shop." I text him and he says he has no idea what I am talking about but is always ready for a party. "This is weird. Who do we have in common who might be warming up a house?"

"Oh, for God's sake. This is crazy. Let's just call the number and see who answers." suggests Bob. He puts the number into his phone and calls the mystery person. It rings a few times and then voice mail picks up.

"Hello, you have reached Maura Jenkins voice mail. Please…" Bob hangs up before the message finishes.

It's About Time

I see the same horrified look on each of us. Maura. Good God. We are speechless.

"Shit. Maura did it. She moved to Old Lyme. Bess, remember she said she was thinking about doing that?" James reminds me.

"Yes, I remember very clearly. That was in my condo before you gave her the boot."

"Have you heard anything from her since the confrontation James?" Virginia asks.

"Nope. Not a peep. It's typical for her to lull me into a false sense of security so I don't see her next assault coming. She never quits." James tells us.

"I am curious who is invited. What if we are the only ones? What if she is plotting to hold us all hostage and torture us in the basement like that movie 'Misery'?" I shudder at the thought. "Or poison us with canapes? James, does she know anyone else in town?"

"Yikes, Bess. Have you been watching true crime again?" asks Virginia. "Those are horrible thoughts. Inviting all of us is super suspect though, considering the ultimatum you gave her?"

"I have known Maura for a long time. She doesn't do anything randomly. I don't know what this housewarming is intended to accomplish, but it isn't anything good. I don't want her anywhere near us or my family." James is firm on that. "She is not someone to be taken lightly." He looks at me and takes my hand. "I say we burn these cards and forget we were ever invited." James opens the grill and tosses in the card. The

Hillary Gauvreau Oat

invitation smolders before bursting into flames. "Why ask for trouble."

Why indeed.

It's About Time

CHAPTER 14

Family Reunion

Bess

I yell out James's back door, "Do you have the cooler?" He replies that it is ready to go in the car, and I suggest that he put it where we can reach it on the road.

We are going on a road trip and I'm excited. James's family reunion is Columbus Day weekend at his sister's home in North Carolina. The weather is perfect and the Blue Ridge Mountains will be gorgeous in October.

Mary, James's sister, whom I haven't met, called a couple of months ago to get his thoughts about an Ogilvie family reunion. Their family is spread across the country and has not gotten together in years. Mary lives in the North Carolina highlands near Blowing Rock where the family migrated after arriving on the shores of North Carolina in the late 1700s. Over the years family members moved away, but Mary's branch of the family tree stayed put. She and her family still live on a 100-acre parcel of land that was given to the Ogilvie family by the governor way back when.

For fun, and to honor their heritage, Mary wanted to create an Ogilvie Highland Games event on the property. James loved the idea and the two of them, along with their younger brother MJ, started making plans. It came together after many video calls, emails, and texts. Fortunately, an annual highland games event is held nearby on Grandfather Mountain which makes it easy to find a pipe band, dancers, and games. Most of those folks were looking forward to joining in the fun, willing to be fed and paid just enough to cover their expenses.

James's excitement was contagious and soon I was offering to make gift bags and researching the Ogilvie clan tartan. My bags included tartan scarves, clan kilt pins for the gentlemen and clan brooches for the lasses. It wouldn't be Scottish if we didn't include a dram or two of Scotch and shortbread cookies. We printed cards with the Ogilvie clan crest on the front. Inside was a traditional recipe for Haggis and a Scottish blessing:

> "If there is righteousness in the heart, there will be beauty in the character. If there is beauty in the character, there will be harmony in the home. If there is harmony in the home, there will be order in the nation. If there is order in the nation, there will be peace in the world."

Amen to that I say. On the back of the card James drew a simplified family tree.

"James, where's the garment bag with your regalia?" Regalia is how I refer to his complete traditional highland dress including a clan tartan kilt, knee-high kilt hose Jacobite shirt, a man purse otherwise known as a sporran, and a jacket. All are carefully and lovingly hung in a garment bag. I'm not Scottish, so while I would enjoy being in the tartan parade, I'll hold back. Being with the Highlander I love is enough.

"Got it!" he calls back. "I think we have everything. Are you ready to hit the road?" It is not the early start we hoped for, but we will only be on the road nine hours to Richmond, Virginia for our overnight stay with my friends. I look around the kitchen for anything I'm forgetting. I always have a tinge of anxiety that I am leaving something important behind when I travel.

It's About Time

"I think we are ready to launch. Have you packed the gift bags?" I look out the back door at James.

"Yes, ma'am." James grins at me. "Don't worry, hon. I think the only thing we haven't packed is the kitchen sink."

"Ha. Ha. Very funny. Okay, I'm locking the door." James is driving the first leg of the trip because I hate driving around New York City. Then we will stop to eat, and stretch. I will take the last leg because I know where I'm going in Richmond. James is already behind the wheel. I get in and buckle up. He looks at me, smiling.

"What?" I ask.

"I am so happy you want to do this with me. And I appreciate your enthusiasm. I know you aren't an Ogilvie but I want to make you feel welcome and a part of the family." James takes a small leather pouch out of his jacket pocket and hands it to me. "Open it."

In it is a 14-carat gold Ogilvie clan brooch, old and worn smooth from use. It is a two-inch circular shape with a lady from the waist up in the center holding a waffle design called a portcullis. Thanks to the History Channel I recently learned that a portcullis is a strong, medieval castle gate that symbolizes strength and security. Engraved on top of the circle is the Ogilvie motto, *A Fin*, meaning to the end. Historically, highlanders are a tough bunch of dudes and I imagine they took that motto literally in combat.

"James, it's beautiful. Thank you. It looks old."

Hillary Gauvreau Oat

"Here, let me pin it on you. It's an antique that belonged to my great-grandmother and was passed to my grandmother and finally to my mother. Mary wanted me to have it and I am giving it to you so you feel welcome in the family. An adopted Ogilvie, so to speak. The family will recognize it and get the message you are one of us and not to mess with you." He kisses me.

"Well, that is good to know. I would hate to be messed with." I smile.

"Oh, trust me, there will be some messing, I am certain of that, but nothing you can't handle." With that, he put the car in gear and we are on our way.

Traffic slows us down in the usual spots, but our conversation flows and makes the delays barely noticeable. James fills me in on the family members I will meet. I am most interested in meeting his sister Mary. From all I hear she seems like someone I will really like. I am also looking forward to seeing Thomas again, James's youngest son. We had a brief time together when he visited from Florida to celebrate his father's birthday. I admit I am a little nervous about meeting the Ogilvie clan. I expect there will be questions about who I am and what our intentions are. While we drive I think about snappy answers to have ready.

We arrive in Richmond early in the evening, and I am happy to see my friends Peg and Frank. They have drinks and food ready for us and we spend a few hours eating and visiting with them. Peg sits next to me and gives me a thumbs-up hidden by the table. I smile because it is good to have the approval of friends I trust. We are tired but wound up from the drive. Around eleven we finally hit the wall and tuck ourselves in bed. With James curled up next to me I am asleep as soon as my head hits the pillow.

It's About Time

In the morning, after a sumptuous breakfast and lots of rich, dark coffee, we get back on the road. It's a five-hour drive to Blowing Rock but we stop at scenic overlooks and get lost a couple of times on mountain roads, so it takes us longer. When we finally pull into the driveway Mary Ogilvie-Dunlap meets us, drying her hands on her apron, with two small children in tow. As soon as James steps out of the car she gets him in a bear hug, kissing his face and pulling on his beard. I like this woman already.

"Mary, I want you to meet Bess. She is important to me, so be nice." James has his arm around Mary and walks her over to my side of the car.

"I know. I know. Like I am never not nice!" She smacks his arm. "Welcome! It is a pleasure to meet you and welcome you to the Ogilvie Games!" We hug like we've known each other our whole lives. The nervousness I was feeling about meeting the family starts to dissolve. With Mary in my corner, I have nothing to fear. She is James's older sister, probably around 62, young-looking, tall, and slender with soft creases on her face from a life filled with smiles. She put an arm around me and walks me up the front steps and into the house. Their home is on New Year's Creek, surrounded by lush meadows and old forests. It is a large clapboard building in a patchwork of colors. The original historic structure is modest and at the center of sprawling additions poking out everywhere. It must be wonderful to be able to live in a place that holds so much family history. The perfect spot for the reunion.

"Mary, this place, your home, it's idyllic! What a wonderful place to live. And to be surrounded by so much family history. Wow"

"Thank you. Yes, that can be a mixed blessing depending on the day of the week. There is constant maintenance to keep it standing. But we love it." She ushers me into the updated country kitchen where people are busily preparing food. "I want you to meet my husband, Graeme." She pulls me by the hand to a white-haired gentleman with a craggy weathered face in his mid-to-late sixties who is making dough for scones.

Graeme smiles as Mary explains who I am. His rich baritone voice welcomes me to Blowing Rock. "I would shake your hand but mine are a bit sticky at the moment. We expect to go through hundreds of scones this weekend so I need to keep at it. Save me a hug for later." I agree to do that.

Mary then points to Isla, their daughter-in-law. She waves hello across the kitchen. "Those two hooligans are Skye and Duncan and they belong to Isla and our son Mal."

"Are they twins?" I ask.

"Yes, and they are quite a delight and a handful when they gang up on me." Mary lures the two children out of the kitchen holding cookies over their heads. They look to be around 5 years old with strawberry blond curls and a sprinkle of freckles. They try to get the cookies away from their Gran and succeed, running off munching. At that point, James comes in carrying the box filled with gift bags.

"Mary, where do you want these?" James asks. Mary rushes over to see what's in the bags. James explains that I did the research, and it was all my doing. I appreciate the credit and add that James was a lot of help with ideas. Mary peeks into a bag and her very expressive face lights up with each item she pulls out.

It's About Time

"Bess, these gifts are absolute perfection! I'm delighted. Thank you so much for doing this. Do we get one too?"

"Of course!" I smile and look at James who puts a supportive arm around me. "It was fun, Mary. And my pleasure."

Mary takes out the scarf and wraps it around her neck calling for Graeme to look. He smiles and nods his approval.

"Why don't you and James take those gifts out to the back porch and set them on the side table by the door? Then come back in here and get yourself something to drink and catch us up on what's going on in your lives." Mary winks at us. "Thomas is coming, yes?" James calls over his shoulder that he is, but Andy can't make it."

After arranging the gift bags, we come back into the kitchen. James gets us two tall glasses of iced sweet tea, and we sit on stools at the busy kitchen island chatting and offering our help. Mary's kitchen is bustling and organized. After an early supper we call it a night. Tomorrow will be a busy day of preparations.

James and I have a reservation at a motel in Blowing Rock not far from Main Street. Our room is furnished with an eclectic collection of thrift store furniture. It gives the room a unique personality, much nicer than corporate hotel rooms that all look the same. After checking in and bringing our bags into the room we take a short walk, stopping in at The Ale House for a nightcap. It's a rustic building with exposed beams, and aged wood that smells like generations of spilled beer. I imagine early settlers stopping in to quench their thirst.

When we get back to our room, I ask James if he has heard anything from Thomas.

"No, not today. He should be on the road early tomorrow morning. He wants to arrive around lunchtime so he can help set up. I can't remember when he last saw his Auntie Mary, Uncle MJ and the rest of them. They will be happy to see him."

"You're going to have to get me a program. All these new people are hard for me to keep straight. Mary is memorable, however. I really like her, James." I slip between the sheets facing James who is already closing his eyes. I brush the hair back from his forehead and kiss him. "I love you, James Ogilvie. Don't snore!" He smiles, mumbling that he never snores.

In the morning, we wake early and walk up the street to a bed and breakfast that has homemade biscuit sandwiches. We order and bring breakfast back to our motel. Temperatures are in the sixties, and the sky is vivid North Carolina blue. Perfect weather for the reunion. The motel's carpet of lush green grass, gazebo, and colorful Adirondack chairs make it a perfect place to eat. James fills me in on what to expect. There will be good-natured teasing at every opportunity, and I shouldn't take it personally. I am warned that Auntie Flora, his father's sister, will talk my ear off if I let her. James is eager for me to meet his eighty-two-year-old father. His mother passed away about 5 years ago but his dad is going strong and will probably be the first one at the caber toss. The caber toss is a traditional Scottish game where the contestant tries to flip a sixteen-foot pole end-over-end. When I asked why anyone would create such a game the only answer I heard was that they must have been "bored as fuck". There are other games as well, all designed for the men, and some women, to show their brute strength.

"We have to hold Dad back at times. He still thinks he's thirty-five. We don't want the celebration to include any EMTs." He

It's About Time

laughs. "The most fun will be the family tug 'o war. I will make sure you are on my team and there isn't too much cheating."

"There's cheating?"
"Always. That's the fun part."

"What do the winners get?" I ask.

"Glory!" announces James. "And bragging rights, of course." To a Highlander that is probably the most coveted prize. It's a short drive to Mary's house, and we will be there by nine ready to help set up.

When we arrive at the house it is already bustling with activity. The rental company dropped off tents, tables, and chairs early that morning. Mary is showing the men where to set things up. What looks like chaos to the casual observer has a plan that Mary is in complete control of. Everything is new to me and I am unsure how to help. We walk around the house to the backyard, getting our bearings. A man, strikingly similar to James in looks, minus a few years and a couple of inches in height, strolls over and grabs James in a hug, spinning him around. They punch each other playfully a few times, excited to see each other.

"Isn't this the best idea ever? Gotta hand it to Mary." He turns to me and extends his hand. "How you do. I am Malcolm James but everyone calls me MJ because we have so many Malcolms and Jameses in the family. It can get confusing until you know us. Then you realize we are nothing at all alike. I am the fun brother. And you must be Bess." His eyes smile along with the rest of his face.

"Yes, I am." James takes possession of my hand. "It is nice to finally meet you after listening in on all the virtual planning sessions."

"Everyone is dying to meet James's new lady friend. Right, big brother?" Before James can answer MJ sizes me up asking if I can handle this crazy family affair.

"I don't know, but willing to try," I assure MJ. That is when he notices the heirloom brooch I am wearing.

"I see you gave Bess Grans brooch to wear! Whoo-hoo this must be serious." MJ turns to me and squashes me in what I now call the Ogilvie bear hug. "Welcome to the family, Bess. It's about time, James." At that point, Mary comes over to see what the excitement is about.

"I see you've met trouble here." She gestures toward MJ. It is easy for me to see how much these three siblings care for each other. There is no pretense, or careful conversation. They are one hundred percent themselves.

"Mary, look. James pinned Bess." MJ points to the brooch. If I had known it would garner this much attention I would have worn it in a more discrete location.

"Oh, Bess. How wonderful." Now Mary is hugging me. "Does this mean you're engaged? Do we have something else to celebrate this weekend?" I am startled and turn to face James, looking for a sign about what is happening.

"We have not specifically discussed that, Mary. I simply wanted Bess to feel like a part of the clan." James explains.

It's About Time

"Well, it seems to me if you want her to feel like a part of the clan you need to make an honest woman of her." Mary suggests.

"Let's see how she feels after the Ogilvie family intensive." James puts an arm around me, and I narrow my eyes into a "what the fuck is going on" look.

"I'll keep my hopes up. Enough talk. We have work to do. Bess, come with me. MJ, show James what to do." I follow Mary wondering what I signed up for coming to this reunion. James wasn't kidding about teasing and being messed with. It will take me a while to figure out who's teasing and who's serious.

 As the day wore on more family members arrived to lend a hand. The property was starting to look like a festival. The games people backed a large rental truck in with a caber tied to the roof. They unpacked a stage for highland dancers and started to mark off the field for games. It's a jovial atmosphere with everyone pitching in. When Thomas showed up the family greeted him warmly. His father pulled me out of the kitchen to say hello to the only other person in the family I know.

"Hi, Thomas. It's nice to see you again." I open my arms to hug him, which he allowed but didn't return. Thomas greets MJ warmly, but barely acknowledges his father. Something is going on but I have no time to think about it because I am called back to the kitchen.

I feel comfortable in the kitchen preparing food with Mary and Isla. We chat as we chop vegetables, make salads, and bake piles of scones. I listen to stories about them growing up, and they ask me about myself. They kid me mercilessly about James and it turns hysterically bawdy. I enjoy these women.

Late in the afternoon, the work is mostly done. James and MJ start a fire in the firepit. We bring a cooler of drinks outside and relax in chairs around the fire. The men joke and drink beer with the games people after they finish setting up. Seeing us sitting down they take it as a sign work is done and join us. Graeme is grilling burgers and hotdogs. After everyone is fed, the inevitable bottle of scotch comes out and is passed around. Stories are told, and I laugh so much my cheeks hurt. After a while, people begin heading back to their homes and lodgings to rest up for tomorrow's festivities. Between the scotch, the hour, and the work, we are tired. As we are getting ready to leave I notice James in a serious conversation with Thomas. When we get in the car to drive back to town I ask if everything is okay. I remind him of the cool reception we received. He isn't sure what is going on but agrees that something is bothering Thomas.

"Do you think he's upset that I am horning in on your family reunion?" I ask cautiously. "Did he know I was coming?"

"Yes, he knew. I gave him plenty of notice and he seemed okay with it. It must be something else. Don't worry about it. I doubt it has anything to do with you. When I have a chance, I'll talk to him and see what's up." James takes my hand. "Did you have fun today? How was it for you?"

"Well, at first, I felt overwhelmed, but gradually I got more comfortable. It helped me to have a job in the kitchen. Mary and Isla are delightful. Just a heads up, those women can get pretty raunchy. And, I have a bone to pick with you, mister!"

"Uh oh. What did I do?"

"What is all this talk about getting pinned and engaged? Is there something you aren't telling me about this brooch? A hidden significance perhaps? It seemed to cause quite a stir."

It's About Time

"Oh, that." James glances at me to check the temperature of the conversation. Was he in a little trouble or deep shit?

"Pinning that brooch on you is an attention-getter, isn't it?" James chuckles. "MJ was messing with you. A little. But it does have significance. It means you're special to me, and I wanted the family to know that. I should have warned you. I'm sorry if it upset you."

"Hmm. So, it isn't like an engagement ring or anything?' I feel a tiny bit disappointed which surprises me. "When Mary asked if we were engaged, I was speechless. I would hate to be blindsided by something we haven't discussed ahead of time. Get my drift?"

"Totally. Absolutely. A hundred percent." He pauses and asks "Would you though? Has it entered your mind at all?"

"What? Getting married?"

"Well not just getting married. Getting married to me. Have you considered that?"

"Jeez James, we just got serious this summer. Don't you think that's rushing things a bit?"

James thought for a moment. "I don't want to rush you, but we've known each other a while now. I know how I feel and I want you in my life, living together, committed, growing old, getting into mischief. We don't have to get married right away. We can have a long engagement. I guess I just want to know if you are open to the idea."

We park at our motel, sit in the car, and look at each other. I open my car door and silently we get out and walk to our room. James has learned to give me time to think. We shower and get ready for bed. I brush my teeth as I look at myself in the mirror. If I'm completely honest, I am open to the idea. He's right. We haven't rushed. We have proceeded carefully, and thoughtfully. Maybe it's time to take the next step.

James was already in bed when I came out of the bathroom. I turned off the light and climbed in next to him.

"James?"

"Uh-huh."

"I am open to a long engagement. You caught me by surprise but I think I have recovered after brushing my teeth for twenty minutes. I made a promise to stay single for the rest of my life, but you are special and I love you. How can I resist? So yes, I agree to a long engagement. Long engagement! Very long engagement."

"Thank God. I was worried you didn't want me. Now that I know you're interested, consider this. I would love to propose here, on Ogilvie land surrounded by my family. What do you think? Can you handle that? Is that too fast?"

"I cannot tell you how relieved I am that you didn't spring a proposal on me in front of everyone. That was a wise choice, Ogilvie. People think a surprise proposal in front of a crowd is romantic. It isn't. Not for me anyway. I'm glad we are talking about it." I kiss him. "I like getting to know your family and this gathering may never happen again. So… if that is important to you and you are proposing, I am saying yes. Let's do this!"

It's About Time

"Really? Oh my *God!* You said yes!!" James kisses me. "I love you so much." The kissing didn't stop there. We tenderly consummated our engagement in The Village Motel, Blowing Rock, North Carolina.

Hillary Gauvreau Oat

It's About Time

CHAPTER 15

Let The Games Begin

Bess

Saturday we are up bright and early. It must be the excitement that got us moving after a late night. James is so handsome in his kilt. I'm wearing a conservative mid-length navy skirt, a gray tweed jacket with navy velvet trim, and knee-high boots. The brooch is pinned over my heart. We get to Mary's in time to have coffee and scones before the opening ceremony. Promptly at 9:00 a.m. the pipe band shows up. There are about 40 family members, a supportive cast of pipers, dancers, and game organizers, and more kilts than I can count. We are gathered around the open center of the yard where the low stage is set up. Mary has a PA system ready to go.

When the pipe band is ready the celebration kicks off. I have chills as the band marches up the driveway playing "Scotland the Brave", an unofficial national anthem of Scotland. People around me stand proudly and eyes are misty.

After they finish playing, they march away to the beat of the drummer. It is quite dramatic and moving. At that point, Mary steps up onto the stage, picks up the mic, and asks James and MJ to join her. The crowd hoots and hollers as the kilted men climb up onto the stage. The men are outfitted in Ogilvie tartan head to kilt. Mary wears a dark dress with a tartan shawl draped over her shoulder, secured with the brooch I gave her.

Hillary Gauvreau Oat

"Wow, I think we need a moment to collect ourselves after that. That was incredible, wasn't it?" Mary encourages a round of applause for the band and then continues. "Welcome to this land that we have grown crops and families on for generations. Even though life has taken us to different parts of our adopted country, we have never lost our connection to each other or our roots. Our history and family bonds are strong. We have a wonderful weekend planned and I am so happy you are here. I look forward to catching up with all of you. James? MJ? Do you want to add anything?" James accepts the microphone from Mary and clears his throat.

"I am thrilled to be here with you all. When Mary had the idea for a reunion, I was all in. It has been way too long since we had a party with the whole family. Bess, raise your hand, please. There she is!" James points in my direction. "I want you to meet Bess, a very special lady I am particularly fond of." I know my face is crimson, and my heart pounds wondering if this is our moment. But James moves on and I relax. "Thank you, Bess, for the wonderful gift bags. Enjoy yourselves. MJ?" MJ takes the microphone.

"Dad come up here and say a few words." We applaud while the elder Ogilvie saunters up to the podium, shaking hands and getting pats on the back. He is dapper in Ogilvie tartan, a shock of white hair, and a tough but tender look to him. I wonder if this is what James will be like at 82. He says something in Gaelic that I don't understand but several people cheer. Then he continues in English.

"As you know my name is Malcolm Thomas Ogilvie. I am the eldest member of this branch of Clan Ogilvie. I wish my wife could have lived to see how wonderful our family has turned out. Of all six of my brothers and sisters, only four of us remain. Come on up here if you would. Malcolm's three younger sisters, wrapped in tartan shawls, make their way to the podium and wave to everyone. Flora, the most talkative of the four, tries to grab the microphone, but the elder Ogilvie holds it tight. Everyone laughs.

"*Mòran bheannachdan*, many blessings on you all." Malcolm steps aside and MJ returns with a tray of whiskey shots. Trays are also circulating through the crowd.

"It's never too early or too late for a toast." When everyone has their whiskey MJ wishes them good health. "*Slàinte Mhath.* Let the games begin.*"* Everyone cheers and downs their whiskey. The bagpipers march back and we are off and running.

I chat with the women, and Auntie Flora does indeed bend my ear. She bluntly asks me questions about myself and shares stories about James and the family. She's a straight-shooting, lively lady and I don't mind at all.

"Come with me and watch me toss a caber!" James takes my hand and pulls me along to the far field where the men have ample space to show off.

"Bess, do you understand the principles here?" James asks.

"No, I don't think so." I suppress a smile.

"Okay, so the tosser is helped to get into position so he can slide his hands under the caber and lift it off the ground. He has to have good balance and keep it upright because it's top-heavy, obviously. If it wasn't it wouldn't flip and land right. It's tricky and first-timers are hysterical to watch, rarely getting past picking the caber up. Once the caber is picked up, the tosser walks, or runs a bit, to get some momentum going and flips the end up so the caber turns end over end. Distance doesn't matter, but form does. It takes a lot of strength. A caber can weigh 90 to 150 pounds, but we're using a lightweight one because we're out of shape." James laughs. "Got it?"

"Yeah, I think so, but what is the point?" I ask smiling. "Is this a skill needed to survive in the wild?"

"Damned if I know. It's just fun." James trots over for his turn. A rowdy crowd starts to gather, yelling encouragement. I notice that MJ and Thomas are also waiting in a group of men. Some experts know what they are doing and make it look easy. Then there are the newcomers with a few beers in them. Only a few of those tossers can lift the caber, and the rest can't flip it over. Harder than it looks, I gather. James steps up to give it a go. He is helped to get the caber in position, manages to lift it, and after staggering around a bit, keeps it upright. I am almost afraid to look. He is red-faced from straining and I hope he survives the game. He struggles, concentrating on balance, takes a few steps, and flips it. Sadly, it doesn't go completely over, landing in front of him with a thud. The bystanders, are good sports and recognize the valiant effort with a cheer.

Next, MJ steps up yelling to James that he will show his big brother how it's done. James laughs at him. MJ is younger, and maybe stronger, but James has better balance. It takes several tries for MJ to carry the caber forward, flip it, and thud. James boos and laughs along with the other men. Now it is Thomas's turn. He is a young man, strong and determined to outdo his father. Thomas lifts the caber making it look easy. He balances, runs, and flips the caber right over! The crowd goes wild. He is one of the few able to accomplish that feat. Thomas struts around celebrating his success. MJ slaps him on the back and says he taught him all he knows. The three men come together high-fiving and laughing. Maybe this will break the ice between father and son. I probably should have some Tiger Balm

It's About Time

ointment ready for tonight when James starts to feel those muscles complain.

Later in the afternoon, everyone gathers for the tug 'o war. It takes a long time to get started because of high level negotiation about who will be on which team, and how many men balance out the women. A lot goes into calculating a winning strategy. For me, watching that is almost as entertaining as the actual game. There is a line drawn on the ground and the objective is for one team to pull the other team over the line. James tells me to stick with him. He calls to Thomas to join us, but Thomas turns the other way and joins the opposition. I guess the ice isn't broken. When we are finally organized, the referee blows a whistle. The first tug almost yanks me off my feet. These people are serious about games. We pull and get pulled, the men grunting while the women and children laugh. I let go at one point to keep from getting dragged through the grass. Others also drop out until it's all men. Grunting and yelling, none of the men want to lose. The women from one team do their best to distract the men on the other team. It's hysterical. Finally, MJ's team pulls our team over the line. The referee blows the whistle. Game over. The competitors collapse on the grass, panting and laughing. MJ's team gets the glory and he will no doubt rub that in.

After a break for refreshments, bagpipes call everyone to gather around the stage. Professional dancers tell us the history of Highland dancing. Basically, it is men dancing after a bloody victory in battle, which is pretty creepy. Happily, no blood is spilled today. We learn a few steps and then they call for volunteers to come up and dance with them. We cheer James's father when he gets up first, along with James, Mary, and MJ. The dancers demonstrate the sword dance which looks a lot easier than it is. James calls me up to dance with him and after tripping over our feet and swords, we start to get the hang of it. Other family members step up to show their agility. Scotsmen are very competitive, it seems. For as long as the band plays, the dancing continues until everyone is worn out.

After dancing comes feasting. Sausages, ribs, chicken, and planks of wild salmon sizzle on several large grills. Roasted sweet corn, salads, baked beans, and a variety of breads fill the tables. Many brought their special dish to add to the feast. James and I find seats at a table with his brother and sister while Thomas avoids us again. I give James a questioning look and he shrugs. Now is not the time for a discussion.

It's dark by the time things start to wind down. Our bellies are full, as are our hearts. Graeme and Mal make a roaring fire in the fire pit, and we drag chairs over. Isla and Mal light sparklers for the kids, and they chase each other around like boisterous fireflies.

The inevitable bottle of scotch circulates. Toasts are made as people stand to say their piece. When the bottle gets to me, I stand up.

"I'm new here and getting to know you is…well…interesting fun." I wink and people laugh and nod, elbowing each other. "You make me feel very welcome. Thank you. I especially thank Mary and Graeme, MJ and James, for all they have done to make today one I will never forget." Everyone applauds. Someone yells thank you for the gift bags and I see quite a few scarves around the fire. That makes me happy. I hold the bottle up and take a swig. "*Slàinte Mhath*". I sit, but James pulls me back up.

It's About Time

"Oh no, we are not done here yet. One more thing I hope you never forget." James turns and takes my hands in his. My heart starts pounding.

"Bess, I am not very good with words so I will simply say that I love you with all my heart. I never thought we would be here when I first scooped you up off the sidewalk." He looks out at the family. "For those of you who haven't heard, the gods threw this lovely woman down on the sidewalk in front of my shop in Connecticut. Actually, it was a couple of skateboarders, but I believe they were sent by the gods." James laughs. "I rushed to her rescue." James looks at me with misty eyes. "Bess, with family as my witness, I promise to love, honor, and respect you for the rest of my life. Will you marry me?" The crowd goes wild, whistling and applauding. Then there's silence as all eyes are on me.

"How could I say no to a proposal from such a handsome man in a kilt? Yes, I will marry you." I smile and James kisses me. Everyone stands and cheers. Mary hugs me. Then right on cue, as if we rehearsed it, the band starts playing. Fireworks light up the night sky. I am sure this was all planned ahead and not because of us but the timing is perfect. James's father hugs me and taps the brooch over my heart saying I am a good sport and he approves, even if I'm not Scottish. That's a pretty special endorsement. It is a perfect ending to a fun day. I have fallen in love, not only with James but with his family too.

* * *

On Sunday, tired and happy people gradually return to the farm where an urn of rich dark coffee, carafes of tea, and piles of Graeme's scones await. Today there will be a time for deeper conversations, sharing pictures and catching up as people come and go. The firepit burns continually, providing a welcome place to gather.

James, MJ, Thomas and I sit together sipping coffee. Thomas is friendly with his uncle but still reticent with his father. At least he's sitting with us. Thomas avoided us all weekend and was particularly bloodthirsty competing against his father in the games. James hasn't had a chance to talk with his son but maybe now is a good time. The strained relationship is becoming obvious and uncomfortable.

Late in the afternoon, I am helping to prep yet another meal in the kitchen with Mary, Isla, and Auntie Flora. God, these people can eat. We are talking about Andy's wedding. Since only immediate family is invited to the ceremony in Montana, Mary wants to plan a family gathering next fall to celebrate. It sounds like a wonderful idea and there is plenty of time to figure that out. Suddenly, we hear loud, angry voices coming from the fire pit area. Mary shakes her head.

"Mix a Scotsman with a bottle of whiskey and fights always break out. I hoped we got through this weekend in peace but I guess not." We head outside to see what's going on.

We find MJ restraining a struggling red-faced Thomas. He is screaming at his father. If MJ lets him go, I'm afraid what might happen. Mary marches up to them and demands to know what is going on. James's jaw is clenched so I don't think words are going to be coming out of him. Thomas on the other hand can't stop spewing accusations.

"You lying bastard! How can you stand here pretending to be so fucking innocent? I HATE you. Auntie Maura told me all about what you did. How could you do that to my mother?" Thomas has had a few tips of the bottle, as they say, and continues to struggle in MJ's grip but is going nowhere. He spit

It's About Time

on the ground in front of James, the ultimate insult. Thomas nods toward me. "Does she know what you did? You lying to her too? I'm sorry you all are finding out what a lying bag of shit my father is." He huffs and grunts while MJ holds him securely. James stands tense and silent. The minute I hear Maura's name I know something bad is happening. There is no telling what she's done to James and his family this time. It seems the games being played are not all on the field.
Mary gets right in Thomas's face and demands he come with her. MJ keeps his grip on Thomas as he steers him toward the kitchen. Mary impresses me. Growing up with two younger brothers she has had some experience breaking up fights. I walk over to James. He collapses in a chair with Graeme on one side of him and me on the other.

"What happened James?" I asked gently. James looks furious and crushed at the same time. A bruise is starting to blossom on his cheek.

Graeme explains that they were sitting around chatting about our engagement and Andy's wedding when Thomas exploded. Graeme wasn't sure why, but he said Thomas was screaming at his father, pushing him, and then punched him in the face. That's when MJ grabbed him, and pulled him off before anything worse could happen.

"I can't believe she would use my son to hurt me. She is lying to him and coming between us just like she did with Caroline and me."

"Who? I don't understand?" Graeme is confused.

Hillary Gauvreau Oat

James tells him it is a long story about a very sick woman he met in college who has been relentlessly punishing him for choosing Caroline over her.

"Maura turned Caroline against me and ruined our marriage. Now, probably because I am with Bess, she is trying to hurt me through Thomas. It's a long ugly story, Graeme."

The kitchen door slams, and Thomas strides out of the house, duffel bag over his shoulder, still looking enraged. He gets in his car and sprays a shower of gravel as he shoots down the driveway. MJ and Mary slowly walk over to us. Mary kneels in front of James and takes his hands in hers.

"Well, that looks terrible. Isla, go get James some ice, please. Looks like the party's over. You want to tell me your side?" He looks at her, squeezing her hands, tears in his eyes.

"Thomas exploded. Accused me of all kinds of horrible things. Maura is the only person who could have put that shit in his head. Thanks for doing what you could, Mary. What did he say?"

"Thomas said a lot of nonsense about you treating Caroline badly, neglecting him, and abusing his mother when she was sick. And now to top it off, you are banning Maura from Andy's wedding after she helped to raise him." Mary stands and pulls a chair over. "None of it makes sense to me. You and Caroline loved each other. You would do anything for those kids. Did you ban Maura from the wedding? Not that I would blame you."

"Mary, I don't want Maura around me or my family ever again. Enough is enough. She did not help raise those boys. Ever. I've told you about her. You know how she inserted herself into our lives. She poisoned my marriage. When Andy said he would invite her to the wedding it was for me, to make me happy. He

It's About Time

thought she supported me in a time of need. He doesn't know the trouble she caused. She threatened to get me fired from my teaching job and ruin my reputation. The boys have no idea what she has done and that was how I wanted to keep it. All I did was tell Andy I didn't want her to be invited and he said that was fine by him. There was no banning. No drama. What if Maura has gotten to Thomas with her lies the way she got to Caroline?"

"Well, I tried to get him to calm down but he wasn't having it. He's a young hot-headed Scotsman. He will calm down eventually. Give him time." Mary patted James's hand.
"I imagine he will, but then what? How do I deal with this? Don't you see? It's a smear campaign. It's her word against mine. The woman is evil and doesn't care who she hurts. There is no better way to hurt me than to turn my son against me. She knows how much I love those boys. I hope Thomas comes around, Mary, but I don't know if he will with Maura influencing him. I can't let her turn my son against me." James bends forward, head in hands.

"Listen, James. I know enough about Maura to share your concern. You have Bess and this family standing with you. Now, what are we going to do about this?" Mary asks. I take out my phone and open voice memos.

"It may not be just your word against hers, James." I find the file and play the recording from my condo when Maura admitted she wants to destroy James. Maura's venom comes through loud and clear.

Mary spits out a potent Gaelic swear that shocks Graeme. "I will not allow my family to be threatened. Evil isn't a strong enough word to describe that witch." Isla hands James an ice pack and a couple of Advil tablets. His cheek is starting to swell and his eye is going to be colorful tomorrow.

"What about Andy? Would he be able to talk to Thomas?" I ask. James shakes his head.

"I don't know. I'll call him when we get home and feel him out. I don't know if Maura has gotten to him, too." James groans and holds the ice to his face.

We hug everyone goodbye and I drive us back to Blowing Rock. We have two more days here before we drive back to New England. Maybe by the time we get home, we will have something figured out.

Sunday night, sleep was difficult. James was worried about Thomas. He texted asking Thomas to let us know when he got to Gainesville but we haven't heard from him. It's a nine-hour drive if he goes directly to Florida, but we don't know that he did that. All we can do is keep trying to get him on the phone and worry. We walk to the B&B, pick up breakfast, and go back to the motel.

James is stressed. I know how I would feel if it was my upset kid on the road. The purple bruise on his face is a reminder of the fight he and his son had yesterday. I offer him a couple of Advil tablets that he washes down with a gulp of coffee.

"What time is it?" James asked.

"Almost 11:00. Why?"

"I'm calling Andy. He should be up by now. I have to do something besides sit here and worry. Maybe he's heard from Thomas." The phone rings a few times before Andy picks up. James puts him on speaker.

It's About Time

"Hey, Dad. How's the reunion going?" Andy sounds normal. Maybe he hasn't heard about the fight.

"Andy, it's wonderful. We miss you." Then there is a long pause.

"Dad? You still there? Everything okay?" James has a pained look on his face.

"Have you heard from Thomas?"

"No. Why? Isn't he there with you?" James fills him in on what happened and how worried he is.
"I've called and left messages, and texted, but I haven't heard anything. He is either not speaking to me, or…I don't want to think about the 'or'."

"Okay Dad, don't worry. I will call him right now and see what's up. Call you back as soon as I talk to Thomas." He hangs up, and we sip coffee waiting. And waiting. When the phone rings we both jump. It's Mary wanting to know if we heard from Thomas.

"No. Not a word. I am sick with worry." James tells her. "I talked to Andy and he is trying to get a hold of him. I thought you were him calling back. Listen, we are ready to drive back to your place. See you in a few minutes." We throw away our half-eaten biscuits and finish our coffee. I agree to drive to Mary's so that James can stare at his phone trying to make it ring. Finally, Andy calls but tells us he couldn't reach Thomas either. He called the landline at Thomas's apartment in Gainesville too, and got no answer. He is going to call around and will keep us posted. James is grim and says if anything happens to Thomas, it's Maura's fault.

"I don't like the thoughts I'm having, Bess. If anything happens to Thomas, I am afraid of what I might do. I understand how people can be pushed to that point and she's pushed it. It's one thing to mess with me, but not my kids."

I reach over and take his hand. "I get that James. I would be having those thoughts too. It doesn't mean you would actually do something to her, now does it? It's just a normal thought. Remember that. Right now, what we need to know is where Thomas is and that he's okay." We pull into Mary's driveway and she is waiting there to meet us. James's phone rings.

"Hello? Yes, this is James Ogilvie." James grips my hand hard. "Okay. I see. Is he alright? Yes, I'll take care of it right away." James gives whoever is on the phone his email address and they disconnect.

"That was the police. Thomas stopped at a roadhouse near Columbia, South Carolina. He picked a fight and the cops were called. He's banged up some, but basically okay, except that he's in jail. The cop is emailing me information. Thank God he's alright."

We walk into the house and sit at the kitchen island. Mary gets us sweet tea while James calls Andy to let him know we found Thomas and he is okay. MJ grabs his keys and tells James to come with him.

"No nephew of mine is going to languish in a shit-hole South Carolina jail. Columbia is three hours away. We will go there and figure this out. We'll need to make bail, and get his car out of impound." James looks at me.

"Go, James. You need to be there for Thomas. I will be fine here. Just be careful and stay in touch, okay?" James hugs me

It's About Time

tight, and they fly out the door. Mary suggests I move out of the motel and stay with them, and I gladly accept her offer. We don't know how long James and MJ will be gone and I don't want to wait alone.

Three days later, James and MJ pull into the driveway looking ragged. Between busting Thomas out of jail and the emotional shit going on, they are worn out. James heads straight to the shower and then comes back to the kitchen wearing clean clothes. He wraps his arms around me and whispers in my ear how grateful he is that I am with him.

"Hey, get a room!" MJ fresh from his shower is toweling off his hair.

James and MJ fill us in on what happened over cups of coffee and scones. A local yahoo gave Thomas some shit in the bar, and that was all the excuse he needed to vent his anger all over the guy. It turned into a melee, and the bartender called the cops. Thomas managed to get away with a broken nose, and bruised ribs. James hired a lawyer and made a sizable donation to the judge's "charity" to get Thomas off the hook with a warning.

"I doubt Thomas will be drinking in South Carolina bars anytime soon," MJ adds.

"Were you able to settle anything with him, James?" Mary asks. James shakes his head, no.

"We got his car out of impound. He got in, said thanks, and headed home to Gainesville." James tells us.

"That kid is as stubborn as his old man. He was happy to see us, grateful for the help, but not letting go of his beef with James. He didn't want to talk about anything." MJ informs us.

I hoped that when James bailed Thomas out it would open the door to a conversation. I can understand Thomas's upset if he believes the bullshit Maura is feeding him. At least we know Thomas is safe which is the important thing. We've had enough drama for the moment and James is giving the whole incident a rest until he has time to think.

"I'll try talking to him when we get home. Maybe by then, he will tell me what's going on. I think we all know where the accusations originated from, but what prompted him to flare up like that now? Since we were talking about Andy's wedding when he erupted, it must have to do with Maura being left out. I prefer not to deal with Maura directly unless I have to. If Thomas isn't willing to listen to the truth, I'm not sure what to do. I can't force him to see reason. There is the recording, but playing that could backfire. I want to do all I can to settle this before Andy gets married. One Vrbo, no matter how spacious, is not big enough for both of us like this." James touches his bruise and winces.

We spend the rest of the day in quiet conversation. James calls Andy to fill him in on what happened with Thomas. He also let Andy know he proposed to me. His son knew that was coming and is happy for us. I can hear him on speaker remarking how we packed a lot into one weekend.

"That's for sure. A lot more than I planned on actually. It will all work out in time. Got room at the Vrbo for one more Andy?" James smiles at me and Andy says, absolutely.

It's About Time

CHAPTER 16

No Place Like Home

Bess

It's late Friday night when we get home from North Carolina. Our bags get dumped on the floor in James's sunroom. We are too tired to do anything but go to bed. It is lovely to travel, but there is no place like home.

We wake up around 7 AM and slowly get out of bed. There is coffee but no cream. I explore the refrigerator and find a few ancient eggs, a green fuzzy something, and a loaf of frozen bread. A trip to the Stop & Shop will be on the docket. I resurrect the bread from the freezer and we make do with toast and peanut butter. While James goes through his pile of mail, I veg out on my iPad until I have no choice but to get my butt moving. I kiss James and tell him I will be back later.

I drag my suitcase to the front door of my condo and rummage through my backpack for keys. When I open the storm door, I see a manila envelope propped inside. I tuck it under my arm, unlock the door, and wheel in my luggage. The first thing I do is open the French doors to let in fresh air. The scent and sound of the sea tells me I am home. Then I unpack. Yes, I am that person who cannot leave packed luggage sitting around. Dirty clothes are deposited in the washer. I sort through the mail which is mostly junk and a couple of bills. The mystery envelope piques my interest. My name is written on the front with a Sharpie marker in neat block letters. No return address.

Hillary Gauvreau Oat

The flap is sealed with package tape and after a moment of hesitation, I carefully cut it open with scissors. Nothing jumps out. No letter bombs or white powders. It seems safe, so I dump the contents on the table. There are pictures from the reunion, a printout of Columbia, South Carolina's police log listing Thomas's arrest and arraignment, and a greeting card sealed with a red heart sticker. After reading the police log, I rip open the bright pink envelope. It's an engagement card to "the happy couple" decorated with hearts, and champagne flutes. I get an ominous feeling as I open it.

Tucked inside the card are newspaper articles about honeymoon murders, domestic violence, and missing persons. That's cheery, I think sarcastically. A sticky note written in the same block letters cautions me to be careful because accidents happen. Isn't that sweet, an engagement threat. How thoughtful. I don't need three guesses to know who is responsible. Maura is the only person on my radar. She is using Thomas, and now me, to get to James. Thomas probably talked to his Auntie Maura when he got home and shared pictures, never giving a second thought to what she would do with them. Why would he? She is, after all, his sweet Auntie. I remember the security camera we installed after the last Maura incident and I open the app on my phone to see who might have a starring role in the video footage. A kid I don't recognize dropped off the envelope. The date stamp is yesterday.

I text Virginia to let her know we made it home, and she immediately invites us over for supper. I confirm we will be there. I pick up my purse and keys, tuck the envelope under my arm and drive back to James's.

"Shit. It has to be Maura." James slams his fist down on the counter causing me to jump. "Who else could it be?"

It's About Time

"Yup. I agree. She is threatening us. What do you think she is capable of, James? Should we get the police involved? She makes my ex-husband Chad look like a saint, which is quite an accomplishment, but not in a good way. Maura seems to believe she is invulnerable and doesn't care what people think. That makes her especially scary." I shiver.

"I'm not sure what she is capable of, Bess. She is manipulative and intimidation is certainly in her wheelhouse. Hell, she's intimidated me for years."

"Yup!" I agree as I put everything back in the envelope. "Make sure your doors are locked. By the way, I remembered the security camera you installed at my condo. It showed a kid delivering the envelope, so she must have hired him. Maura is smart. I'll hand her that. Have you checked your camera lately? Just curious if anyone has been skulking around."

"Nope. I forget it's there. Usually, I see a possum or two. But, on the off chance that someone has been skulking, good word by the way, let's look." James opens the Nest app and zips through videos from the last two weeks.

"Whoa, slow down. Go back. What is that?" James backs up the video and pauses the frame. "Holy crap, is that a bear?" I ask.

"Yes, and a big healthy one at that. I guess the possums have friends. I heard there have been a lot of bears around the lake this year." James continues reviewing the footage until he stops cold.

"Oh my God. Take a look at this." James shares the screen and presses play. Maura steps up on the deck, tries the door, which thankfully is locked, then looks up at the camera and blows a kiss.

"Holy shit. Well, she's not a bear. Thank God, you changed the locks. I think we should call the police. Let's put it on their radar." I suggest. James says he doesn't want to overreact.

"Let's wait and see what happens," he says.

"Oh, you mean like assault?" With hands on my hips, I glare at him impatiently.

"She's just trying to scare us. We can always get a restraining order if we have to."

"Ha. Do you think a little piece of paper will stop Maura? I have my doubts."

"A piece of paper that is backed by the powerful hand of the law, missy. It's like on Law and Order. Did you watch that show? That serious voice tells us that police investigate the crime and the DA prosecutes. I wouldn't mind seeing her defy it and get carted off to jail." James hums the theme song.

"Please take this seriously," I beg. "She scares me."

"You think I'm not serious?" James barks. "You're being threatened, Thomas is being coerced, I am being stalked, and it's all *my fault*." James throws his hands up in the air. "What would you have me do, Bess? Roll back time and undo my stupidity?" I slip my arms around his waist and look up into his face.

It's About Time

"James, honey, none of this is your fault. Full responsibility is on Maura for being a demented bitch. All you did was fuck an attractive and willing girl in college. How could you know it would turn into this? You okay talking with Virginia and Bob about it?"

"Sure. The more people who know the safer we are. Right?"

"If you say so." I say, but I have my doubts.

* * *

The autumn leaves are vibrant in shades of red, yellow, and orange. A chill is in the air that hints frost won't be far off. Virginia has stacks of homegrown pumpkins arranged on the deck next to corn stalks tied with colorful ribbons. It's the full glory of fall in New England. Our friends welcome us back with warm hugs and good food.

"Yum, I smell lasagna," I comment as we hang our jackets on the hooks by the door.

"You guys want wine?" Bob asks.

"You have to ask?" I tease.

"I always ask, smarty pants, because I'm an excellent host!" Bob teases back, always able to dish it out as well as take it. We settle around the fireplace with glasses of lush, Pinot Noir.

"So, how was it? Did you have fun?" Virginia asks.

"We had a blast! And we got engaged." I laugh watching Virginia's jaw drop. She jumps up and grabs us both in a hug.

"It sure took you long enough!" Bob says hugging me and shaking James's hand. "Good going, James."

Virginia looks at my left hand and remarks that she doesn't see a ring.

"Nope. I have a brooch!" I point to the brooch, and James tells them about his great-grandmother's heirloom.

"James's brother noticed the brooch immediately. His sister asked if we were engaged, and James had a good story to cover his ass. At first, I was annoyed because it felt like there was plotting going on behind my back. Thankfully there wasn't, but it opened up a conversation about our future. The more I thought about it, the better I liked the idea of a future with James. It all worked out. Right, James?" James smiles and nods yes.

"Oh, my God. This is fantastic. Okay, details. Tell us everything." James and I fill them in on the reunion activity, the teasing, games, food, and sitting around the fire with the family. I show them pictures on my phone.

"This looks like so much fun. You even had a bagpipe band? Wow. Quite the gathering." Bob notes.

"Yes, and you should have seen James throw a pole in the air." I giggle.

James looked incredulous. "It's called a caber, and I did quite well." James defends.

It's About Time

"Here's a picture I took just before he tossed it. A lot of those dudes couldn't even pick the thing up. James was amazing, but Thomas was the winner! Here's a picture of James with his father, sister Mary, brother MJ, and Thomas. Remember you met Thomas last summer?"

"They all look similar. Must be related." Bob jokes.

"I love the kilt, James! You look so handsome," adds Virginia.

"You both would love Mary. She is organized, energetic, and kind. But tough too. She broke up the fight." I tell them.

"Wait. What fight?" Virginia wants to know.

James butts in. "Before we get into that, I have to tell you about my romantic proposal. Sunday evening the family was sitting around the fire pit drinking whiskey and toasting everything under the setting sun. When the whiskey got to Bess she stood up, raised the bottle, and thanked everyone for making her feel welcome. Then she sat down. That was the moment I was waiting for. I pulled her up, vowed undying love, and asked her to marry me. She said yes. I knew she was willing because we had already talked about it. She pointedly informed me she would not appreciate a surprise proposal in front of a crowd. Good thing I didn't try that or we might not be having this conversation." James laughs. "You want to see the video my sister took?"

"Are you kidding? Of course, we want to see it!" Virginia and Bob crowd next to James on the couch to watch.

"I agreed to a very long engagement so don't you be asking about dates and wedding plans," I tell them right before I hear the hooting and hollering at the end of the video.

"We will plan a party to celebrate," Virginia informs us. "This is so wonderful and exciting. How could there be a fight amid such joy? What happened?"

"Mary said it is rare for Scotsmen and whiskey to get together without a fight breaking out, but this was a little different," I explain that something was going on with Thomas, and he was distant until he exploded, yelling accusations and punching his father. "James had a pretty colorful shiner as a result. Mary marched Thomas into the kitchen to calm him down and despite her best efforts he got in his car and flew down the driveway. We were worried about him driving to Florida in the state he was in." I tell them.

"I would be worried too. What was that about?" Bob asks. James and I respond at the same time with one word. *Maura!* Virginia rolls her eyes, and Bob groans.

"We suspect Maura has been filling Thomas's head with lies. He has known her since he was young and I have shielded him from all the crap she has pulled. I'm guessing that Thomas listens to his Auntie Maura and believes what she tells him. And what she tells him are lies about me, his mother and God knows what else." James pauses, looking down at his tightly folded hands.

"Is there any line that woman will not cross? Using a child to hurt you is despicable." Virginia is outraged.

"But that's not all. Go on James." James tells them about the roadhouse, and Thomas getting arrested.

It's About Time

"Thomas was cruising for a fight. He was primed and ready when he stopped at a bar in South Carolina. After a couple of drinks, he picked a fight with a local that resulted in a brawl. The police were called and Thomas was arrested. My brother and I drove to Columbia to get his ass out of jail. It cost me a bundle for the lawyer and a generous donation to the Judge's charity but we got Thomas off the hook with a warning. He appreciated the help, for sure, but wasn't willing to talk to me about anything. I still don't know exactly what's going on. But I can guess." James tells them.

"James is giving Thomas time to settle down before he talks to him again. We hope to get the air cleared before Andy's wedding next June." I add.

At that point, the timer buzzes and Virginia goes to the kitchen to take the lasagna out of the oven.

"Come eat and finish your stories at the table," Virginia suggests. We are hungry and the lasagna smells delicious. We follow Virginia into the kitchen settling in around the old oak table.

"Man, I missed you! This looks fantastic." I compliment Virginia. Bob pours more wine, making a joke that it isn't wrapped in gold but is acceptable. Salad and steaming squares of lasagna trailing strings of melted cheese fill our plates.

After dinner, we sit around the table talking. Bob clears our plates, and I get the envelope.

"And the story continues." I open the envelope and dump the contents on the table beside the grated parmesan. "When I got home this was at my front door." Virginia and Bob explore the contents shaking their heads in disbelief.

"What is all this? Let me guess. Maura again?" Bob asks.

"I don't know, but who else could it be? Maura is local now so she has access to my condo. She and Thomas have a connection. It had to be her because there are pictures from the reunion."

Virginia is horrified. "She is threatening you! Do you get that?"

"Oh yes, believe me, I get it and it scares the crap out of me," I say. That is when James tells them about her taunting him in the Nest camera while we were away.

"Something needs to be done. This can get out of hand. Someone could get hurt." Bob warns.

"Agree. I wanted to go to the police but James thinks we should wait. Do you have any suggestions? Aside from a restraining order?" I ask Bob. I shove everything back into the envelope.

"You have evidence that she is menacing you. Recordings, video, this envelope. If I were you, I would see what a lawyer suggests." Bob advises.

"That's not a bad idea. Do you know someone, Bob?" James asks. Bob pulls a card out of his wallet. "This guy helped me out when I was having problems with an employee I let go for stealing. He's right in town." He hands the card to James.

It's About Time

"I don't understand. What does she hope to accomplish? She can't possibly think this kind of behavior will endear her to you. Why doesn't she just move on with her life? Find another rich old guy and leave you alone." Virginia wonders.

"Yeah, well that's what a normal person would do. Maura is not normal and believes she has every right to punish James for rejecting her. She probably enjoys it."

"There isn't anything she can do that will change how I feel about Bess or my boys." James leans back in his chair and closes his eyes. "But she can make our lives miserable."

"I think you're right, James. People like her don't think ahead to an end game. She's just doing what satisfies her in the moment. That keeps us off balance and looking over our shoulders."

"What blows my mind is how long she is willing to keep this up. It has been years, for God's sake." Bob adds.

"She won't give up. We have to stop her by refusing to be intimidated and stand up to her threats. We will handle whatever happens. People who know James will stand by him." I smile at James and cover his hand with mine. "Strength in numbers, eh, 'Jay-Jay'? Now can we please talk about something else?"

We move on to more enjoyable things, like engagement parties, and grandbabies. Before long the tension dissolves, and we are laughing and telling reunion stories.

Hillary Gauvreau Oat

After dinner, we drive back to James's house. It's Saturday night and we are usually together in one place or another on the weekend. But now that we are engaged James thinks that makes things different.

"We need to get organized and figure this out Bess," he tells me.
"Figure what out?"

"Where we are going to live. Are we keeping two homes?" James is getting way ahead of me.

"You want to live together? Like, now? We just got home. Give me a minute to catch my breath, please." My eyes are wide with surprise.

"Yeah, of course. But don't you?"

"Well, a lot is going on. I haven't had a chance to think about it. Remember the long engagement promise?"

"Well, let's talk about it tomorrow, okay? See what we can agree on." James suggests. I can see he isn't going to let this go without a discussion.

"Yes, okay. We can do that." We pull into his driveway. "But tonight I need to go home."

"Why? You're already here. I will make pancakes." He cajoles.

"James, I'm not prepared. I didn't bring anything with me. My laundry is still in the washer. I haven't been home in almost two weeks and I have a full day of clients Monday."

It's About Time

"Okay, I get that. This is exactly why I want to talk about our arrangements. I don't like taking care of two places, never having everything we need, and feeling nomadic. I want to get annoyed about your girlie stuff all over the vanity and see your clothes in the closet. I get it, you're right. That's what I want. I need to know what you want. But tonight, considering what's going on, I don't want you to be alone. I'll grab some stuff and meet you at your place. Okay?"

"Sure. That's reasonable. I can live with that. See you in a few." I get out of his truck and into my car to drive home.

James helps me fold laundry, and his dorky jokes about my "delicates" make me laugh. I like having him around and want to trust that I can rely on him. That will require the test of time. Sure, it's easy at the beginning when it's all hearts, flowers, and chemistry. But what about later, when it's routine? When we disagree? When one of us gets sick? Then what? Will he still be here?

James tosses a pillow at me. "Hey, what are you thinking? I can tell when the wheels are turning."

"You really want to know?"

"Of course." He looks at me quizzically. "Unless you want me to sleep on the couch. Then, no, don't tell me."

"I was just thinking how nice it is to have you here, helping me with stuff. That will take a little getting used to. I've been doing things myself for a long time. Like since I was four and I figured out I was on my own." I toss the pillow back at him. He smiles.

"What do you mean you were on your own?" James asks, sitting on the edge of the bed.

"Well, my father worked a lot and wasn't around. Asking my mother for help just pissed her off." I sat next to him on the bed. "I was four when I promised myself I would never ask for help again. I remember it clearly. If I am too independent and you feel like I don't need you, nudge me. Because I want to learn how to let you help me."

"Okay. I can do that."

We finally get to bed around 10:30. James snuggles up next to me, brushes the hair away from my face, and kisses me softly on the cheek.

"I'm sleepy, James."

"I know. Close your eyes." James props himself up on an elbow, kisses my eyelids, and softly traces the contours of my face with his finger.

"That tickles."

"Does it?" He runs his hand slowly down my neck to the little hollow of my collarbone and kisses it.

"James . . . I . . ."

"I know . . . shhh. Indulge me. If you want me to stop I will." James attends to every part of my body with exquisite care. The way he touches me is tender and unfamiliar. I'm used to meeting needs, not receiving this kind of attention. I'm not sure how to respond. Is responding something to think about or simply allow? I feel self-conscious and shy. The tension that

It's About Time

is always in my body starts to melt. Gentle kisses track down my arm to my fingertips. James massages the palms of my hands. Slowly, I relax. Masterfully he explores every responsive nuance in me and like tiny embers, ignites them. James loves me slowly in a way I have never experienced before.

"James . . . ?"

"Mmm?"
"Thank you." Tears spill down my cheek and I don't even know why. It is like every cell in my body released a lifetime of tension.

James brushes the wet from my cheek with his thumb. "You're crying. Good tears?" he asks.

"Good tears. I love you so much it scares me."

"Why is that scary?"

"Because I won't be able to bear losing you."

"I'm not going anywhere."

"You can't promise that. People die."

"Like your mother?"

"Yes."

"You're right. Someday that will happen. I will do all I can to make sure it's no time soon." James kisses my salty wet cheek and protectively drapes his arm over my body. I snuggle up close listening to his breathing.

In the middle of the night, we are rudely awakened by the doorbell.

"What's going on?" I ask James.

"I don't know."

There is pounding on the door. "Open up. Police." comes a loud voice.

"What the fuck?" James curses. He quickly puts on shorts and we run to the door.

"What's going on?" I stand close to James holding on to him. The policeman looks us over and says he is responding to a report of a domestic disturbance at this address. One cop asks James to step outside, and the other one, a woman, asks if she can come in. When she gets inside, she looks around and asks me if I am safe or if I need help. Now I am fully awake, I tell her I am fine and safe.

"What's going on? There must be a mistake. We were sleeping." I tell her. She glances around the room one more time turns, and walks out to confer with her partner. James comes back inside, shivering from the cold, shirtless and barefoot. The police apologize for disturbing us and leave. We lock the door and secure the chain.

"Holy shit. What was that about?" I ask. "What time is it anyway?"

It's About Time

"It's about 3:30." James looks grim. "I'm going to call that attorney tomorrow, Bess. I think Maura called the cops to harass us. The guy said a woman called in the report saying she heard screaming coming from the condo."

"Is she stalking us? How did she know we were here?"

"I don't know, but we will find out." James puts his arm around me and steers me back to bed.

* * *

The aroma of coffee finally rouses me. It took a long time to get back to sleep after the cops left. I can't believe it is almost nine o'clock.

"Good morning, Pancake Man!" I kiss James.

"Are you ready for some delicious blueberry pancakes? I hope you had no plans for the blueberries in the refrigerator because I used them up." James flips the pancakes onto plates and pours coffee. We sit at the table to eat.

"I could get used to this. How long have you been up?" I ask James.

"I couldn't get back to sleep after the cops left. I might have dozed a bit but basically I was up most of the night. Once the adrenaline gets going it's hard for me to sleep. I read for a while. You have some interesting books on the shelf. Did you read *Hamilton* or is that there to impress me?"

"Yeah, James, it's all about you." I laugh. "I read some of it. It was interesting but pretty dense. I plan on going back to it but it hasn't happened yet. What did you end up reading?"

"The book about surviving narcissistic abuse. I thought it would put me to sleep but I found it riveting. Can I borrow it?"

"Oh, I know which one you mean. That's a good one. Take it. I want to hear what you think when you're done."

After James finishes his last pancake and washes it down with strong coffee he asks me about my mother.

"What happened, Bess?"
"Well, when I was a toddler, she was diagnosed with breast cancer. She died when I was twelve. Growing up I fretted every day about her dying. I might have worried more about it than she did but I was young so she didn't share much with me. And my father wasn't a talker. In therapist speak, it has created some attachment issues for me."

"Yes, I picked up on that last night."

"Oh. I'm sorry. I hope it wasn't too much."

"Oh my God, no. You're perfect. It makes sense that you would worry about losing someone you love. Losing me." James smiles saying those words and kisses me. "Oh, I left a message for that attorney. I'd like to see him tomorrow if he's available. Can you come?"

"I wish I could. My day is booked catching up with clients. Can you handle it?"

It's About Time

"Yeah. It will just be a consultation. What do you want to do today?" James asks.

"After last night, absolutely nothing except maybe a nap. How's that sound?"

"That sounds good. We were going to talk about living arrangements too, remember?"

"Yes, I remember, but I don't think I have the energy for that today. Can we talk next weekend?" I suggest expecting it to be a long, drawn-out negotiation.

"Next weekend? We aren't going to talk until then?" James looks horrified.
"This is an important conversation with a lot of decisions to make. I need time to figure out how I feel." He accepts that but I can tell he's disappointed. "Let's play it by ear, okay? Maybe it will be easier than I think."

We let the cleaning up slide and get comfortable on the couch in front of the fireplace to read. James stretches out with his head in my lap. In short order, his book falls to the side and he is making little snore-y sounds. My hand rests on his chest feeling the beat of his heart. I want to live with him, but there are so many details to sort out. Do we live here, at his place, or find our place? I love living here at my condo. Suddenly I realize I don't have to have all the answers. Duh. Being together is the important part. The rest of it we will figure out.

James finally opens his eyes. "Hey."

"Hey. Feel better?" I smile down at him.

"A little. I probably need about six more hours though." He yawns, stretches, and sits up.

"James, while you were napping, I was thinking. Maybe the moving-in-together conversation isn't that complicated. I want to live with you and I know we will be able to figure it out. I'm thinking about what I am comfortable with now.

"Okay. So, what is that, exactly?"

"For now, I'm comfortable moving some things into your house and will make space for your stuff here. I will provide all the bathroom girlie stuff you can stand. I'm not ready to make a complete move yet, though. Let's see where we end up spending most of our time and if the condo or your house doesn't work for us, then we will look for something else. Together. In the meantime, I want to spend lots of time with you. Can we take this one step at a time? Ease into this?"

"I guess so. I'm disappointed we aren't living together now, but I hear what you're saying. I'm okay with your plan but I don't want to wait too long. Let's keep talking about it. Do we agree to that? And I'm staying here tonight, just so you know."

"Deal." I smile and we seal our agreement with a kiss.

CHAPTER 17

It's The Law

James

Monday morning, I unlock my shop and step inside. It's just as I left it but so much has changed it seems unfamiliar, like a past life. I sit at the work table drumming my fingers on the aged teak wondering where to start. Maybe I will run next door for coffee. The phone rings saving me from my dilemma. It's the attorney's office letting me know they have a 3:00 p.m. opening. I confirm I will be there.

My thoughts drift to Bess. Our living arrangement is okay for now, I guess, but I'm eager to figure out a permanent solution. I don't mind staying at her place and happy to share my house, but it feels like sleep overs. We're back and forth like nomads. I want stability, a place for us to set down our roots. Not that I'm complaining. Too much. Okay, yeah, I'm complaining. I need to be patient. Bess is probably right that in time we will have a better idea of what works and where we want to be. Bringing my attention back to the task at hand, I sort through a stack of work orders. I start on an easy repair that I can get out of the way. It's reassuring to get back to clocks, something I understand and can fix.

Knock knock. The door opens with the cheery tinkle of the bell.

"Bess! I was hoping you would stop by."

"I'm on a lunch break. Want to share my grinder?" Bess holds it out like an offering.

"Yes, I'd love to! How does it feel to be back at work?" I ask as Bess unwraps the Italian grinder.

"I like being back. It's a full day of catching up though. I'm tired, but so far so good. What about you?" Bess says.

"It's taking me time to get organized. I'm not sure where to start because I am a bit distracted. The lawyer's office called, and I have a meeting at 3."

"Great! I can't wait to hear what he says. Are you coming over for supper tonight?"

"You bet I am. Then I can fill you in on my meeting."

"That sounds good." Bess wraps up the remains of her sandwich and gets ready to head back to her office. I give her a salami-flavored kiss and will see her after work.

Clocks aren't holding my attention today. My mind wanders all over the place thinking about Bess, worrying about Maura, and preparing psychologically for meeting the lawyer. I don't want him to think I am a whiney wimp who can't handle his women. I burst out laughing. That's my father's voice echoing in my head. He's a tough Highlander, always in charge, and never lets anyone see him sweat, especially not the ladies. He thinks boys need to be toughened up. His parenting style is old-timey man training. I finish fixing an anniversary clock with a sticky torsion pendulum and leave a message for the customer to come and get it. Then I make a list of questions I have for the attorney. Maybe if I get them out of my head, I will be able to concentrate on other things. At 2:30 I wash up and decide to walk to the lawyer's office a few blocks away.

It's About Time

The office is in an old Victorian house that was elegant in its day. A conservative black and gold wooden sign on the front lawn announces the office of Eric Cunningham, Esq., Attorney at Law. I walk up the steps to the antique front door, turn the polished brass knob, and enter a hallway that is like a tunnel going back in time. The original mahogany woodwork is ornate. The gleaming hardwood floor creaks a welcome as I walk in. A staircase to my right leads to the second floor. The old plaster walls are painted a relaxing shade of sage. There is the scent of lemon oil mixed with that indefinable old building smell. The hall is about twenty feet long leading to a bright open room, so I head in that direction. An older woman dressed in a navy suit with a white blouse buttoned up to her chin sits at a tidy desk and smiles. She looks like she came with the house. Several doorways are spaced out along the walls. One of them opens into a good-sized conference room. The rest of the office is filled with neatly organized office equipment and cherry filing cabinets.

"You must be Mr. Ogilvie." She gets up, shakes my hand, and leads me to the conference room. "Please, make yourself comfortable, the attorney will be with you soon. Would you like water?" I say that would be nice and sit down toward the end of the polished conference table. Ms. Prim, as I call her, brings me a cold bottle of spring water and places it on a coaster. The woman moves like a cat, silent and stealthy. In stark contrast, a man bursts through the doorway at maximum speed making me jump. He slaps a legal pad down on the table.

"Mr. Ogilvie, may I call you James? And please call me Eric." He booms and comes at me like a bullet train, gripping my hand and shaking it vigorously. "Welcome to my office. Or maybe not. People who come here are usually not all that happy about seeking the advice of a criminal attorney."

Hillary Gauvreau Oat

Eric is not what I was expecting. He's probably in his fifties, about five-feet-eight-inches tall. Short in stature but large in presence. He sports a Lacoste polo shirt complete with crocodile logo circa 1970, and well-worn jeans. If we weren't sitting at a conference table, I would swear he was going out to mow the lawn. Wire-rim glasses are stuck to his forehead and shaggy grey hair is sticking up in a lot of different directions reminding me of Einstein and Jerry Garcia. This man is the exact opposite of "Miss Prim".

"I understand you got my name from Bob Wilson. He is a good man. Hard worker and talented. How can I help you?" Eric talks fast, wasting no time.

"I'm being harassed and threatened. It's a long story but basically, I want to know what my options are to get this person to leave me and my family alone." Eric lowers his glasses and looks at me. His affable nature shifts to all business.

"James, how long has this been going on? How are you being harassed?" Eric clicks his pen a few times over the legal pad, never taking his eyes off me. I collect my thoughts and begin my story starting with college and ending with the latest developments including the police coming to the house.

"There is much more to the story including lies and manipulation. She threatened to pay high school girls to lie that I had sex with them to ruin my career as a teacher. I was a chemistry teacher at a private school in Hartford then. She said she would ruin my reputation and my boys would be taken away from me if I didn't keep her happy. Keeping her happy means cooperating, including having a sexual relationship, which I did not want. I am so ashamed about caving to her threats that I never talked about this with anyone. Even my kids don't know what she has done. She destroyed my marriage and now she

It's About Time

is turning my youngest son against me. As a result of her lies my marriage fell apart. After we filed for divorce, my wife was diagnosed with cancer. She died eight years ago. We never got the divorce, but our relationship never recovered. After that, I didn't care about anything except my kids. I let Maura push me around. I gave in to all of her demands. But things are different now. I have a life worth living, a woman I love and I want to be free of this harassment. It might sound like I need a therapist instead of an attorney but now that I am with Bess things have escalated. We considered calling the police but Bob suggested I talk to you first." The attorney makes notes while I talk.

"Bob gave you good advice James. There are potentially serious legal issues here. It is illegal to falsely report a crime to the police for starters. That's the easy one, so far. Harassment, threats, and stalking are also crimes. We would have to prove it, however. Do you have any evidence to back up your claims, aside from your testimony?"

"Well, I have a video of the woman showing up at my house while we were away. My fiancé has an audio recording where the woman admits to wanting to destroy me."

"Did she get permission for that recording?"

"No, she didn't."

"Well, the information will be useful to us but inadmissible in court. But that's okay. Go on."

"And there is this envelope that was left at Bess's condo. We just got back from my family reunion in North Carolina. The pictures are from then. The police report is about my son. He was angry at me because he believed the lies Maura told him.

Hillary Gauvreau Oat

He was pissed off during the reunion weekend and on the last day he exploded accusing me of all kinds of ridiculous shit. Maura's name was mentioned so I knew where the lies came from. He drove off in a fury and got in a fight at a bar that landed him in jail. The card and newspaper clippings with the post-it are what scared Bess." I hand Eric the manilla envelope. He dumps it out and pokes through it with the tip of his pen. He puts on nitrile gloves and slides the card from its envelope, looking at the news stories and the note telling Bess to be careful. He examines both envelopes to see how they were sealed.

"This person was at the reunion?" He asks as he pulls off the gloves. "I'm assuming other people have handled this by now." He comments.

"No, she wasn't there but she and my son Thomas have contact. He was there. He talked with her and shared reunion pictures. The envelope was handled by me, my fiancé, Bob, and Virginia, and now you."

"This is a circumstantial connection to your woman unless we can get fingerprints or some other evidence from it. Just because you know it came from her isn't enough to accuse her of anything. I know that's frustrating. We have to prove it somehow. Does the woman have a name? It's easier to refer to her if I know that."

"Her name is Maura Jenkins. At least that is her maiden name. I'm not sure what she goes by now. She has been married and widowed a few times." That perked Eric up.
"She just bought a house in Old Lyme so there are property records."

"Hmm. And what do you know about these husbands? Anything?"

It's About Time

"No. Not much other than they were old and rich. Maura has become quite wealthy as a result."

"Well, that's interesting. Sometimes we have to look sideways to get where we want to go. So where do you want to go, James? Do you want to press charges, get a restraining order, or sue her for damages?"

"I want her to stop and leave me and my family alone. What would be the best way to do that?"

"Good question. That depends on her of course. Some people back off when they have to cough up a large sum of money. Sounds like she has bucks so suing for damages might not work. Others get a grip when they are threatened with arrest. The charge that could stick is calling in a false incident report to the police. That's easy to check into. Police can ID the caller. They don't like false reports but usually don't pursue a single incident. If we bring this to their attention in the context of harassment they will take it seriously. We might have a criminal case as well. You need to know that if we push her, she might push back. Has she ever threatened violence?"

"I have never been afraid she would shoot me if that is what you're asking. She has acted out, pushing, slapping, and throwing things. I never really felt threatened because I'm much bigger than her."

"Does she own a firearm?" Eric asks. I think for a moment.

"Yes, she did, anyway. Not sure about now. She was living in New York City and got it for protection."

"I'm not saying you should be worried, but I don't want to overlook anything. Sometimes people surprise us, and not in a good way. Here is what I suggest. Hold on a sec." Eric gets up and rushes out to the other office. When he comes back, he is carrying a folio of paperwork.

"So, let's get business out of the way. Then you can decide how you want to proceed. If you want me to pursue this, I require a $5000.00 retainer. I charge $350 an hour plus expenses. I like to keep the chit-chat to a minimum for your sake. But do not hesitate to call me if you need to, okay?" He smiles. "I need all the evidence you have including dates, names, and contact information. Write down everything you remember. Once I have looked it over and done some investigating, I will have a better idea of the best course of action. If any. Sometimes these things are awful but there isn't much that can be done legally. I know that's frustrating. It frustrates me too, knowing what's going on and being unable to prove anything unless something terrible happens." Eric sets his pen down on the legal pad and sits back waiting for me to decide.

"Eric, I want her to stop. I am happy to know there are legal options. I want your help." I sign the agreement and promise to drop off the retainer and get all the evidence together within the week. He hands me an information sheet that includes instructions for sending him electronic data.

"I'm going to photograph everything in the envelope before you leave. I will send you copies. Then I will bag the envelope and see if the lab can get any information from it. Agree?"

"Yes, absolutely." I'm impressed by this guy already. Hopefully, something good will come of this. Eric puts gloves on again and lines up all the items from the envelope on the table. He takes digital photos and then tucks everything back into a sealed

It's About Time

plastic bag labeled with my name, and his information. We both initial and date the label and he gives me a receipt.

"Okay, that's it for now. It's good to meet you, James. I'm sorry you're going through this and hope we can resolve this mess." I shake his hand and feel relieved that I am finally taking action. He moves his glasses back up to his forehead and shows me out.
I walk slowly back to the shop lost in thought, wanting to call Bess to tell her about the meeting but I know she is with clients. It is almost time to close up anyway. When I get to the shop, I organize things for tomorrow and lock up. Then I go home and pack some things to bring to Bess's. Strike while the iron is hot as they say.

At home, I dig a suitcase out of the closet and fill it with clothes, an extra charger for my phone, and the book she loaned me. I add a couple of bottles of wine to the mix. I am going to need a set of toiletries so the next stop is CVS. I may need more things but this will get me started. It's now around five o'clock so I text Bess to see when she will get home. She texts right back that she is finishing up. The next stop is The Dock to pick up fish and chips.

Bess is already home when I pull into a parking place in front of the condo. Between the wheelie bag, CVS supplies, and the food, I have my hands full. Bess comes out to help, kissing me in full view of the neighbors. Bess kissing a man bringing a suitcase into her home will cause a delicious buzz. I smile.

"I see you are wasting no time getting your stuff here." Bess laughs. "You afraid I will change my mind?" She takes the bag of food, unpacking it at the table

"Change your mind? Ha! Never! I am just eager." I leave my stuff in the foyer and get beverages from the kitchen. "I'm dying to tell you about the meeting with Eric."

"Wow, you're already on a first-name basis?" Bess asks as she dips a French fry in ketchup and bites off the end. "Tell me all!" I join her at the table bearing frosty mugs of ice-cold beer.
"Well, the guy isn't into formality. We were immediately on a first-name basis. I like that. He seems unpretentious and knows his stuff, at least as far as I can tell. Remember I watch Law and Order." Bess shakes her head at me.

"Seriously, I'm really glad Bob suggested him. I never considered legal ways to deal with Maura. She had me convinced that no one would believe me, and I was powerless. Eric asked what result I was looking for, and I told him I wanted her to leave me and my family alone. Whatever it takes to accomplish that, short of a hitman, I'm in. Anyway, he said we can bring criminal charges against her if the evidence is there. The police can ID her call Saturday night, and that's a clear-cut crime. The other option is civil, and we sue her for harassment. There is also the restraining order option. He wants me to get all the evidence to him so he can review it and see what the best option is. Bess, I feel so relieved to have help with this. I wish I'd known I had legal rights years ago. I owe Bob, big time."

"I'm relieved too. What do we need to do? Did he mention a fee?" Bess asks.

"Oh yeah. I need to give him a retainer of $5K. He charges $350 an hour and said we need to keep the chit-chat down for my sake. He's very practical, which I like. Honestly, I would have offered him more to get Maura off my back. He gave me instructions for sending him digital information so I can get the video, and your recording to him. He has the envelope. Oh yeah, I forgot. He is sending that to a lab to see if we can get

It's About Time

any evidence from the contents. He asked me who touched it, and he used gloves when he photographed all of it. I'm telling you the guy knows his stuff. I kind of doubt we will get anything from it, but who knows? Maura would never expect me to actually do something, like get a lawyer. So maybe she licked the envelope and we get finger prints and DNA." James grins. "Eric is covering all the bases. Is there anything else you can think of to give him?" I'm revved up and ready to go.

"I can't think of anything right now, but I'm kinda fried. It was a long day. Sounds like you handled it." Bess gets up from the table and tosses her trash away. "I am really happy you had such a productive meeting, hon. Maybe we can be done with her for good without hiring a hitman. Murder for hire is such risky business."

"Wouldn't that be wonderful! I'll clean up. You relax." I make us tea and turn on the fireplace, before joining Bess on the couch. "Hon? Eric asked me if I thought Maura could be dangerous. He says when we push her, she might push back. I remember she used to have a pistol for protection in New York. Not sure if she still has it. He said we need to be aware that sometimes people surprise us. I have never felt physically threatened by Maura, but I can't put anything past her. This is the first time I've pushed back. She thinks she has total control over me. When she finds out I am bringing charges against her, I don't know how she will react. Once the ball gets rolling, I don't want you, us, to live alone. That will accelerate our living together plan, at least temporarily. I don't want you at risk. Me either for that matter. If this is all too much for you, and you want to back out of our engagement, I will hate it but understand."

"Thank you for telling me that, James. I figured she might try to get even but wasn't sure if you knew that. I agree with Eric, things could get dicey. I love you, and we are in this together.

If we break up then she wins. I will not let that happen. So yes, I think you should move in here. Your place is more isolated, and here we are surrounded by people. That makes me feel safer. Why don't we move stuff this weekend and make space for you here? What do you think?"

"I am relieved to hear you say that and agree. I think we should get an alarm system installed here too. I will do a little research on that." Bess sits up and puts her arms around me. I kiss her and hold her tight.

"We are going to be okay," she whispers in my ear.

"I know. This was a long time coming and I could not have done it without you."

Bess kisses me and stretches out again on the couch as I call Bob. "Bob, hey it's James."

"James, how are you? It's good to hear from you."

"I had to call and thank you for the referral to Eric. We had an incident here Saturday night. Did you hear? Police came knocking at 3:30 in the morning. It pushed me to finally do something."

"Maura called the cops on you guys?" Bob asks.

"Yeah, we think so. They said someone called in a domestic abuse incident. Fortunately, they believed us, that nothing was going on. We were sleepy and confused although there was nothing like a police presence to wake us up. It was upsetting. I don't want to deal with this shit anymore. So, I had a meeting with Eric today, and it's promising. I didn't know there was so much I could do legally to get Maura to back off. I owe you!

It's About Time

Bess and I will take you guys out to dinner. Anywhere you want to go."

"Miami? I love Cuban food." Bob teases with a laugh. I tell him I will see what I can do after I pay off the lawyer. We chatted for a few minutes about my impression of Eric and what the next steps might be. After we hang up Bess smiles and tells me she likes that I am getting friendly with Bob. Friends are good to have.

"Bess, I know I just talked about moving in, but will you be okay here if I head home tonight?" I have a million things I want to get organized for Eric. The sooner this ball is rolling, the better.

"No problem. I am wiped out and looking forward to an early night. While things are peaceful, go do your thing."

"Don't forget to lock up and have your cell phone close, okay?" Bess salutes and says yes, sir.

So far everything with Bess feels easy. Sure, we have disagreements and negotiations but there are no tantrums. I think we have a good shot at a comfortable life together. Fingers crossed.

It is only 6:30 but already pitch dark outside. I love the cool colorful days of fall except for early nightfall. I climb into my truck and head home. Bess was right about giving our living situation time to reveal itself. I never thought safety concerns would be the deciding factor but here we are. I get to my house and unlock the door. I'm comfortable at the condo and coming home to a dark house doesn't feel as nice as it used to.

Hillary Gauvreau Oat

I toss my jacket over a chair in the sunroom and decide to start a fire. That always makes it feel homey. I turn on the kitchen lights over the island and open a beer. There is enough wood stacked by the stove to get me through tonight. The paper and fat wood ignite easily and when it is drawing air up the stove pipe I place a couple of small logs on top. While the fire is catching, I rummage through my desk to find a notebook, pen, and checkbook. I unplug my laptop and carry all of it into the sunroom. The instructions Eric gave me are still in the truck. I open the sunroom door cautiously looking for bears. The motion sensor light clicks on and the coast is clear. It is a beautiful night on the lake. I walk down to the water and sit on the dock. I will miss this place if we give it up. But the memory of Maura being here does taint it. I'd rather not think of her when I sit in the sunroom.

After I retrieve the instructions, I settle in on the couch and put my feet up on the coffee table. First things first, I write a check to Eric. Then I review the instructions for sending him digital media. I have the video and the recording Bess made on my laptop. I send them off. Done. It was then that I remembered Caroline's journal. Not knowing if that is useful, I save it on a flash drive and will ask Eric about it. It is all hearsay as far as I know because it was Caroline's thoughts. There is no way to prove anything. I am the only one besides Maura who knows the lies it contains, and the trouble those lies caused. I'll let Eric decide.

I open a blank Word doc and start listing everything I remember, highlighting the things I think Eric can use. Every memory stimulates me to remember more. The lies, threats, and manipulations are adding up. Things I forgot about, now seem crucially important. I can see how I tried to deny and minimize the abuse from the beginning which did me no good. Time passes quickly and the fire is now embers. The beer is gone. I close the laptop and stretch. Being able to take action

It's About Time

makes me feel less victimized and that energizes me. Although remembering all the shit that's happened has put me on edge. I will bring all this stuff to Eric tomorrow and get this moving. Crap is liable to hit the fan once we take action but I hope the result will be positive and permanent.

I lock up, take a quick shower, and get into bed feeling cautiously optimistic. James Ogilvie is not silent anymore and can see the light at the end of this very dark experience.

Hillary Gauvreau Oat

It's About Time

CHAPTER 18

Moving On

James

I gathered all the evidence I had against Maura and sent it electronically to the lawyer. On Wednesday I dropped off Caroline's journal on the flash drive with the retainer. Ms. Prim, also known as Margaret Wiseman, inquired how I was doing. She is allowed to chit chat apparently and I appreciated the touch of human warmth. I told her I was okay and eager to get this mess behind me. Obviously. Who in their right mind would want to drag this out? She nodded in agreement and wondered if I included texts and emails in my documentation. Since I never imagined taking legal action documenting any of this was not on my radar. I deleted Maura's texts quickly like I was sucking venom from a snake bite. The few random emails I found didn't seem helpful. Maura is careful about not putting anything in writing that reveals her true nature.

While I wait to hear from Eric, I check out home security. Bob, thinks ADT has a good system so I call them to schedule a consultation. I decide to change my passwords on everything, especially online banking. I have no idea what information Maura might have in her possession, so better safe than sorry. Cleaning me out financially is something I can see her doing. Sometimes I wonder if I'm overdoing it with these precautions. It's hard for me to accept that Maura would cause harm or damage. Then I remember what she has already done and Eric's warning. Why can't I keep that on the front burner of my mind? Part denial maybe, and partly years of her mind fuckery.

Hillary Gauvreau Oat

Reminds me of the frog in the pot of boiling water. The water was warm when I got in, so I never noticed the heat being cranked up to a boil. This is the first time I have ever pushed her, and I have no idea what she will do. She might not shoot me but that doesn't mean she isn't dangerous. I keep busy but nothing takes my mind off of what might happen next.

During the week the clock shop doesn't leave time for anything else. This weekend I will move into Bess's condo, check on my house, and mow my lawn. Bob is willing to help. Then we will have dinner together. I am so happy to be moving in with Bess, but sorry it had to be under these circumstances.

Friday, I lock up the shop and get home before Bess. I turn on the fireplace, get wine ready to pour and keep a pizza warm in the oven. I check the refrigerator and find enough green stuff to make a salad, so I feel less guilty about eating pizza again. As I toss the salad I hear the key in the front door. Bess looks tired but smiles when she sees me. She drops her bag in the foyer and we wrap our arms around each other.

"That feels good. Please tell me this week is over. It was a bear." Bess complains. I kiss the top of her head. "People are going through some terrible stuff. I want to help but mostly all I can do is listen and care."

"I know you and your caring is a healing balm. Trust me. Hungry?" Bess says she is and picks a cucumber slice out of the salad. After supper, we get cozy on the couch by the fireplace.

"It's debriefing night. Whatcha got? Unless we are not doing that anymore?" I ask.

"Since you are here all the time now, I don't think we have to leave it to Friday night. It will be impossible not to notice when

It's About Time

I get cranky. But hey, I'm open to hearing what's on your mind. Are we set for the weekend?" Bess asks.
"Ah, the weekend. Well, I have a long to-do list. There is moving in which I am excited about. We have to make space here and Bob will help me move stuff. Then, as planned, we will have dinner with them here. You're in charge of the menu. Right? I need to mow my lawn and get a few things at the hardware store. The ADT security guy is coming to take a look and offer us ideas. I think it might be good to have security installed at my house too since I won't be there every day. What do you think?" I was moving fast through the list and unsure if Bess was keeping up with me.

"That sounds good. I have already moved clothes out of the extra closet in the bedroom so it's all yours. Have you gotten any updates from Eric?"

"Nope. He said it will take him some time but I'm impatient now that I've taken this step." We sit quietly holding hands. "I wish I had seen half of this shit coming years ago. I was so hurt by the way Caroline was acting, plus I had my hands full teaching and taking care of the boys. The tiniest comfort that came from anywhere was like rain on a parched desert. Maura maneuvered her way in and capitalized on my pain. I forgot who she was because I needed help so badly, and she had no trouble reeling me in. Putting the information together for Eric, I was shocked by how much abuse I accepted as normal."

"I guess that's why they say hindsight is 20/20. Don't be too hard on yourself. No one teaches us how to deal with people like Maura. They only tell us to share our snacks and not run with scissors. The rest we learn from experience, I guess. No one wants to believe people can be cold and cruel. That's why I never saw it coming. Neither did you."

"You can say that again. I can't believe she continues to punish me for falling in love with Caroline. Jeez we've all been dumped. It sucks, then we move on. Not her. Oh no. This is personal. She is obsessed with making me pay. Forever. No one leaves Maura Jenkins! I get it now. It wasn't anything I could have prevented or fixed. It's who she is."

"Yup. The dangerous part is the complete lack of empathy. If she ignores the pain she causes other people, she has no problem inflicting it. Maura seemed to zone right in on your vulnerability. I shudder to think what her husbands went through." Bess linked her arm through mine and rested her head on my shoulder. "But now we know. That's the important thing."

* * *

Saturday, I leave early to mow the lawn at my house and organize things to move. I turn onto Lonely Hollow Road and pull into the driveway. I add 'tools' to my list of things to pack. I get the gas can out of the back of the truck and walk toward the garage at the back of the lot. When I get to the back deck I am horrified. I set the gas can down and stare. There is a hammer lying on the deck. Furniture is smashed and thrown off the deck in a jumble. The motion sensor light is smashed. Black paint has been sprayed on the Nest camera lens and "FUCK YOU PERV" is scrawled across the siding in giant letters. I call the police. Then I call Eric and leave him a message. I hate to bother him on a Saturday but he needs to know about this. I leave a message for Bess, telling her what's going on. It isn't clear on the Nest camera app who did this before they obscured the camera. I'll send it to Eric anyway. Maybe he can process it and get a clearer picture. I take pictures of the whole mess and send them to Eric and Bess.

It's About Time

There is nothing else to do until the police arrive, so I get out the lawn mower and cut the grass. I am almost done when a cruiser pulls into the driveway. A couple of town cops get out and I show them the vandalism. They ask questions, take photos, check out the light and the camera, and make notes. They want to know if I recognize the hammer. I don't. They ask if I'm the clock guy, and don't seem too disturbed by the damage saying it was probably kids. This is small potatoes for them but I know the backstory. It wasn't kids but I didn't get into that with them. After they leave, I carefully slip the hammer into a Ziploc bag just in case Eric wants it, and toss it into my truck. When I finish the lawn, I drive to Hardy & Son Hardware in town with my list. Both Bess and Bob are waiting for me on the deck when I get back from shopping.

"Hey, hon." I kiss Bess. "What do you think of the artwork?"

"James, this is awful," Bess says.

"I hate to break it to you, old man, but you're going to have to replace those cedar shingles unless you want to put about 4 coats of paint on them. Probably be worth it to put in a claim with your homeowner's insurance."

"I think that makes sense Bob. I will put it on my expanding to-do list. Today I want to get the light and camera working. Did Bess tell you ADT is coming to give us a quote? After this, I'm definitely getting security here too."

"Not a bad idea. At least until you get a handle on the Maura problem. I assume she was involed in this? Last I heard bears don't use spray paint." Bob says.

Hillary Gauvreau Oat

"I am leaving this in your capable hands, guys. Virginia is coming over to help me make an apple pie." After Bess leaves, Bob and I get the most immediate repairs done and make sure everything works. Then we load boxes of stuff, my dresser, a desk chair, and the antique walnut desk that my family brought from Scotland into the trucks. I tuck a bottle of Talisker under my arm for toasting, and I am set to go. Everything else can wait. Bess and I will clean out the refrigerator another time. It's not like I am moving across the country and it will be good to check on the house occasionally.

Bob and I stow the damaged deck furniture in the garage and I change the code on the electric door opener. When all is secure, we drive out of Lonely Hollow Road to my new home.

The condo is warm and smells like apple pie. A man could not ask for a better place to land. Bess shows me where she made space for the dresser and desk in the spare room. After Bob and I carry the furniture in, I pile computer stuff around the desk and hang clothes in the closet. When we finally have everything in the house I pull out the Talisker and propose a toast.

"Are we using glasses, James, or doing this Scottish style straight out of the bottle?" Bess asks with a grin.

"I will get you amateurs glasses. You're company after all!" Scotch is poured and I raise my glass. "To friends! Thanks for the help today, Bob. I am grateful to know you. To my new home! Thank you for making pie ladies. And to Bess. I have no words to describe my love for you. *Slàinte Mhath!*"

"Or as they say in English, down the hatch." Bob laughs and swallows the whiskey. "Oh dear, what is this stuff? It tastes like I swallowed a bonfire." I fill Bob in on the Isle of Skye distillery and how the smoky taste is highly regarded in Scotland.

It's About Time

"Oh, so the more you drink the better it gets?" Bob grimaces and they all laugh. I shake my head at the lot of them.

"Okay let's get all the talk about Maura and lawyers out of our system before we sit to eat. After that please God let us find something else to talk about." Bess pleads. "Maura craves being the center of attention. Let's not give it to her!" We raise our glasses in a toast to peace with friends.

I agree with Bess although Maura is still the main thing on my mind and I find it hard not to talk about the situation. Bess brings a delicious pot roast, mashed potatoes, and garlicky green beans to the table. Bob, our sommelier, opens a bottle of Merlot.

"Merlot, Bob?" I ask. "I'm surprised. Isn't that a tacky wine?"

Bob works the corkscrew into the bottle and explains how the movie *Sideways,* ruined the Merlot industry for years, but it's finally recovered. "There is nothing wrong with a nice mellow Merlot my friends. See for yourselves." He pours a small amount into James's glass. James hams up the tasting, inspecting the color with one eye closed, and gives it a sniff before swallowing it down.

"It's a soft, sensual wine. This bottle is a good quality wine from France, velvety and plummy. It pairs nicely with pot roast and apple pie." Bob describes the Merlot with a snooty accent. We all laugh, and Virgina smacks his arm.

"What? I'm just trying to educate the masses." Bob pouts.

"You're such a clown!" Virginia kisses him on the cheek, "I love that about you." I want us to be like Bob and Virginia in 30 years, provided we live that long.

The rest of the weekend is uneventful, thank the gods. I cross things off my to-do list. Bess and I organize my stuff and it fits. I still have a house full of stuff but first things first. Monday morning Eric calls.

"You had an eventful weekend James," he says. "Yes, I want the hammer. Can you come by my office this afternoon? I want to go over the next steps."

"You got it. I'll see you later. I know this vandalism has to be connected to Maura. As long as I have lived here nothing like this has ever happened in that neighborhood."

"You could be right." Eric hangs up. He is all business.

I arrive at the old Victorian a little before two. I can see Eric in the conference room looking through papers and making notes. When he hears the floor creak he looks up and waves me in.

"Sit, James. I have news." I choose a chair next to Eric and place the hammer sealed in a Ziploc bag on the table. "Thanks for bringing that. Good news. We were able to isolate fingerprints on the contents of the envelope. Maura Jenkins's prints were all over it. She enrolled in the Department of Homeland Security Trusted Traveler Program so her fingerprints are in the database. I thought we would have to get DNA testing done but we got lucky. Since she was the only one you did not see handle the envelope it suggests she sent it. I followed up on the false police report as well." Eric shuffles papers and pulls out a report. Police ID'd the caller even with a blocked number. It was Maura's cell phone. Bingo. It was a rookie mistake. People think if they block their number, they are

It's About Time

safe from police detection. Not true. The vandalism video footage is trickier because it was dark. My tech guy was able to enhance the image and get facial recognition that identified Maura Jenkins. Man, she is all over you. So we have her on stalking, harassment, filing a false police report, and vandalism. I think we start by getting you a restraining order, and I'm going to see about getting an arrest warrant on various charges. Did you get security set up?"

"Wow, you must have worked all weekend. Okay, all that sounds good to me. I got an ADT security system but it needs to be installed. I will get to it tonight."

"I find this kind of work to be challenging and fun. No way I would put it off until regular working hours. With your permission, I will pull the trigger on this, so to speak." Eric slides his glasses down from his forehead and looks at me intently. "I will need you to go to court with me tomorrow morning to ask for the restraining order. Your sons are over 18 so they are not included in this. If they need protection, they will have to file where they live. Once the judge signs the restraining order Maura will have to stay away from you, your immediate family, residences, and workplaces. She cannot legally communicate in any manner, and she must turn over any firearms she is in possession of. I doubt she would try to kill you but asking for that ensures safety, and it's also a dramatic touch that will get the judge's attention. After all, we don't know what she is capable of. How does that sound to you?"

"It sounds great. I don't care if she goes to jail, I just want her to leave us alone. If this the way to make that happen then count me in."

"Good. I will get the ball rolling. I will talk to the prosecutor today. Tomorrow in court I will do the talking, and the judge will ask if you agree. It's a simple process. Then Maura will be served and after that she will have to keep her distance. The prosecutor will review the criminal charges, and if she believes there is a case, Maura will be arrested and arraigned. That is usually enough to scare people to stay away for a good long time. For sure she will lawyer up with the best money can buy and post bond. The prosecutor may offer her a deal, we settle, she gets a slap on the wrist, and we never go to trial. That is what I would like to see happen. I want to scare the pants off her. Maybe she will decide that revenge isn't worth jail time. Questions?" I shake my head no. Eric leans back, folds his hands over his belly looking satisfied. "You know, she has screwed herself. She is going to discover she isn't as smart as she thought. I'll see you tomorrow morning at the courthouse." Eric gets up, vigorously shakes my hand, and walks me out of the conference room. This is all new to me. My heart is pounding with fear and excitement. After I leave the office, I text Bess. She is home, so I call on my way to the shop to let her know what's happening.

"Bess, I have to go to court tomorrow to get the restraining order. Can you come with me? I admit I am nervous about all this legal stuff. I hope I am doing the right thing and not poking a hornet's nest as you like to say."

"James, I am so glad you are taking action. It's about time Maura finds out she can't get away with this shit. Yes, I will be there with you."

"Thank you, hon. I love you! I'll be at the shop this afternoon. Do we have dinner plans? Want me to pick something up?"

"*No*! I've had enough takeout. I'm making dinner. Ever since North Carolina, I can't fit in my clothes." Bess informs me.

It's About Time

"Gotcha. I'm feeling a little chubby myself. See you after work." I hang up and unlock the door to my shop hoping work will distract me from thinking about tomorrow. Even in the face of the physical evidence, I am afraid no one is going to believe that I, a big strong man, need protection from a woman. Just thinking about that makes my heart pound. Maura drummed it into my head that no one would ever believe anything I said. My shame stopped me from getting support that would have offered another perspective to challenge her. I now understand that coercive control has no gender boundaries and men are just as vulnerable as women. Before we go to court tomorrow, I need to know, for my peace of mind, that Eric is aware of how I feel. It's usually women entering the courtroom seeking protection from a guy who beats them up. I'm going to testify that non-physical abuse can be just as harmful and leaves no marks. I send an email to Eric telling him my thoughts and concerns. After I sent it, I started to breathe better. Focus on clocks James. Focus. Later in the afternoon, Eric emailed me all the court forms that he filled out asking me to look them over. I approved them and sent him a picture of Maura to give to the Marshal.

~~~~

Tuesday morning, I dress in dark pants, a collared shirt, and a blue crew neck sweater.

"How do I look? Believable?" I ask Bess.

"You look quite credible. And handsome." She kisses me and I hug her tight.

"Thank you for coming with me. I can't believe how nervous I am. I expect to be laughed out of the courtroom."

"Yup. That's normal for what you have been through. I am with you, hon. I get it. Whatever happens, we are okay. You ready to go?"

"I guess so. Can't wait to get this over with." Bess is driving us to the courthouse.
She parks the car and takes my hand as we walk to the entrance. We pass through the metal detectors and meet Eric outside the courtroom.

Once we seat ourselves inside, I sign the forms I reviewed yesterday. Eric gives them to the clerk who passes them to the judge. Now we wait for the judge to call my name. This is nerve-wracking and just the beginning.

When it's our turn, we stand in front of the judge.

"Mr. Cunningham, are you representing your client in this matter?"

"I am, Your Honor."

"Mr. Ogilvie, you are requesting a restraining order against Ms. Maura Jenkins, is that correct?"

"It is, Your Honor." The judge looks over the forms and signs them approving our request. I start to breathe again.

"Mr. Ogilvie, this is a temporary order. There will be a hearing in seven days to decide if it will be extended. Mr. Cunningham here will make sure you have everything you need."

"Thank you, Your Honor."

It's About Time

That was it. Outside the courtroom, Eric tells us a State Marshal will serve Maura and she will be required to immediately surrender her firearm. I feel a rush of relief and euphoria. I have help. I am going to finally be free. That's all I care about. Being safe and free of Maura.

The clerk approaches and informs us the hearing is scheduled for next Wednesday. I'll meet with Eric to be sure we are prepared. Maura will probably be there, and I need to prepare myself for that. I picture beautiful Maura, dressed impeccably, looking vulnerable with maybe a tear in her eye. A slick expensive lawyer dressed in an Armani suit stands by her side reassuring her. Then there is me, a burly Scotsman asking for protection standing next to Jerry Garcia. What will people think?
As if reading my mind, Eric reassures me. "Remember this isn't about the optics. It's about the evidence. We have that. Don't worry."

Still, my anxiety is through the roof. Bess agrees to come with me for support and as a witness, if needed. Eric got depositions from the cops. I keep telling myself it will be okay. One step at a time. I want this to be over, just keep focusing on that.

On the home front, aside from constant talk about lawyers and court, Bess and I are adjusting to living together. That's the best part of all of this. I am feeling less like a guest and more like I belong at the condo. The ADT security system is installed and I am reassured we have it if we need it. If anything sketchy happens we get a call and take action. Bob gave me a very fair estimate for the shingle work at my house. I'll help him do the work, and he is only charging me for materials. The insurance adjuster approved the claim and the check is in the mail, as they say. Things are moving along and no new issues have come up. I am surprised Maura didn't call to scream about the restraining order. Maybe it's a good sign. I hope so, but can't be sure. Maura is predictably unpredictable and that is part of the problem.

It's About Time

CHAPTER 19

Taking Care of Family

James

On Wednesday, Bess and I cook together like old times. As we chop and roast, sauté, and toss, I fill her in on my afternoon meeting with Eric and let her know she may be called as a witness. "You okay with that?" I ask

"Sure. I have nothing to hide. She has nothing on me."

"Great. Thank you. I know this isn't what you signed up for. He wants to meet with both of us on Monday to make sure we are prepared for court. He reminded me that the worst that can happen is we don't get the extended restraining order. I'm not being judged. It's not life and death and I'm not going to jail. I guess it's good to keep that in perspective." I place my palms flat on the cold granite counter, leaning in for support. "I feel like I'm consumed with lawyers and focused on Maura problems. Wouldn't she like hearing that? She wants the focus on her, positive or negative. Doesn't matter." I huff. I turn to look at Bess. "I hope this isn't too boring for you. Lenny Bruce keeps coming to mind. He stopped being funny once he started obsessing about his legal woes.

"Lenny Bruce? Really? James, you've never been that funny." Bess laughs. "Just kidding sweetie. You have a delightful sense of humor. But I haven't thought about Lenny in years. He was obsessed?"

"Yeah, I saw a documentary about him. He was always a little rough around the edges, but after his legal troubles, it was all he could talk about in his act. People stopped going to see him because he wasn't funny anymore. Just angry and sad. He was a very funny guy before that." I explain.

"Well, I don't see you being obsessed, just appropriately concerned. So what if you talk about it? If you get boring, I'll let you know." Bess reassures me. "It would be good to mix it up with some fun though. Did I tell you that Bob and Virginia are planning a Halloween party?"

"They are? That's great. Costumes too?"

"Absofreakinlutely. What do you want to go as?" Bess finishes plating our dinner of sauteed chicken and roasted acorn squash. I carry the green salad to the table and pour wine.

Now I'm thinking about costumes which is a nice reprieve. "Hey, Halloween is just a few days away. How are we going to get costumes so fast?" I ask as I savor the tender, perfectly seasoned chicken.

"No problem. Halloween is busy for people, with trick-or-treating, kid's parties, and all. They decided to avoid all that and have the party the weekend after Halloween. Smart, huh?"

"Yeah! I like it. Plus, costumes will be on sale. Shall we do a couples theme? Antony and Cleo? Romeo and Juliet? Fred and Wilma? Bonnie and Clyde?" I ask.

Oh, I like the Bonnie and Clyde idea. But what do you think about Gomez and Morticia Adams? That's kind of Halloweenie." Bess suggests.

It's About Time

"Great idea. Maybe we can put together costumes. All I need is a dark suit and a mustache. Right? Let's go to the thrift store and see if they have anything we could use. I like creating a costume rather than buying one everybody has."

"Me too. This will be fun. We can go shopping this weekend while everyone else is eating candy. Oh, candy! We need to pick up treats for the kids." Bess reminds me.

It is a relief for both of us to have a light-hearted conversation and something to look forward to. Just as we are finishing dinner my phone rings. I look at Bess. "It's Thomas." I exhale slowly and press accept.

"Thomas. I'm glad you called." Bess starts cleaning up dinner to give me a little space. I move to the couch in front of the fireplace, switching the call to speaker. I haven't talked with my son since bailing him out of jail. We've exchanged texts but nothing of consequence. I called several times and left messages but Thomas didn't returned the calls.

"What the fuck, Dad?" My passionate and volatile son is blasting me again. I brace myself to listen the best I can. "Why do you have it out for Auntie Maura? I just got off the phone with her, and she was sobbing. She said you got a restraining order against her. Why? Are you crazy? What did she ever do to you? She's right, ya know. There is something wrong with you." As much as I wanted to school my adult son to respect his elders, this was probably not the time. At least I know more about what's going on, even if it's coming at me in a torrent. Maura was no doubt sobbing crocodile tears for dramatic effect to get sympathy from my son. It's a classic Maura number. She is throwing her shit on me and hoping Thomas will believe her.

"Yes, that's true about the restraining order." I figured Maura would find a way to get back at me for taking legal action and I hate that she is using my son to do her dirty work. "Tell me more, Thomas. What is it you think I've done? Why are you so upset with me?"
"Auntie Maura is like a mother to me. She was there for me when you were too busy or too depressed. Or too drunk."

"Ouch. You knew I was depressed? I thought I kept that hidden."

"You tried, but it was pretty obvious you weren't yourself. I thought you missed Mom, and I didn't want to add to your trouble so Maura and I would talk. Mostly we shared memories of Mom and the fun we used to have. Now, she says I'm old enough to know the truth. It was hard for her to tell me because she didn't want me hurt. At first, I couldn't believe what she said, but then the pieces fell into place. I understand now why Mom was gone so much and how things changed in our family. You fucked Mom over and I hate you for that." Thomas's pain hurt my heart. He is an emotional kid, a lot like his mother, and Maura has manipulated him.

"Thomas, of course you're upset. I would be too. Is this why we got in that fight at the reunion?"

"Yeah. I saw you being all happy and warm with Bess and the family, and it just blew my mind. How could you be two such different people? When you guys started talking about Andy's wedding, I lost it." Thomas confessed.

I pause, trying to stay calm, even though everything in me wants to rant about all Maura's done. "That's a really good question to ask Thomas. Am I two different people? What did Maura tell you about me?" I was genuinely curious to know how bad the damage was.

It's About Time

"She said you lied to Mom and us, you neglected us, and drank too much. Mom stayed away because she was afraid of you. Maura said you were charged with domestic abuse. Mom was afraid to leave because you threatened to take us away from her. How could you do that and then say you love us?" I could hear Thomas sniff and blow his nose. At that moment I wanted to kill Maura. This was the same pack of lies she told Bess over Chinese food. I clench my fists to stay in control. This isn't Thomas's fault. It's mine.

"Thomas, I have made mistakes in my life, but hurting our family is not one of them. Your Mom and I had our disagreements, sure. But there was never abuse. Ever. Maura is the one who lied and is still lying."

"Oh, sure. Perfect. Auntie Maura said you would deny everything and blame her."

"Thomas I am not going to tell you what to believe, but I am asking you to be open to hearing me out, okay? Let me ask you this, what do you remember? Do you recall times when I was horrible to you or your mother?" Thomas was quiet.

"I was young. I don't remember a lot, and it gets confusing. I know Mom wasn't around a lot."

"That's true. Your mother was an amazing creative spirit with a bright future in music. It took her away from home which made her miss us every day. And we missed her. But I wanted her to be happy, so we made that sacrifice. I liked being home with you guys so it worked out. For a while anyway. Thomas, you were fifteen when your mother died. There must be some things you remember."

"Well, I remember Auntie Maura being around when Mom was away. She took us to see "Toy Story" and bought me a Buzz Lightyear action figure. I remember you cooking macaroni and cheese and taking us for ice cream at that Frosty place. You came to my baseball games. When Mom was sick you and Gram took care of her." Thomas sounds confused. "Maybe I don't remember the bad stuff because it was so scary!" He offers. That sounds like something Maura would have suggested to him. I am being careful not to cause him to defend Maura. The last thing I want is for it to be my word against hers. She is much better at convincing people than I am, and I don't want Thomas to have to choose sides.

"Maybe that's true. Or maybe it didn't happen the way Maura tells it." Silence. "Maybe it's time to talk about the past. Would you be willing to Zoom with me and Andy? I would like him to be in on this conversation. If he's available we could set it up tonight. What do you say?"

"Yeah. Whatever. Send me a link." Thomas hangs up. I have a death grip on my phone.

Bess sits down next to me. "You okay? That was intense. Are you ready for this confrontation?"

"I don't know that I'll ever be ready, but it's here. I can't believe Maura called him to cry on his shoulder. No, I take that back, I can believe it. She is playing the victim card and manipulating my son." I am pacing and ranting. "After years of keeping quiet, it's time to talk about this. I just hope the boys believe me."

"They love you. Thomas especially, that's why he is so angry. All you can do is tell them the truth." Bess kisses me. "Do you want me to go out so you can have privacy?" Bess asks

It's About Time

"No. Please stay. I may not be able to remember everything clearly and your observations are important to me."

I text Andy asking if he is available to Zoom tonight, adding 'It's important'.

An hour later the three of us connect on video. Thomas looks miserable with his arms crossed over his chest. Andy wants to know what's going on.

"Thomas and I just had a conversation. Thomas, do you want to tell Andy why you are upset?"

"Sure. I called Dad to find out why the fuck he got a restraining order against Auntie Maura. I'm upset because she called me sobbing." Thomas says.

"Wait. A restraining order? Why? What happened?" Andy asks.

"Maura has been causing trouble. I met with an attorney to file charges and get a restraining order. This is a long story that I hoped I would never have to get into it. Maura has threatened, harassed, and stalked me. She vandalized the house too."

"Really Dad? Seriously? You expect us to believe that? Auntie Maura says you lie about everything. Prove it." Thomas is irate and I don't blame him. He has been groomed by one of the best liars I have ever known.

"Okay. When we got home from North Carolina there was an envelope at Bess's condo." I share the pictures of what was in the envelope. I decide to stick to current events. No sense rehashing ancient history unless I have to. "Did you share reunion pictures with Maura, Thomas?"

"Yeah, So what if I did?" he snaps.

"Well, this is what she used them for. We were able to connect this to Maura. I figured you had contact with her. No one else at the reunion did. Maura also added the police log and implied Bess is not safe. That scared us so I brought it to a lawyer to find out how to stop it. This isn't the first time I've had issues with Maura. Like I said, it's a long story."
"How do you know it was her? Anyone could have gotten those pictures off Facebook or somewhere." Andy asks.

"We know it was her because her fingerprints are on it. Then, a few days later, she called the police in the middle of the night to report a fake incident at Bess's condo. Can you imagine how scary it is to be awakened out of a sound sleep at 3:30 in the morning by police? Maura was identified as the caller. Not only that, it means Maura was watching us and knew we were together at the condo. She is the one who vandalized my house because she was in the security footage before painting over the camera." I share photos of the deck.

"Oh my God, Dad. This is awful. Why is she doing this?" Andy demands.

"I wish I had a clear answer, Andy." I share a sanitized account of my ancient history. I want to clarify and strengthen the bond with my sons. It isn't necessary to make a case against Maura as much as I want to. "As near as I can figure, Maura never forgave me for loving your mother and wants to make me pay. Maura and I dated in college until we graduated and I met your mother. Now that Bess is in my life it seems to have set Maura off all over again." I frown and hope they will understand.

"Dad, I had no idea. So that was why you didn't want her at our wedding?" Andy asks.

It's About Time

"Yes, it is. I didn't want to get into all this at the time. I was hoping to spare you guys all the gruesome details." I confess.

"Oh, so Dad banned Auntie Maura from the wedding because she is a psycho? Right. Sure." Thomas challenges.

"Thomas, there was no banning. I was inviting Maura for Dad's sake and he asked me not to. It was as simple as that. I am not close to her, she isn't family, so I agreed. Jeez, where did you get that banning shit from Tom?" Andy is annoyed with his brother. I keep quiet. Thomas looks confused, which might mean the truth is getting through to him. Confusion is what happens when lies collide with truth and we don't know what to believe.

"Andy, are you covering for Dad? Don't you remember how Auntie Maura took care of us when we were growing up? She loves us. None of this makes sense."

"I swear. I am not covering for Dad or anyone else. I haven't heard from Maura in years. How come she's all over you, Tom?" Andy asks a good question. Thomas is thoughtful, trying to reconcile new information with what he believes.

"I want you to listen to something. The last time, and I do mean *the last time*, Maura was here and stayed at the house, I put my foot down and told her I didn't want to see her or have her near my family ever again. That pissed her off. I changed the locks on the house to keep her out. That also pissed her off. She went to see Bess and told her lies about me. Similar lies to what you heard Thomas. Bess recorded the conversation for me to hear. I want to play it for you." I open the file on the computer. Maura's voice comes through loud and clear saying she wants to destroy me.

"Oh my God, Dad...what's wrong with her? Why would she say that? No wonder you want to protect yourself." Andy believes me. Thomas is chewing his lip, processing.

"I don't know. I have to ask Auntie Maura about this." Thomas says.

"Thomas, Maura has no problem lying if it serves her purpose. Her lies drove a wedge between me and your mother. I didn't know the full extent of her manipulation until recently. Andy, when I was searching for the song you wanted, I came across a computer journal your mother was keeping. At first, I didn't open it because remembering her still hurts. When I finally read it, I was shocked by the lies Maura told your Mom. I can't explain why your mother never asked me about them and wish that we had a chance to sort it out. But we didn't and that was when our trouble started. You were kids and I wanted to protect you from all of that."

I continued, "Maura admits to wanting to hurt me, and what better way than to come between me and the people I love? Thomas, you are a lot like your mother, trusting and openhearted and I wouldn't want you to be any other way. You both are the best things your mother and I ever created. It would kill me if Maura ruined that for us. She thinks she is in control and above it all, so I doubt she expected me to take legal action. She won't like that and will do whatever she can to get even. Including lying to you guys. So, yes, I have a restraining order and I will do whatever I can legally to stop her from messing in our lives. I am telling you the truth."

It's About Time

The room was still and silent until Andy spoke. "You said it's a long story. I'm having a hard time understanding how Maura got into our lives. How did this start?"

Andy is my scientific analytical son, more like me. It doesn't surprise me that he wants more information.

"When I was in college I met Maura. She was, and is, beautiful. When she showed an interest in me, I was flattered. She has a talent for making people feel special when she wants to and that worked on me. Gradually she controlled more and more of my time. She was possessive and jealous but I didn't do anything about it. I figured when school ended our relationship would be over. After we graduated Maura moved to New York City, and I fell madly in love with your mother. Maura went ballistic. When things calmed down, she said she was happy for us and wanted to stay friends. I regret allowing that. She inserted herself into our lives under the guise of friendship. While she was influencing your mother's opinion of me, she was comforting me. Invited or not, every time your mother left the house, there was Maura. I asked her to back off. That's when she threatened to ruin my reputation, get me fired from the job I loved, and even have you boys taken away. My fear that she could do that made me cave to her demands. Then your Mom got sick. Maura's husband passed away and after your mother died, she believed we would live happily ever after. I refused."

"Wow. Why can't she let this go?" Andy wondered.

"Some people hold grudges forever, I guess."

Andy said he loved me and supported my decisions. Thomas still looked confused and I could understand that completely.

"Thomas, are you ok? I know this is a lot." He looked at the camera and shrugged. This will be challenging for him. His attachment to Maura may overrule the information he now has. I can only pray that eventually she will show him who she is and he will believe the truth.

"If you need anything, I am here. Please call if you want to talk more about this. I imagine you will have questions and I'll keep you updated from my end. I love you both more than I can ever express." We disconnect our call and I stare at the blank computer screen wondering if I created a bigger mess.

"James?" Bess looks concerned, inviting me into her arms. She holds me. Words are not needed at this moment. Everything that I had been holding on to, the fear, shame, stress about lawyers and court, love for my children, and anguish for all the mistakes I made found comfort in Bess's embrace. No more secrets. I feel a burden I didn't know I carried lift off me. We sink down on the couch. I feel accepted in my brokenness. Bess knows every horrible mistake I have made, every gut-wrenching pain I suffered, and still loves me.

"You done good, Ogilvie. That was tough." She whispers in my ear.

"Thanks." I stretch out and close my eyes, exhausted. When I wake up Bess is sitting on the floor leaning back against the couch reading. She had covered me with a blanket and stayed by my side. I rest my hand on her shoulder. She turns and smiles at me.

"Ah, you're back. How ya doing?" She strokes my hand.

"Well, I'm worn out, but other than that I'm relieved the truth is out there. I'm worried about how the boys will deal with this.

It's About Time

Especially Thomas because he is still in Maura's clutches. There isn't much I can do about that."

"Yup. All you can do is love 'em and stay available."

"You know it doesn't surprise me that Maura called Thomas after she was served. She's in trouble if she contacts us. Like you said, she zones in on vulnerability and Thomas is the vulnerable kid. Hearing him struggle I know exactly how he feels. I want to make Maura pay for that. Or at least hold her accountable." I confess.

"Maura is cold and dead inside, James. That is what scares me. I hope Thomas eventually sees through her. In the meantime, all you can do is take care of yourself, stay close and love him."

* * *

On Saturday, I meet Bob at my house to replace shingles. The physical work feels good. As I rip off shingles I mention my conversation with Thomas.

"I'm worried, Bob. Maura has done so much damage, and she gets away with it every time. Not only that, she seems to get rewarded. Look at the cash she raked in from dead husbands."

"Hey, you don't think she accelerated their demise, do you?" Bob asks only half kidding.

"Who knows? Just so long as she doesn't accelerate my demise!" I laugh. "Hey, do you need help for the party next weekend?" I ask. "We are looking forward to that."

"Sure! Virginia is a huge fan of holidays so we have decorations for every occasion including Groundhog Day, believe it or not." Bob rolls his eyes. "You want to come over later and carve pumpkins? We can eat and hand out candy to the treaters."

"That sounds like fun. I'll let Bess know." I pull off the last shingle. Now comes the hard part. Bob lifts bundles of cedar shingles from his truck along with a couple of nail guns.

"After we get this set up it will go quickly." Bob tells me. We replace the old tarpaper with Tyvek and set up a rail guide to keep the shingles from looking like rolling waves. Soon we hear the rhythmic sound of nail guns, bam, bam, bam. At around four o'clock we finish and clean up.

"Thanks, Bob. Knowing what you're doing helps!" I load the extra shingles into Bob's truck as he picks up everything else. "I'll clean up and we'll see you in a bit. Can we bring anything?"

"Surprise us! I think we have food. It won't be fancy." Bob says as he climbs into his truck to head home. I wave goodbye and make sure the house is secure before I leave.

* * *

The weekend goes by too fast. Carving pumpkins with arms elbow deep in pulp, adorable trick-or-treaters, and quiet time on Sunday offers us a break from thinking about lawyers and court. Monday morning, Bess and I drive to Eric's office to be briefed on the hearing scheduled for Wednesday. Eric greets us in his usual all-business manner, ushering us into the conference room and shutting the door.

"Okay, so this is a hearing. It's not the same as a trial. I don't know if I will need you to testify, but if I do you will be sworn in and then I will ask questions. I imagine Maura will be

It's About Time

represented by counsel and they may also ask questions. Please answer the questions honestly and concisely. Do not offer more information than what is asked for. People get in way over their heads when they talk too much. Got it? We simply want to make a case for a restraining order. We are not trying to prove anything else. At least not yet. Questions?"

Bess and I shake our heads, no questions. This process is intimidating but Eric is very capable. We're in good hands.

"Okay. Bess, tell me what you remember about the night the cops showed up." Eric's pen is poised over the legal pad.

"Well, we were asleep when we heard knocking at the front door. Then we heard a man say, "Police, open up!" So we opened the door. The cops spoke to us separately. The woman cop asked me if I was safe or if I needed help. I said no, I was fine, we were asleep. I asked what this was about but she didn't answer me. James was outside with the other cop. It was scary especially since we had no idea what was going on. The cop told James someone reported a woman screaming for help. I don't know who that was, but it wasn't me." Bess describes the experience exactly how I remember it.

"What do you remember, James?" Eric asks.

"Just like what Bess said. We were asleep. It was around 3:30 in the morning. Cops pounded on the door and said they got a call about a woman needing help. One cop told me to step outside and asked me if I had been drinking, and wanted to see my hands. I told him we were asleep and asked him what this was about. He said a woman called to report screaming at the condo. At that point, the other cop walked out and talked with her partner. Then they apologized for bothering us and left. It shook us up."

"Good. Now what about the envelope? Bess, that showed up at your place, yes?" Eric is furiously writing notes.

"I got home from our trip to North Carolina. It was Saturday morning. I opened my front door and the envelope was inside the storm door. When I opened it, it scared me. There were pictures from the Ogilvie reunion, the reason we were in North Carolina, and a police log referring to James's son's arrest. But what scared me most was a card congratulating me on my engagement. Tucked inside were news stories of horrible things happening to people on their honeymoon. There was a note that told me to be careful because accidents happen. I put everything back in the envelope and took it to show James."

"Did you show anyone else?" Eric asked.

"Yes, our friends Virginia and Bob Wilson. Honestly, I felt threatened not just by the note but also that someone was watching us."

"I will bring the envelope into evidence. James, tell me about your house."

"Okay. I went to my house to mow the lawn and pick up things to move into Bess's condo. We were concerned about what was going on, and I didn't want Bess to be alone. When I got there, I saw the vandalism on the back deck. The security camera had been spray painted, the motion sensor light was smashed and graffiti was painted across the back of the house. I called the cops. They came and filled out a report."

"I will submit photos of the vandalism into evidence including the photo of the vandal and the facial recognition analysis.

It's About Time

Bess, I want to play the recording you made. Do I have permission to do that?"

"Yes, of course."

"Great."

We rehearse answers to the questions Eric will ask us if we have to testify. Eric takes the role of Maura's attorney challenging us and trying to put us on the defensive. It does shake me up so I'm glad we are doing this preparation.

"I may not need you to testify. We'll see how it goes. Questions?" We again shake our heads no. "If you think of anything, let me know. Otherwise, I will see you both Wednesday morning in court. Try not to think about it too much." Eric shakes my hand, thanks Bess, and we are on our way.

"Well, that was interesting," Bess tells me. "I get what you mean about no chit-chat. He seems to know what he's doing. I hope this goes well, and we can be done with all of this. I am ready for normal life." I put my arm around Bess as we walk to her car.

"Me too." I agree. "Me too."

Hillary Gauvreau Oat

It's About Time

CHAPTER 20

Order in the Court

James

Wednesday morning, I try to calm my nerves. Drinking more coffee is not going to help. Court doesn't scare me as much as coming face-to-face with Maura. Knowing her and the captive audience, she will nail an Academy Award-winning portrayal of victimhood. That's after she shoots a flame thrower of hate my way. My nervous system is on high alert. I dress in a button-down shirt, conservative tie, dark dress pants, and my lucky tweed jacket given to me by Caroline many years ago. Bess wears a tailored suit with a white blouse that warns people not to mess with her. She looks like a beautiful warrior for justice. We drive to the courthouse and meet Eric outside the courtroom. I am hypervigilant, scanning the hallway for Maura.

"You ready?" Eric asks. We are as ready as we can be. We march into the courtroom trying to look calm and confident while feeling anything but.

My hands are cold. My mouth is dry. My leg won't stop jiggling, bouncing around to the beat of my quickening pulse rate. I hold Bess's hand like it's an anchor keeping me from flying off into space. The courtroom doesn't look like anything in the movies. It's just an average room with tables and chairs on either side of a center aisle. The walls are painted a creamy white and the woodwork is the color of honey. The tangy scent of nervous sweat and the aroma of coffee permeates the air. We are assigned the right side of the room which reminds me of a wedding. Groom's family on the right. Maura will be on the left with her attorney. This is a marriage of justice and accountability, concepts foreign to Maura. The door opens behind us and I hear the familiar clicking of stiletto heels on the worn hardwood floor. My heart is pounding. Bess squeezes my hand. Maura cannot hurt me when I'm surrounded by law enforcement. Breathe. Bess has an eye on me, aware of what I am going through. Eric is leafing through notes after handing off evidence to the Court Clerk. I don't look at Maura because Eric advised against it. But I can feel her, smell her expensive Chateau Krigler #12 perfume, and hear her talking. She laughs quietly with her attorney. I turn to look at Eric and he smiles reassurance. We are okay.

The bailiff asks us to rise. "Court is now in session. The honorable Justine Brown presiding." The judge marches to the bench in front of the room.

"Good Morning Ladies, and Gentlemen. This is a hearing regarding the extension of a restraining order against Ms. Maura Jenkins by Mr. James Ogilvie. Are both sides ready?"

Eric stands and says we are ready. A female voice from Maura's table says they are also ready. Interesting that she has a female attorney. Knowing how calculating Maura is, I'm certain that is not a random choice. I guess she figures beauty will give her an edge over brawn. Somehow, I doubt the black woman sitting on the bench will be swayed by designer clothes and blond hair. It's the luck of the draw ladies. Maybe next time you'll get a paunchy middle-aged judge susceptible to flirting. I glance over at my Jerry Garcia lawyer who tamed his hair for the occasion and is wearing a suit, his tie slightly askew. I smile because I like this man. He is real and I trust him.

It's About Time

"Mr. Ogilvie, you are represented by Mr. Cunningham, is that correct?" the judge asks. Eric and I stand.
"Yes, Your Honor, that is correct."

'Ms. Jenkins. You are represented by Ms. Shapiro?"

"Yes, Your Honor." I automatically look in the direction of that voice. Maura wears a soft cream-colored cashmere sweater, a brown tweed skirt, and stiletto boots. What looks like casual dress is anything but. I know she put a lot of thought into looking soft and pretty but not too beautiful. Approachable and vulnerable. I nervously adjust the knot of my tie wondering if I should have paid more attention to my clothes. Attorney Shapiro is statuesque and crisply professional in a Gucci navy blue suit. Her long blond hair is twisted into a neat bun at the back of her neck. I have an image of her pulling out a pin and blond hair falling over her shoulders in slow motion causing the courtroom to be transfixed. The judge speaks bringing me back to reality.

"Great. The gang's all here, let's get this show on the road. Mr. Cunningham, please present your evidence." Judge Brown says.

It is a blur of evidence, testimony, and depositions. Bess's recording plays and I hear Maura and Ms. Shapiro whispering. The police depositions are read into evidence as are the photos of my house. Eric hands the manilla envelope to the Clerk to pass to the judge. Eric elaborates on the chain of custody and the process of fingerprint identification.

"Anything else Mr. Cunningham?" Judge Brown asks.

"No, Your Honor."

"Ms. Shapiro. Your turn." the judge cues the defense.

"Thank you, your honor. I call Ms. Maura Jenkins to testify."

All heads turn as Maura slowly walks up to the front of the courtroom and is sworn in by George the bailiff. He's a big guy with a silly grin, who is clearly mesmerized by Maura's presence. Thank God for Judge Brown. Ms. Shapiro proceeds to ask well-rehearsed questions. It is a slick presentation only missing power point slides. She is playing up Poor Maura, the victim, as I knew she would. I avoid eye contact. She and her attorney review our history from the moment we met. She talks about my cheating and implies there was sexual abuse and drunken binges that led to physical violence. It's another version of the same old story Maura likes to tell. She has told it so often she might even believe it. I wonder if her lawyer believes her or if it even matters. She sighs, whimpers and blots fake tears. I'm surprised there is no symphony violinist playing background music for this sad tale. I hope the judge doesn't buy this charade. Ever since I have known Maura, I have been afraid no one would believe me. People tend to side with the rich and beautiful.

Eric jumps up and objects. "Your honor this is all hearsay. Where is the evidence?"

"Sustained. Ms. Shapiro, do you have evidence to support these claims?" the Judge wisely asks. I am starting to like Judge Brown. She is not easily dazzled.

"Your Honor, the testimony speaks for itself. This poor woman has been harassed and intimidated by this man for years. She was only protecting herself. And yes, there were times when she may have gone too far, but she was terrified and distraught,

It's About Time

Your Honor." That last part caught the attention of Eric. Is she admitting to wrong doing? It sure sounds like it.

"I can appreciate that, Ms. Shapiro. However, evidence is required to substantiate claims in a court of law, as you are aware. Tales of woe are not enough. Mr. Cunningham, cross examination? And let's move this along. This is a hearing not a trial." From my untrained perspective it appears that Maura's attorney was unprepared for the evidence we have against her. I'm positive Maura thought her beautiful presence would be enough to sway the judge.

Eric stands and slowly walks to the front of the room in a Peter Falk-Colombo-esque humble display of ineptitude. "I'm a little confused Ms. Jenkins. Nice boots by the way. Are they Christian Louboutin?" Maura lights up at the compliment.

"Why yes! Yes, they are! You have a good eye." She says coyly trying to win over my attorney. It's pathetic.

"I thought so. My wife would love a pair of those. Now, where was I? Oh, yes, it sounds to me, and I could be wrong, that Ms. Shapiro here . . ." he nods to Maura's lawyer, "just said you admit going too far." Colombo is gone, replaced by a no-nonsense attorney. "Would that be when you vandalized Mr. Ogilvie's property? Or are you referring to the fake police report? Fill me in."

"I need to explain. You have to understand how frightened I was." Maura dabs at fake tears.

"So that's a yes? You are aware that you crossed a line?" Eric pushes.

"Yes, but . . ." Eric didn't give her time to finish.

"Ms. Jenkins, did you have this envelope delivered to the condo owned by Ms. Bess Parker?" Eric holds up the manilla envelope. "Remember you are under oath."

"I . . ." Maura is fumbling, and it makes me happy to see her squirm. I have been waiting years to see Maura being held accountable. Eric pushes on.

"Ms. Jenkins, did you call the police with a false report on the night of October 14th?" Maura straightens herself up and looks indignant.

"I am not saying another word. You can speak to my attorney." Judge Brown reminds her she is under oath and will answer the question. Eric speaks up saying it's not necessary, that he has enough testimony from Ms. Jenkins. Eric turns and walks back to our table. He whispers that we can relax because he won't be calling us to testify.

"Ms. Jenkins, you may step down. Is that all the evidence you have Mr. Cunningham? Ms. Shapiro?"

"It is Your Honor." Both counsels agreed.

"Okay then. Mr. Cunningham, you are asking for an extension to your restraining order. In light of the evidence presented that motion is granted. The restraining order is extended for one year to be reviewed at that time if further protection is required. Ms. Jenkins, you are not allowed any form of contact with Mr. Ogilvie. Got it? That means no funny business, Ms. Jenkins. No texts, calls, stalking, or harassment. If you have issues with this gentleman, I encourage you to try legal solutions as Mr. Ogilvie has done. Please see the Court Clerk to take care of fees and

It's About Time

paperwork. Court is adjourned." The gavel pounds down, and we all stand until Judge Brown leaves the bench.

I'm ecstatic. I can barely contain myself. I hug Bess and over her shoulder, I see Maura shooting daggers out her eyes at me. I look away. Eric and I shake hands enthusiastically. Oh, what the hell, I hug Eric too. I am so relieved. For once Maura is being held accountable and that is something to celebrate. We walk out into the light of day. The sun is shining, the sky is the bluest blue I have ever seen.

"Bess, let's take the rest of the day off. Want to go somewhere nice for lunch to celebrate?" I hold her in my arms and spin her around. I can't stop smiling. "Eric, you want to go to lunch with us?"

"I wish I could. You go. Have fun. I'll be in touch." Eric shakes our hands again and walks quickly down the street to his car.

"That guy is good. A bit of a workaholic, but he knows boots." Bess chuckles. "I am starving. Let's do this!" We end up at an Indian restaurant in Old Saybrook that we have mostly to ourselves. The food is spicy and delicious, and the company is even better. I haven't felt this relaxed in a long time. We toast with glasses of house wine and chat nonstop about the hearing and the upcoming Halloween party. Just as we start in on our spicy Aloo Mater and Chana Masala, my phone rings.

"It's Eric. I better pick up." I tell Bess. "Hello, Eric. What's up? I didn't expect to hear from you so soon." I get up and walk outside to take the call on the sidewalk in front of the restaurant.

"James, I am letting you know the police and prosecutor have decided there is enough evidence to issue a warrant for

Maura's arrest. The trouble she caused you has turned around to bite her on her designer-clad ass. I knew calling in a fake report to the cops would trigger them and getting the judge to agree to the restraining order helped too. So, heads up. Maura will be getting a call from her attorney asking to turn herself in by Monday. Make sure your security is working and be careful, okay? Sometimes getting arrested can make people a little squirrely."

"Thanks for the call, Eric. We will be careful. Does this mean she will go to jail?" I ask unsure how I feel about that.

"Probably not. She'll get booked and released to wait for a court appearance. I'm not sure how they will handle this. Most of the charges are small but they piled up. I made the case that she could be a danger to you. That's not an exaggeration so keep it in mind."

"Okay. Let me know if there are updates. Thanks for everything. You have been a great help. I haven't felt this relaxed in years."

"Yeah, well don't get too relaxed just yet. We still have a ways to go. With her back against the wall, she may decide she has nothing to lose. Be careful." Eric hangs up and I slip the phone back in my pocket and return to lunch.

"What's up?" Bess asks.

"Eric wants us to know that there is an arrest warrant for Maura. They are asking her to turn herself in. I have mixed feelings about her getting arrested. I mean, she certainly has earned an arrest considering all she's done. But I feel sorry for her too. It's like she is her own worst enemy. Know what I mean?"

"I do, yes. Remember she is also *your* worst enemy, hon. It's great you feel compassion but don't let it cloud your judgement.

It's About Time

Maura is a block of ice who would throw you under the bus in a heartbeat. When is this supposed to happen?" Bess wants to know.

"She gets served today and has until the end of the day on Monday to turn herself in. Eric says we need to be careful because she may feel she has nothing to lose."

"That's a scary thought. What do you think, James? Would she try something?" Bess wonders.
"I honestly don't know. I hope she is smarter than that. All we can do is stay alert. We have security. I'm not getting too worked up about it. For the first time since I met Maura, I feel vindicated and supported. I'm going to enjoy that at least through lunch. If she decides to do something stupid, it's her funeral. I mean that metaphorically, of course."

We continue to enjoy our lunch and talk about more pleasant things. At least I try. I don't want to worry Bess, but Eric is right. Maura could do something stupid. She is known for retribution.

* * *

Saturday night Bess and I transform ourselves into Gomez and Morticia Adams and drive to Bob and Virginia's house ready to party like it's 1999. It is so much fun we hate to leave. Everyone we know from town is there including Bess's son Matt and his family. There is Halloween candy and spooky treats. The most fun is the relay race where we balance an eyeball on a spoon and carry it to a caldron, dropping it in. The first team to get all their eyeballs in the cauldron wins. We team up, guys against gals. After a couple of adult beverages, it is hysterical fun. The women have more finesse and get the prize.

I needed a good laugh and this party provided many. After helping to clean up we get in Bess's Honda to drive home. Bob and Virginia's house seems like it is out in the middle of nowhere but it is only a few miles from downtown. The narrow country road is dark and drizzle absorbs our headlights making it difficult to see. I am grateful we only have a short drive down Four Mile River Road before getting to civilization. Suddenly headlights come up fast behind us, a vehicle is hanging on our bumper.

"Yikes." Bess squeals. "What the fuck are they doing?" She turns around to see what's going on and is blinded by high beams. "Just let them go by, James. Maybe they're drunk." I slow down a bit hoping they will pass us.

"They seem to want to hang on our bumper. I wish I could find a place to pull off and get out of the way." The road is narrow and there isn't much of a shoulder.

The vehicle pulls out like it's going to pass us. The dark SUV stays next to us and a little too close for comfort. Tinted windows make it impossible to see who's driving. The SUV inches closer until it makes contact with the side of our car. Metal on metal screeches. I am gripping the wheel to stay in control and speed up hoping to get away. No such luck, they are determined.

"What the fuck? Are they trying to kill us?" I lean on the horn while wrenching the steering wheel to push against the SUV and stay on the road. There isn't much of a shoulder and no matter what my speed the vehicle stays against us. Before I can slam on the brakes the SUV smacks into our car pushing us sideways. The size and weight of the SUV are no match for Bess's Honda HR-V. We are forced off the road bouncing down a steep embankment. Our car rocks as it slides down the steep muddy slope. Bess screams. I hear glass breaking. I wrestle

It's About Time

with the wheel, stomping on the brakes but there is nothing that slows us down. We scrape against a tree trunk and drop down into a ditch, before crashing into a stone wall. Airbags explode in our faces. Then quiet. The SUV is gone. Rain is coming down.

"Bess? Bess, are you okay?" I shout, panic stricken with adrenaline surging through me.

"I think so. Are you?" She is shaking.

"I'm banged up, but it could be worse." I feel blood dripping into my eye. I try to open the driver's side door but it's jammed. Bess's door is up against the stone wall pinning us in the car. There is nothing to do except wait for help. Thank God my cell phone is still in my pocket and didn't go flying. I push the deflated airbag away and call 911. Before long we hear sirens in the distance. Bess is in shock. I reach for her hand and she cries out in pain.

Before long flashing lights show up. Cops and rescue units arrive. They pry open my door and carefully help us out of the front seat to the waiting ambulance. The EMT checks us out and gets us in the ambulance to be transported to the Emergency Room. Bess's wrist is broken. I have a laceration over my eye and a possible concussion. The cops ask if I've been drinking. We are dressed like the Adams family for Christ's sake so we were obviously at a party, but not drunk. He decides to give me a breathalyzer test anyway and I pass. Thank God I didn't have that last beer.

Bess and I are wheeled into the Emergency Room of Lawrence Hospital. Thankfully it isn't jammed. Nurses get us checked in, IVs are started and radiology is called. Bess is in pain, and her wrist is swelling. My head is pounding. A PA sews up my laceration and we wait for the radiology techs. The cops ask us lots of questions. We tell them about the dark SUV forcing us off the road. It happened fast in the dark so we didn't see the driver or the license plate. We tell them it seemed deliberate, not like an accident. They will let us know where the tow truck takes our car and if they need anything else. I hope they get the asshole who did this. God, my head hurts.

Finally, we are released from the ER. Bess calls her son Matt to pick us up. She doesn't know where her purse is and I don't know where my keys are, probably somewhere in the car. Fortunately, her son Matt has a spare key to the condo. We will figure all this out tomorrow.

Matt comes rushing into the ER. "Mom! Are you okay? What happened?" Matt wraps his mother in a frantic hug.

"Gentle, honey, I'm a bit sore. My wrist is broken. Want to sign my cast?" Bess slurs from the effects of the pain medication. I fill Matt in on what happened after we left the party. Matt had the kids with him so they left earlier than we did.

"Do you have keys to the condo, hon?" Bess asks sleepily. "I think I need to go to bed now."

We are released, loaded into wheelchairs and Matt picks us up at the ER entrance. He walks us into the condo and makes sure we are okay. Bess hugs him and it makes me wish my boys lived closer. Matt is a good guy and I like him.

"Thanks for coming to get us. Sorry, we had to get you up at this hour." I say.

"Don't worry about it. I'm just relieved you're both okay." Matt says.

It's About Time

I close the door and look around for Bess. She is already in bed and sound asleep. I feel a little wired so I stay up, taking a couple more Tylenol tablets to ease the pounding in my head. Mild concussion they told me. I would hate to have a bad concussion. I open my iPad and the New York Times app. It is all basically the same news. Nothing good. I play a game of sudoku and do a crossword puzzle. At least my brain still works. My thoughts go back to what happened. It was not an accident. I don't know if whoever did this wanted to kill us, or just scare the shit out of us. I didn't say anything earlier but my thoughts keep drifting to Maura. Unless this was some sort of outrageous, unrelated incident by some jerkoff, the only person I suspect is Maura. Did court and the arrest warrant push her over the edge as Eric warned? Is this an extreme measure to scare us into dropping charges? Maybe. I suppose it wouldn't be hard for her to get her hands on an SUV. Or maybe she hired someone to do her dirty work. Whatever it is, I am not going to find an answer tonight. I get up slowly because I am feeling sore everywhere, and limp to the bedroom. I gently slide into bed without waking Bess. I lay my arm over her waist and softly kiss the back of her neck. After what happened, I half expect her to tell me to beat it because there is too much baggage to deal with. I wouldn't blame her if she did.

In the morning, everything hurts. We discover seat belt bruises and pain in parts of our body we didn't realize were bruised. I load up on Tylenol and offer Bess the prescription pain medication the hospital ordered. Bess settles in on the couch and I make us oatmeal for breakfast. It is the most comforting thing I can think of. We sit on the couch, wrapped in blankets, eating.

There are calls to make. The kids need to hear from us before anyone else tells them what happened. We also have to call Virginia and Bob. Then there is the insurance company. I'm not sure how much of this will get done because the pounding in my head is relentless. Before I do anything, I have to call Eric.

"Eric. Remember you said to be careful? We had an incident and I can't help but wonder if Maura is responsible. I'll call it an accident but it didn't seem like one. If it was a random event, we are the unluckiest people on the planet." I fill Eric in on what happened and ask if he can check with the cops to see what they know.

Later the police show up at our door to check on us and to return our keys and Bess's purse. They give us the business card of the garage where our wreck was towed.

Other than that, it is a quiet day punctuated by groaning. We let the kids know we are okay. Early in the afternoon Virginia and Bob come to see us, and we tell them about what happened.

"Who would do something like this?" Virginia demands. "You could have been killed for God's sake."

"Yeah, well thankfully that didn't happen," I tell them.

On Monday we are doing a little better. My head still hurts and Bess's wrist is throbbing. She has an appointment with the orthopedist to be evaluated. While she is there, I drop in on Eric to get his opinion about this latest event.

"Eric, I imagine Bess's car is totaled. Plus, we were dressed like Morticia and Gomez Adams! We had just left a belated Halloween party at the Wilson's. Have you heard anything?"

It's About Time

"Not yet. I'm waiting for them to get back to me. How ya feeling?"

"I've been better. Mild concussion, but I would hate to have a bad one. Bess broke her wrist and is at the orthopedist right now. We're banged up but it could have been worse. Nothing personal, Eric, but I hope we can break up soon." The attorney raises his eyebrows and nods in agreement.

Back at the doctor's office, I wait for Bess. It's good news. She doesn't need surgery but the cast will stay on for several weeks.

"While you were in there, I went to see Eric. He's going to check with the cops and see what he can find out. I hope it was a horrible random event and not someone who has it out for us. You know who that would most likely be!" Bess looks pale and not in the mood to talk. When we get home, I tuck her in on the couch with a blanket, medication, her phone, tea, and the TV remote.

"I'm going to go to my house to check on it and then pick up some groceries. You okay here on your own for a little while?"

"Yeah. I think so. Probably going to nod off. That pain med makes me sleepy."

"You will be off it soon." I kiss the top of her head and tell her I will be right back. "Text me if you need anything. Okay? I'm so sorry this is happening. I know it isn't what you signed up for."

I dash out the door so I can get back quickly. My house is in good shape. The lawn is shaggy but it can wait. I walk through the house looking for things I want to bring home with me. That's interesting. I just called the condo home. I guess it is starting to feel that way. I lock the door securely behind me. At the grocery store, I pick up a few things to get us through a couple of days. From there it's a short trip down Route 1 to the garage that has Bess's car. The mess of twisted metal is parked in the back. It's totaled for sure. I have a key but decide to check in with the owner before I go rummaging around.

"Hey, that Honda HR-V. It belongs to my fiancé. Okay if I go through it and take our stuff out?" I ask. The owner shakes my hand, saying we were lucky from the look of the wreck. After showing him my ID, he asks if I need a box to put stuff in. "Sure, that would be great. Thanks." I gather Bess's stuff and load it all in my truck. My head is pounding. I'm done for the day.

"I'm back" I call as I unlock the condo and come in with the box, groceries, and flowers. Bess walks out of the bedroom looking better. Her color is good and her eyes are brighter than when I left.

"Ooo, flowers. How nice!" Bess kisses me, and I am relieved to see how good she looks. She looks better than me right now. I show her the pictures of the car.

"Holy crap. It looks terrible. My poor sweet car. I hope the insurance claim doesn't take too long. I need a car."

"Well, you can't drive yet anyway, and I'm happy to chauffeur you around. You're looking better. How do you feel?"

"Better. I stopped taking those pills. I am sticking to Tylenol. My wrist hurts a little more but I feel like myself again."

"You look like your lovely self, too." I wrap her in a careful hug. As we put stuff away, there is a knock at the door. Police. "Sweet Jesus, what now." I open the door.

It's About Time

"Mr. Ogilvie?" I nod yes and invite the two cops inside. They nod to Bess "Mrs. Ogilvie." We let correcting that go for now but I did like the sound of it. "We came to check on you and let you know that we found the car that hit you."

"That's great," Bess says. "What can you tell us about it? Do we need to do anything? Press charges? Were they drunk?"

The cops take off their caps and ask if we can all sit down. We show them into the living room and take seats. "We are unsure exactly what happened, but the driver wasn't drunk. We know that much. The driver," the cop looks down at his notes "is a woman. She crashed her vehicle about four miles past where your accident happened. She was going at a high rate of speed and missed a curve, rolling the vehicle. Damage and paint matches, so we know it's the vehicle involved in your accident."

"Oh my God." Bess is shocked. "Is she okay?"

"No, she's in critical condition at Lawrence Hospital. She is still unconscious so we haven't been able to question her."

"Can you tell us who she is?" I ask softly, not sure if I want to know.

"The vehicle is registered to…" the cop checks his notes. "Francisco Alglada." Bess and I look at each other and shrug. The name isn't familiar. "According to her ID, the driver was Maura Jenkins."

"Man, I was afraid of that." I blurt out.

"There is an arrest warrant for her. We understand that there has been some trouble and you recently got a restraining order against her. Correct?"

"That's correct," Bess says.

I feel sad that we have come to this point. What the fuck is wrong with Maura?

"Okay, well for now there is nothing to do. When she regains consciousness, we will interview her. We are glad you two are doing okay." The cops stand and I walk them to the door while Bess sits processing the new information. After I close the door, Bess asks me if I think Maura was trying to kill us. I shake my head and tell her I don't know. I'd like to believe she just wanted to scare us, but at this point, I'm not sure of anything.

I call Eric. When Margaret answers, I ask to speak to Eric. "Eric, the cops were just here. Maura was the driver who forced us off the road. They told us she crashed her SUV after the accident and is in the hospital. Can you check on her? See what you can find out?" Eric agreed and will call when he knows something.

"I'm glad I'm off the pain meds because I think I want a drink. How about you?" Bess asks.

I agree. Please God let this be the end of all this. I am not the kind of person who wants anyone, including Maura, to be harmed, but right now I don't know what to wish for.

It's About Time

CHAPTER 21

What Goes Around, Comes Around

James

Eric calls on Tuesday morning to confirm Maura is still unconscious in the hospital. I put him on speaker so Bess can hear what he says.

"Pain in the ass HIPAA keeps us from knowing the medical situation with Maura, but when she recovers, she will be in deep legal poop. Vehicular assault is a felony. She must have been sure no one would figure out who hit you. I'm sure crashing her car was not in her plan. People like her think they are bulletproof and smarter than everyone else, but in fact, are just stupidly arrogant. So now we wait for her to regain consciousness. But don't hold your breath. The cops hinted that she had a pretty severe head injury. I'll let you know if I hear anything else."

"Thanks, Eric. I appreciate your help."

"Well, that's interesting. I guess what goes around, comes around. Eh?" Bess comments.

"Yep. Maura is in deep trouble and is probably looking at jail time. Who knows when that will be, and isn't it just like Maura to keep everyone waiting. At least she can't hurt us for now. What she did was over-the-top stupid, even for her." I hold Bess close. "Bess, when we started getting to know each other, I had no idea any of this would happen. Is it too much for you? I can move out if you want to rethink our engagement." Making this offer is the right thing to do, but as I say the words I feel the bottom drop out of my stomach.

"I won't tell you it hasn't crossed my mind. Life was peaceful before you and that damn turkey showed up on my doorstep." Bess steps back and looks at me. "We've both been through the relationship wringer with screwed up people. If my ex-husband was like Maura, we might have two crazy people after us and be in witness protection! Fortunately, Chad cares about how the world sees him and wouldn't risk wrecking his stellar fake reputation. He finds subtle, but poisonous, ways to get even." Bess smiles. "Loving you means knowing we are here for each other. None of this is your fault. I'll let you know if it gets to be too much. The possibility is that Maura may have taken care of our problem, all by herself." Bess stands on tip toes to kiss me.

"I am going to the office today. Starting slowly with just a couple of clients. Do you still operate that clock shop or have you given it up? How's your headache?" Bess raises an eyebrow.

"Ha. Ha, smartass. Head still hurts, but it's better. I am going to do some work today too. Want me to pick up groceries later?"

"Sure. I can go with you. I just can't lift anything heavier than an egg." Bess grimaces. "I keep forgetting I don't have a car. I'll walk to my office. Pick me up after work, okay?"

I agree and leave for my shop. As I unlock the door my phone rings. I let it go to voicemail. I flip on the lights and turn up the heat. I have a list of phone calls to return from customers wanting repairs or wondering where the hell their clocks are. At the top of the message list is an unknown number. I listen to the message and have to sit down. It's from estate attorney Mark Grosman in Greenwich who wants to talk about Maura's durable power of attorney and health care proxy. What do I have to do with any of that? Okay, the first call of the day to another freaking attorney. Before long I will be able to pass the Bar Exam. I place the call and connect with Attorney Grosman's paralegal. Mr. Grosman wants to meet with me today, if possible.

"I don't understand. Power of attorney? What does that have to do with me?" I ask.

"Yes. Attorney Grosman will explain everything. As you know there is a need to have someone in charge of Ms. Jenkins' affairs under her current circumstances."

"Um, yes, I am intimately aware of the circumstances." She can't see me roll my eyes.

"Wonderful. How is 2 PM for you? Attorney Grosman will be in his Guilford office this afternoon, and I think that is more convenient for you, isn't it."

"Yes, that would be easier. I can be there at 2."

"Perfect. The office is right on the green. I will email directions. Is your email the same? Ogilvie@itsabouttime.com?"

"Yes, that's correct. Thank you." I slump in my chair wondering why Maura put me front and center in her estate planning. Has she alienated every other person in her life? Or is it another manipulative scheme to keep me hooked? I guess I will find out. I call Bess to tell her about my trip to Guilford and she volunteers to come along.

Hillary Gauvreau Oat

Interstate 95 is the usual hell hole of traffic and construction. I don't know how people drive it every day. We use GPS to get to Grosman's office. Parking is in an open space of crushed stone at the side of the building. The office is in a simple, two-story, repurposed gray house with a pointed roof and white gingerbread trim. Bess and I walk to the front door across patchy brown grass. The building isn't impressive by Greenwich lawyer standards but maybe my expectations are skewed toward Maura's need to impress. Inside the office, there is a small waiting room. A middle-aged woman, neatly dressed, stands to greet us warmly.

"Mr. Ogilvie, I presume?" she asks as she shakes my hand. "I am Attorney Grosman's paralegal Diane Smith. He will be out in a minute. Did you find us easily?"

"Yes, we did, thanks. Nice to meet you." We sit in the waiting area talking quietly until a man saunters into the room on soft as-butter Italian leather shoes. He's wearing a perfectly tailored suit, a white shirt open at the collar with no necktie. I never understood the point of neckties, maybe he doesn't either. That might be all we have in common. The man is forty-five-ish, tall, tan, and athletic with close-cropped dark hair lightly touched with gray. He fits the picture of who I would expect Maura to hire.

"James? Ouch, what happened to you? I wonder what the other guy looks like." the attorney winces.

"We were in an accident." I say and Bess raises her cast into view.

"That seems to be happening a lot these days. I'm so sorry. I'm Mark Grosman. I hope you don't mind first names." He shakes my hand and asks Bess if she is Mrs. Ogilvie. That's the second time this week!

It's About Time

"Hello," says Bess. "Not yet. My name is Bess Parker and I'm James's fiancé. It's nice to meet you."

He leads us into a messy office stacked with papers, files, and assorted coffee cups. He clears off a couple of chairs and invites us to sit.

"Sorry about the mess. It's been hectic. So, Ms. Jenkins gave you, James, Durable Power of Attorney in the event she could not take care of her business and named you as her healthcare proxy. I have copies of everything including her living will here for you. Were you aware she made this decision?" Grosman asks.

"Well, actually no. I'm surprised." I am more horrified than surprised wanting to describe Maura as the bane of my existence but I hold back.

"Well sometimes people don't mention it, that isn't unusual especially if an attorney is involved. That's me," he says smiling wide and exposing perfect white teeth. "Maura told me you were the only person she wanted making decisions for her. She believed you would take good care of her affairs if the need arose. Her current situation puts you in charge of her property, assets, and healthcare decisions. I have a list of her accounts and a checkbook that is yours to pay expenses. There is no shortage of money so don't hold back getting her all the care she needs. These are keys to her house in Old Lyme and her car. Passwords for her accounts are written on the back page. You are responsible for paying bills while she is incapacitated. Got it? Questions?"

"Yeah, I think so. But why me? Isn't there anyone closer to her that should have this responsibility?"

"She was clear that you were the only person she trusted. Are you aware of her background James?" the attorney asks.

"I met her in college but we never really talked about her past. We just moved forward. Sort of."

"That doesn't surprise me. She didn't want anyone to know about her past. Her childhood was brutal. She didn't know her father. Her mother worked her ass off to provide for Maura and was never home. When Maura was ten her mother married an asshole that was not a great stepfather, to say the least. She left home at sixteen and finished growing up on the streets. She fought to survive and was good at that. She gave the impression she was born with advantages but that was more a wish than a reality. I give her a lot of credit for surviving, but the brutality, and insecurity took a toll on her as a human being. It made her cold, calculating, and suspicious of everyone. So, when she said she could trust you, I knew you were special and connected with her in a way she didn't allow many others to do. So here we are. How are you doing so far?"

"I am speechless. I don't know what to think."

"I can imagine. Well, I'm here to help. She ensured that all my expenses through her death, whenever that occurs, are paid. I am at your disposal."

"Okay, I appreciate that. I don't know where to start. You have suggestions, I hope."

"Of course. First, you should show the doctors the health care proxy and her living will. That will put you in charge of healthcare decisions, rehabilitation, and long-term care if needed. As I said, spare no expense. If, God forbid, she does not regain consciousness, it will fall on you to decide about maintaining life functions or not. I don't envy you there. I

It's About Time

recommend you go to her house and make sure it's secure. Go to the banks, show them the DPOA, and sign in to the online accounts."

"I have a question. I get that someone has to make healthcare decisions and that someone is me. But all this financial stuff? Can't someone else manage that, like you?"

"Yes, of course, but she appointed you. Like I said, I'm here to help in any way I can." Grosman writes his cell phone number on a business card. "I don't give out my number to everyone. My wife hates it when clients call my cell. But I want you to know I am here for you. Feel free to call anytime. Questions?"

"Um, no, not yet. I'm still in shock." I can feel Bess tense up next to me. She hasn't said a word.

"I'm sure you are. It is a big responsibility." Mark hands me keys and a fat folder with Grosman Law Offices embossed on the front. We shake hands and leave.

When we get in my truck, I look at Bess and she does not look happy. Ok, that's an understatement. She looks pissed.

"What the fuck, James. What are you doing? Are you seriously going to be a good do-bee and take care of Maura? Possibly forever? REALLY?" Bess raises her voice to levels I rarely hear from her.

"Excuse me? What the fuck?" I snap back. "I haven't had time to consider anything. Maura is a monster. I know that. First, she tried to kill us and now she wants me to take care of her. She is right about one thing though. I am trustworthy. I would never do anything to hurt her as much as I might want to."

Hillary Gauvreau Oat

"James! Come on!" Bess glares at me. "After everything she has done, do you really think this is all about trusting you? And what about us? If you do this, how does it affect our future? I have had just about enough of this woman. Why haven't you?" Bess stares straight ahead, mouth tight, arms crossed bringing attention to the cast on her arm.

"Bess, calm down. You are the one who always needs time to think. This just hit me. I have to think. Could you give me that?" Now I'm annoyed.

"Calm down? Really? Well, Mr. DPOA, If you are determined to do this, she owes me a new car! Want to write me a check?" Bess huffs. We drive home in silence.

That night we get into bed to read, as usual. We haven't talked since Grosman's parking lot. Before long, Bess slaps her book down hard on the nightstand and rolls over, obviously still upset. I look at my book, but I'm not able to concentrate. Finally, I surrender, close the book, shut off the light, and get up. I pour myself a shot of whiskey and sit in the dark living room looking out the French doors. I doze off on the couch, waking up when I hear Bess in the kitchen making coffee. I shuffle into the kitchen to pour myself a mug.

"Hey," I say.

"Hey," Bess says back. "Why did you sleep on the couch?"

"I couldn't sleep so I got up, had some whiskey, and dozed off. Do you have a few minutes to talk?" I ask. She is already dressed for work.

"Of course." Bess pours more coffee and we sit at the table.

It's About Time

"It's this whole thing with Maura. I'm sorry it upset you, and I understand why. I couldn't sleep thinking about it. Despite what the lawyer said, knowing Maura, I believe her decision to put me in charge has more to do with control than trust. Even incapacitated she wants control. It is so Maura."

"Yup. I don't trust her at all." Bess says. "But her intentions are unimportant. What matters to me is what you intend to do."

"Well, the last thing I want is to take care of Maura, especially if we are looking at forever. I want to talk to the doctors about her. Find out what the prognosis is, ya know? Is this going to be a period of recovery or a long-term care thing? They may not be able to answer that question but their opinion counts. She didn't know this would happen to her, but I feel set up anyway. So, I find out what's going on medically, sign off on whatever it is she needs as far as care, then throw it all back into the attorney's lap. I don't want any part of this. I owe her nothing. Does that make me selfish? Cold? Uncaring? Please be honest." Bess reaches across the table with her good hand, resting it lightly on the arm.

"James, the last thing anyone would ever say about you is that you are cold and selfish. I have been thinking too. Remember you said you would understand if I needed to break off our engagement?" I nod yes, and feel a knot tighten in my chest. "If you hadn't come up with this plan to wash your hands of Maura, I knew I couldn't be with you. You, me, and Maura, forever? No way. That breaks my heart. You have no idea how relieved I am to hear your thoughts. Just to take it a step further, I don't think you have to talk to the doctors. Just wash your hands of the whole thing. Clean break. How's that for cold-hearted?" Bess raises her eyebrows and tilts her head challenging me.

"You're right. I think Grosman is more fond of Maura than I am. He will do right by her, especially at his hourly rate which I assume is pricey. I don't need to do anything except unload this responsibility." I take a deep breath feeling relief as the dead weight of Maura slips off my shoulders.

After Bess leaves for work I call Mark Grosman telling him I don't want any part of power of attorney or Maura's healthcare. I fill him in on the current situation, the restraining order, arrest warrants, and how she forced us off the road.

"That's why she is in her current situation. I cannot in good conscience take care of her. It's a huge conflict of interest for me."

Grosman quietly says he understands and promises to handle it. There is the inevitable legal paperwork that needs to be signed and then I will be off the hook.

"I have another question, Attorney Grosman. Since Maura was responsible for totaling my fiancé's car and injuring us, is it possible to get financial compensation from Maura's assets?" I figure I may as well ask.

"You say the police positively identified Maura as the driver of the car that caused the crash?"

"Yes, absolutely. Eric Cunningham, my attorney, can substantiate that and answer your questions. I will text you his contact information."

"Okay. And you are willing to waive all future claims?"

"Yes, of course."

It's About Time

"I believe a financial award for damages is reasonable to ask for. Let me talk to your attorney and get back to you."

"Thank you. I appreciate your help with this."

"No problem. I am sorry you went through all that. I'll be in touch."

* * *

Life is becoming normal for the first time since I met Maura. Bess's wrist and my concussion healed. I was freed of all responsibility regarding Maura's care. Weeks have gone by and I hear through the grapevine that she is off life support but has the conscious awareness of a carrot. I thought about going to see her but haven't. At least for now. There are things I want to say for my benefit, not hers. Attorney Grosman sent a check for $250 thousand which was more than we expected but not nearly enough to cover the damage Maura caused in my life. We accepted it and released her from any further responsibility. Bess got a new electric car that is like driving a computer and a lot of fun. Eric and I kid that we are enjoying a trial separation. If things change with Maura's condition and she is tried for her crimes we will reconnect. Maybe we'll get a beer together one of these days. It's a relief not to be looking over my shoulder all the time.

Our families, kids, and grandkids, got together here for Thanksgiving. It was the first time we were all together. Andy and Emily flew in to join us and connected seamlessly with Bess's family. Thomas brought his girlfriend Lydia. The boys and I continue to talk and slowly sort truth from fiction. This has taken a toll on Thomas's ability to trust. We're not the Brady bunch but we're doing okay. I think the car accident scared all of us and we realize anything can happen so take advantage of the moment. Wasn't it John Lennon who said "Life is what happens to you when you are busy making other plans"? Ain't that the truth?

Bess and I are figuring out our next move regarding marriage and where to live. We are solid and happy so there's no rush. We aren't using my house, so we'll clean it out and sell it. I loved it there but don't intend to live in it ever again. Every time I'm there I am haunted by memories of Maura.

Christmas is coming, so aside from spoiling Bess's grandchildren with presents on Christmas Eve, we welcome a quiet day at home counting our blessings. I'm surprising Bess with an engagement ring this Christmas. It's another 'it's about time' moment. Andy's wedding is next June and we hope to have things worked out with Thomas by then. I look forward to a joyous celebration with the people I love. Mary, my dear sister, who worried sick about us during the Maura debacle, is planning another get-together to celebrate Andy's wedding. Life moves on. After so much strife it is a relief.

It's About Time

CHAPTER 22

The Final Chapter

Bess

The soft glow of the bedside lamp illuminates the emerald ring on my left hand. I remember Christmas thirty years ago when James gave it to me. We had a lovely quiet day after a boisterous Christmas Eve ripping open gifts with the grandchildren. Sadie, my daughter Cait's toddler, was more thrilled by the flying paper and ribbons than the gifts. Her four-year-old brother, Barrett, was enthralled with his older cousins, as they set up the video game console to play Mario Kart. It was great fun but after that, we wanted a quiet, romantic day together. It was our first Christmas together after getting engaged at the family reunion. The fireplace warmed our bodies and spirits. Christmas music played softly in the background. We sipped eggnog and agreed the only thing that could make that day better would be a touch of snow. Our family ornaments, collected over the years, combined to make the Christmas tree spectacular. Christmas is always a holiday of extraordinary expectations, but that year it came through for me. I close my eyes and am transported back to that day.

* * *

Christmas Thirty Years Ago

"So, do we open presents now?" I ask. James and I promised each other not to go overboard with gifts. We reserve going overboard for the grandchildren. I hand him a large box wrapped in snowman paper and gold ribbon. "Open it! I can't wait any longer," I beg.

James rips open the gift and folds back the tissue paper, revealing a Shetland wool sweater handmade in Scotland. I searched long and hard to find the perfect blue color. Tucked inside the sweater is a framed photograph of us when we got engaged. "Do you like it?" I ask excitedly.

"Bess, the sweater is beautiful! It's so soft, and I love the color." James pulls the sweater over his head and strokes the soft wool. "Thank you so much." He kisses me and holds the photo. "Where did you get this picture? I never saw it before."

"Your brother took it on his phone and slipped it to me so I could surprise you." I kiss James. "Merry Christmas."

"I love it!" James carefully places the picture in the center of the mantle. "My turn," he announces. He hands me a rectangular box wrapped in green tissue. "Sorry about the lack of artistic wrapping. I am not good with that stuff."

"No need to apologize, hon. It's what's inside that's important." I shake the box. "It doesn't rattle. Or tick! Is it a tie?" I laugh. James rolls his eyes and shakes his head. I peel off the tissue and lift the cover of the box. Nestled inside is a pair of socks. "Socks?" I ask, trying not to sound disappointed.

"Yeah. You said not to overdo it. They're good socks. Darn Tough and made to last. You like them?" James grins like a Christmas Cheshire cat. "Try 'em on!" he urges.

"Okay." I want to be a good sport but can't help feeling a bit let down. How much thought goes into socks?? I pull one sock on and agree it is very comfy. When I pull the other sock on my toe

It's About Time

catches on something hard. I pull the sock off and reach in. Tucked inside the Darn Tough sock is a beautiful emerald ring. "Oh my God James!" I excitedly leap up, grabbing him in a bear hug. "You sneaky devil, tricking me with socks. It's beautiful. Emeralds are my favorite."

"Wait! Before you put it on." James gets down on one knee taking my left hand in his. "Bess, I love you more every day. You're funny, warm, and smart. I'm not perfect, you already know that, and I have fucked up a lot of things in my life. But knowing you...I can say without exaggeration, you brought me back to life after a very dark time. I promise to love, protect, and care for you for as long as I live. Will you marry me? Still? Even after everything?"

I said yes, of course, and James slipped the ring on my finger where it stayed all these years. It was perfect and still is.

* * *

"Mrs. Ogilvie? Are you in pain?" my caregiver, Faith Blahsim, a gentle lady from Haiti, asks. "You were mumbling. Do you need anything?" I smile at her.

"No, I'm fine, just lost in a fond memory." Tomorrow is my eighty-fifth birthday. These days are unpredictable. This could be my last day so I try to make the most of it. I have been in Hospice care for several months but still hanging in. Jimmy Carter lasted a year in Hospice and I am willing to let him have the record. He won't get a challenge from me. Although I do like to get my money's worth. Faith stays with me at night and takes good care of me. From my perspective, there isn't much difference between night and day. I prefer to be awake as much as possible to savor every minute. Nights are quiet and give me time to remember. The photo of our engagement that I gave James on Christmas is standing in front of me.

When I first got into Hospice, my children gathered special photographs and placed them all around my bed. The number grows every time they visit. Tiny fairy lights weave around the frames. Some pictures make me laugh. Some make me cry. Always I am grateful. My memories are especially vivid in this bardo between life and death. Often, I chat with people long gone as if they are alive. Maybe they are alive somewhere. I guess I will find out. Wherever they are it's quite lovely to visit with them. Bob Wilson has been gone a while now, but yesterday he visited looking sprightly and wishing me a happy birthday. We had a nice chat. I wish I thought to ask him where he was. The beach outside the open French doors is dark but I can smell the salty scent of the ocean and hear the gentle waves. God, I love this place.

When James moved into my condo, we assumed it would be temporary, but as the days passed, we got comfortable and never left. It was a huge job cleaning out James's house and neither of us wanted to do it again. Our home became an interesting combination of periods and styles. Everything we kept was meaningful and made us happy. After James died, I would often sit at his antique desk, and run my hand over the smooth wood, remembering him sitting there.

My eyes rest on a photograph from Andy's wedding in majestic Glacier National Park. Andy wore his Park Service uniform. Emily wore jeans, hiking boots, and a white fisherman knit sweater. They did the wedding their way. I remember how we worried about Thomas after Maura coerced him with vicious lies. We did everything we could to repair the rift between Thomas and his father before we flew to Montana. After Maura forced us off the road, Thomas had to face the hard truth that Maura was not who he thought she was. By the time we arrived in Montana, he and his father had patched things up enough to be together without a fight breaking out. It took time and love to heal the rest of those wounds. Gradually, we became a family.

I wish I didn't have to remember Maura, but as it turned out she was sort of an angel in disguise. It was a pretty solid disguise though. After her accident, she wasn't able to speak or care for herself. Is it snarky to say that was a blessing? I laugh to myself. James would approve of that comment. Mark Grosman, her attorney, managed her long-term care until she died. For me, her death was a relief. That may not be the politically correct thing to say but that was when my Maura nightmares finally stopped. The weird thing is that she left her entire estate to James and we will never know why. I doubt she had altruistic intentions or was trying to make anything up to him. Knowing her, there was probably some ulterior motive. Maybe she wanted to stiff someone else in her family or keep her memory alive to haunt James. We had long talks about the best way to handle her estate. James sold her house in Old Lyme and the villa in Barcelona immediately. Bob Wilson was thrilled to get her wine collection. Her car went to a family in need.

The rest of Maura's estate we used to create something good. First, we made sure that there were trust funds for our children, grandchildren, and future great-grandchildren. James was determined to help people who have been abused but also to help abusers. Instead of just repairing damage we wanted to do what we could to prevent it. It doesn't make sense to punish people for the suffering they cause if they are also victims. We created *Metta Support*, a foundation based on the Buddhist concept of love and kindness. Our mission statement is the quote from Martin Luther King, Jr that hate cannot drive out hate. Only love can do that. Metta Support has provided shelter, therapy, medical care, legal counsel, and education to hundreds of people for twenty-five years. There should be enough funding for it to continue long after I am gone. I wonder what Maura would think about that.

They say the best revenge is a life well lived. I like that idea. Wanting vengeance is human. But then what? I didn't want my life to be poisoned by anger and bitterness. James and I chose a life well lived and found a love that exceeded expectations. I have no regrets.

After Andy's wedding, James's sister Mary, invited everyone to North Carolina to celebrate. It was wonderful and no fights broke out this time. Mary and Graeme are gone now. James was close to his sister and her death hit him hard. Mary's passing brought James and his brother MJ closer, and he came to visit us often. MJ adores his nephews so we could usually count on him joining us for holidays. We never made the trip back to North Carolina. It was too painful for James to visit the house and not be greeted by Mary standing in the driveway waitng. Thankfully, Mal and Isla took over the homestead so it stayed in the family. I think the younger generation will keep the family legacy safe.

My eyes scanned photographs of weddings, births, and graduations, before finally resting on a picture from our wedding. We got married here on the beach, barefoot, surrounded by family and our closest friends. The wedding was informal and sweet. The young ones played in the water and made sand castles while we vowed to love each other through whatever came. And come it did! Midway through the ceremony, a fast-moving thunderstorm sent us scrambling. We took it as a blessing from the Gods, running inside the condo drenched and laughing. The picture was taken when we got inside, looking like happy drowned cats.

Four years ago, James and I celebrated our twenty-fifth wedding anniversary. Virginia arranged a catered affair

It's About Time

including authentic barbeque with all the fixings. She toasted us with wine Bob had reserved for special occasions. Bob passed away two years before from cancer. Drinking his wine brought him to the celebration. I've enjoyed many parties on the Wilson's deck, but that one was special. I never thought I would get married again, or celebrate it lasting 25 years. Turns out the third time's a charm. I got lucky when I fell on the sidewalk in front of It's About Time!

A month after that, James had a severe stroke. We were walking on the beach in front of the condo and he collapsed. Paramedics raced him to the hospital. I never left his side, reassuring him, and praying. Lots of praying. He was on life support when his boys arrived. He never regained consciousness, but we thought he smiled slightly when they entered the hospital room. Doctors said he wouldn't recover and it was my responsibility to tell them when to let him go. I struggled mightily with that decision.

No part of me wanted to say goodbye, but we all knew James would be pretty pissed off if we held onto him out of selfishness. We stood around him when the machines stopped. My heart broke and I did not know how I could go on. We helped each other through that difficult time. Everyone, family, friends and people from town, attended the clock man's memorial service. His sons created a ceremony to honor him. The centerpiece was an old anniversary clock that James had kept in the window of his shop for years. Andy read a poem and when he finished, the clock stopped.

I placed the clock on the mantle and didn't wind it again. Andy took some of his father's ashes to sprinkle on the tallest peak in Glacier Park. He said it would give his Dad a head start to heaven. Thomas spread ashes on the green at the UMass campus, James's happy place. I gave ashes to James's brother, to sprinkle at the homestead in North Carolina. I spread the last portion on the beach where we were married. I owe all the love and joy in my life to a turkey and a stubborn Scotsman. I almost didn't let James in. Think of what I would have missed. I start to cry. It feels like yesterday.

"I'm here Mrs. Ogilvie." Faith gently blots my tears and places a tissue in my hand.

"More memories, Faith. Did I ever tell you about our wedding?" I point out the photo, and she sits with me while I reminisce.

Next to our wedding picture is a picture of Thomas's wedding. They had a traditional ceremony with all the trimmings in the Baughman Center at the University of Florida in Gainesville. The place is stunning in its simplicity with natural wood, a vaulted ceiling, and a view of trees through tall arched windows. Of course, there was Thomas's and Caroline's music. His wife, Lydia was lovely. Sadly, they split up after about three years. I don't know the details of their break up but knowing what Thomas had been through, I can empathize. I am certain he will have another chance at it just like James and I did.

I hold photos of my babies, Matt and Cait, fanning them out on the blanket. Cute as little buttons they were. Now they are accomplished people with families of their own. I look up searching for the framed photographs of our family at Christmas. Each year I attempted to get pictures of the kids decked out in their holiday finest. One year when Matt was about eight, he refused to wear his Christmas sweater. He insisted on wearing his favorite Teenage Mutant Ninja Turtles tee shirt. I wanted him in the picture so after a struggle I couldn't win, I surrendered. Now that picture is one of my favorites. He is grinning from ear to ear. Cait however gave her brother several withering looks as I remember. She was adorable in her

It's About Time

long red and green plaid taffeta dress with an organza bodice that was scratchy. She kept it on all Christmas day despite how uncomfortable it was. The time goes by so fast. As the children became adults with their own families, we still managed to get together for a family photo around Christmas. The last one we took included James with his sons.

I must have drifted off because when I open my eyes it is light out. Virginia is sitting next to me.

"Hey, birthday girl! Are you ready to party? I hope I didn't wake you. I was muttering while reading another political tell-all book. They get me so riled up. I'm not sure why I bother." At 81 years old Virginia is still funny. Thank God we didn't lose our sense of humor as we became old crones.

"No, you didn't, and I know why you read that stuff. You love getting riled up. Keeps your blood pumping." Virginia helps me raise my head and gives me a sip of water. "Yup, I'm ready to party. Bring it on. Eighty-five is the new forty I hear."

"So, what do you want? Coffee? Scotch? Cake? We've got it all, and it's your day."

"What time is it?" I look around for a clock, although time doesn't much matter to me these days.

"9:30 in the morning. How was your night? Have a sexy dream?" Virginia teases.

"Ha. I wish. My night was good. Lots of memories. They are like beautiful pearls that I hold and admire, one after the other." Then I chuckle.

Hillary Gauvreau Oat

"What's so funny?" Asks Virginia.

"Oh, I just made a joke in my head. I was thinking about how we are still here, at least for now, and so many people are gone. Bob, James, Mary, and Graeme . . . all gone. That didn't make me laugh though. I told myself that Chad died when he exploded from an over-inflated ego. That made me laugh." I laugh again. "Don't they say laughter is the best medicine? If I keep this up, maybe Hospice will fire me."

"Ha! That is probably true on both counts my friend. Party on!" Virginia gets up to make way for the Hospice worker. I ask her to go easy on medication because I want to be alert. She helps me slip James's Christmas sweater on over my nightgown. The soft Shetland wool still smells like him. Welcome to the party, James.

My son Matt arrives with his family, followed by my daughter Cait and her husband Bart.

"Happy Birthday, Ma." they kiss me on the forehead and chat, filling me in on their week. I ask them to sit with me before the party gets too busy and we miss our moment.

"I know today is a party and I don't want to get morbid. I just want you both to know how much I love you and what a joy it has been to be your mother. I know I'm not perfect. I regret the times I wasn't there when you needed me. I hope you can forgive me. I am so proud of you." I squeeze their hands.

"Ma, we both have kids so we know how hard it is to be a parent. Some days I have no patience. I wish I was half the mother you are." Cait says. Matt nods in agreement.

"Yeah, Cait sucks at parenting." Matt laughs and Cait punches his arm. "Ow. But seriously, Ma, I think we also need to

It's About Time

apologize to you for all the times we worried you sick. We're probably even. We make up for all of it with a lot of love and forgiveness and that's what counts. Right?"

"I taught you well! That is true. I like that you two always give each other a hard time and me the benefit of the doubt!" People wander over and gather around me. Lots of pictures are taken and I don't even care that I probably look like hell.

My granddaughter Rose struggles to get through the door weighed down by bags and carrying a special bundle.

"Happy Birthday Mema." I have always felt close to Rose, Matt's middle child. Being a girl sandwiched between two brothers helped her stand out and become a confident woman able to hold her own just about anywhere. The bundle she carries is her new baby. My second great-grandchild. "Mema, this is Grace." Rose sits on the edge of my bed cradling the tiny infant so I can see her beautiful face.

'Rose, she is gorgeous." Grace's huge blue eyes search around finally finding my face. I smile at her. "Gracie, you are in for the ride of your life. This isn't the easiest place to be but the rewards are great. I'm so happy to meet you." Grace makes those newborn faces that may be smiles or gas, no one is sure.

"Do you want me to tuck her in next to you so you can get to know each other?" Rose asks.

"I would love that, yes." While Gracie and I get to know each other, the family decorates the room with streamers, signs, and pictures. Andy and his wife Emily arrive. Thomas trails along behind them. The table is loaded with food and drinks. Soft jazz plays. Children snuggle with me in my bed and chat non-stop.

Thomas approaches slowly asking to have a few private minutes with me. He sits and holds my hand in both of his like his father used to do. Andy looks a lot like his father but Thomas has James's heart.

"Bess, when you came into our family, I was too stubborn, to accept you as my stepmother. But over the years I came to love you. You have always been kind and patient even when I was a total asshole. It was obvious you loved my father. He was happy and you were so good to each other. Now I feel lost." Tears well in Thomas's eyes. "Mom and Dad are gone. It makes my heart hurt to think of losing you, too." Andy, who had been standing nearby, puts a gentle arm around his brother, saying nothing.

"Thomas, I know you and Andy have experienced a lot of losses. It hurts like nothing else. My mother died when I was young, too. Did you know that? My, how that pain lingers. Maybe it's wishful thinking but I believe that we are never really alone. Your father and mother may not be alive, but they're with you. Always. I know that's not the same, though, so consider the people in your life now who love you. One has his arm around you. Plus, there's MJ, Mal, my kids, your niece, Emily, and probably a cast of thousands knowing how wonderful you are. My advice, for what it's worth, is to try to let them in. Focus on the love you have rather than the losses. That doesn't mean you don't miss people. I miss your father every single day. But we take the love that is offered wherever it comes from and give back as much as we can. Know what I mean?" Tears run down Thomas's face as his brother hugs him. Seeing the hugging, others are drawn in as if by magic. The hug-huddle expands with Thomas in the center. I hope he can let himself feel the love. From somewhere in the huddle, I hear a voice.

It's About Time

"Are we ready for cake?" It's Matt keeping us on track. The crowd cheers.

"Bring it on," I say. "What's a birthday party without cake?"

I am presented with a chocolate whipped cream frosted cupcake. A question mark candle sits in the middle of a creamy cloud.
"What's with the question mark?" I ask, teasing.

"We couldn't remember how old you are." They tease back. Matt lights the candle.

"Make a wish Mema!" chant the grandchildren in a chorus of voices. I think for a minute. What do I wish for when I have almost everything? I wish James was here but I will keep that between him and me.

"I wish you all happiness! And for some help blowing out this candle!" The little ones gather around, we all take a deep breath and blow. A spoonful of sweet vanilla ice cream melts in my mouth. "Where's the whiskey?" I ask. "It's not a celebration until the bottle is passed around,"

Andy retrieves the last bottle of Talisker James brought into the house. Everyone gathers around me and passes the bottle from adult to adult, offering toasts and birthday wishes. It's fun watching those new to Talisker. There are winces as they swallow the smokey Scotch. I know James is close by, enjoying the fun.

The youngsters are getting tired, so their parents pack them up to go home. There are long lingering goodbyes. Finally, Virginia and my four children are the only ones left. I am suddenly quite tired and nodding off, the pain medication is doing its job.

"We love you, Ma. We are having a sleepover here with you tonight," they whisper, tucking my favorite blanket around me. Through the open French doors, I can hear the sound of waves lapping the beach. The sun has set, the sky is dark and the stars sparkle. I feel like part of it all. Faith passes out blankets and pillows. Quiet conversation punctuates spaces of silence. I did okay as a mother. Virginia holds my hand and tells me stories of our adventures together.

"Remember when we did reconnaissance?" She asks and chuckles. "Then we barged in on James and I didn't know what was going to happen. It all worked out. Even in the worst of times, we had fun. When you get wherever you go after this, save me a seat, okay? And tell Bob we drank his wine." Virginia chuckles again and stretches out in the recliner next to me. She is my best friend forever. I close my eyes, held in the love of my family.

"Happy Birthday, Bess," James says. I open my eyes and he is leaning over me, radiant, exactly as I remember him on our wedding day.

"James. What are you doing here?" I can't believe my eyes.

"I'm here to take you out for your birthday. There is an amazing beach I want to show you."

"My birthday wish came true. I wished you were here." I tell him, astounded.

"I know! And here I am. Ready?"

"Yes! I'm ready. Let's go."

It's About Time

James takes my hand and effortlessly lifts me into brilliant sunlight. The sky is deep azure. The white sand is soft under my bare feet. James's hand is warm and solid. I am so happy and full of life. We wade in the warm crystal-clear water talking and laughing. I tell him about the kids, and our new great-granddaughter, Gracie and how much Thomas misses him. We kiss and he tastes sweet like birthday ice cream. Clumps of beach grass sway in a gentle breeze. Flowers bloom bright and fragrant at the edge of a dune. Heliotrope trees, with crooked trunks and canopies of green leaves, offer shade. Colors are vivid, scents are rich, and the air sparkles. "This is a gorgeous beach, James. Where are we?"

"We're home, honey. We're finally home." James smiles and puts his arm around me. "Walk with me. I have so much to show you."

Hillary Gauvreau Oat

ABOUT THE AUTHOR

Hillary Gauvreau Oat grew up in Schenectady, New York which is the city Kurt Vonnegut and General Electric put on the map.

Fascinated by our strange and wonderful world, Hillary studied science when in school. She worked in cancer research and clinical labs after she graduated and then attended a graduate program in social work where curiosity about healing led her to The Barbara Brennan School of Healing.

Her desire to understand people, in addition to thirty years as a Healing Science Practitioner, brings compassionate depth to Hillary's writing—and she believes that love always wins.

Hillary lives in Niantic, Connecticut and adores her five brilliant and energetic grandchildren and her sweet grand dog. *It's About Time* is her first novel.

https://hillaryoat.com
hillaryoat@gmail.com

Hillary Gauvreau Oat

Made in United States
North Haven, CT
04 June 2024